GENERIC
LITERATURE

by
Rock Boulder

Published by MANIA PRESS ■ 4225 Redwood Place ■ Boulder, Colorado 80301 ■ (303) 443-7391

If you are a teacher, order this book for your class . . . .

If you are a reviewer, review this book for your publication . . . .

And if you are a sucker, spend $3.95 and buy this book. And lotsa luck . . . .

CONTENTS

Adam

. . . and the adventure. The excitement. The grandness of it all. To take a trip
AROUND THE WORLD! Softly now . . .
The world is turning
And I am burning
To see it
To free
     myself.
Hands keep on packing. Make ready for the great trip, for the exploration of the
outside world that will further expand my inner consciousness. To know. To know! As
of now my eyes are opened but a crack, they see but a sliver of the beauty that is, and my
spirit, my spirit, my spirit is a trembling ball of crystal that would explode into
eternity . . .
The world is turning
And I am burning
To be as one
With all that the sun
Illuminates . . .
Ahhh. These useful youthful most willing bones
Of mine that carry me about here, there,
Everywhere, why they sing with the music
That a young man calls his own, I am, 'I
AM!' is what they proclaim, as do robins
In the spring, and to be alive. To be . . .
Why simply 'To be' That's all a man needs.
—"Adam. Don't forget to pack at least half a dozen underwear."—
     My mind is like a river. It goes and flows. Why the world is like a river, it too goes
and flows, runs on and on, always keeping the spirit active and alert by giving it
something new to feed upon, by changing the scenery. And yet the river that is the
world also keeps the spirit safe and secure by providing a constancy of motion, by
making the spirit feel that he is standing still, protected and sheltered, while the world
goes sweeping on by him for his enjoyment and inspection, and Life can be a cruise. A
car-ride. I mean there's nothing finer than going for a spin in a car.
Or in a train.
Or even in a boat or aeroplane.

1

O yeah. I like it when the world flows on by me, providing action and stimulation and exoticness and yang, while I get to rest within the womb of yin e.g. the back seat of a moving car. —"Adam!? Did you hear me?!" my mother asks. She is now standing in my bedroom doorway.

"I have eight pairs of underwear in my trunk," I reply.

"I wasn't sure if you heard me—"

"Of course I heard you," I interrupt. And I did hear what my mother said. I mean even though it sounded like her voice was coming from far, far- away . . . and that's the way her voice always sounds . . . I still heard her.

"Are you excited about the trip?" she asks.

"Ummm-hmmm."

"It'll be a good chance for all of us to be together," she continues. Pursuing. I mean Mom has this idea of bringing the family back together again by having all of us take this trip together. I *should* tell her not to get her hopes too high. Why I should and I should
But I won't I won't

"It will be a good chance," I say.

"Your father and I," she sniffles, the tears coming to her eyes, brought on by the salty wreckage of her marriage.

"It wasn't *your* fault,"
I return.
Halt! Halt!
Bring guilt and anxiety
To a halt!
In these days of Circumstance . . .
—It's nobody's fault.

"Dear Jesus," she petitions.
She is a Jesus Freak.
She always speaks
His Name
Be she in triumph
Or in shame . . .
—"I so hope that things can be the way they used to," she runs on.

'What's THAT?!' my memory asks me. He does not recall an idyllic past, nosirreee, not for our family.
And yet my mother
Beneath the covers
Of her mind
Would swim in nostalgia
Sentimental nostalgia
A fantasized sentimental nostalgia
Of something that never really was
—" . . and even so, it's good that we all have an opportunity like this," she runs on and on. "We're all getting such a deal. Not many people ever get the chance to take a trip around the world."

"At half the normal fare," I continue. Mom is a teacher and she will be teaching for something called 'Semester on the Waves.' It is a program that takes college students around the world on a boat. They take classes while they sail and they get college credit while having one helluva good time. Since Mom will be a faculty member on this cruise we her immediate not-so-loving-and-or-together-family get to come along for half price i.e. twenty five hundred dollars a piece— which isn't bad—to see the world
—And I have to dance
—Since I have the chance
To see it all
To know it all
To be it all
—"Don't forget to take plenty of socks," my mother reminds me.
"Of course."
"Would you like to come to the meeting tonight?" she slips in. Mommy is a Jesus Freak. She's going to a fundamentalist-revivalist hand-holding group therapy session. Everyone there will feel and sing:
O Jesus You're My Friend
You will always be there
Through the bitter end
And I am not alone
And I am not afraid
You make everything alright
You make everything okay
You're my Big Brother
My Eternal Mother
Yes Jesus You're My Friend
I'll Hallelujah it again!
Yes Jesus You're My Friend!!
With You it all makes sense
All this modern nonsense
And I am peaceful happy quiet still
Cause now I know that all that happens
Is nothing more than Your Divine Will
(Why before I met you
There was no hope
It was a fact
That I could not cope
Living as I was
At the end of my rope
But YOU took care of all of that!
Yes Jesus You're My Friend!
Let's Hallelujah it again!!
. . . and deep down, my mother is very happy. She has Jesus, Jesus has her. And she wants to share with me her son the Peace she has but I don't know. I am human,

3

I am frail, I want the Peace oh so badly
Oh so madly!
But I also want Truth. I don't know. There's something phony about all this Jesus Freak stuff. I mean they are so certain that they have a lock on ABSOLUTE TRUTH but come: Is it not true that any mortal who claims to know immortal truth lives a mortal fantasy?

—"No, no, not tonight. Give my regards to Brother Grand."

"Adam," she persists.

"I'm not going to the Prayer Group," I reply. Emphatically.

"*He* can make you so happy," my mother offers.

"Mom," I say gently. Looking for the tolerance that is just not within her. I throw some T-shirts into the trunk. She's driving me away from her by insisting that I become a Jesus Freak just like her.

She drove away her husband (my father) that way.

She drove away her daughter (my sister) that way.

The stupid bitch.

Sometimes I hate her

—But she is my mother

Sometimes I hate her

—But she is mommy

"Alright, alright, do what you want. Have it your way," my mother exclaims, throwing up her hands, leaving the room, offended that I her son and child have a mind of my own. That I have an existence of my own.

Me! Me! Me!

Must be Me!

Me! Me! Me!

Must be Me!

I'm eighteen!

'I' must be seen!

And I am alone. She has left the room and gone back downstairs. I can hear her footsteps on the stairway as she goes trailing away . . . away . . . but something is close to me. Something is rising. A certain tingling. A certain feeling. I'm trembling. I know what my body wants.

—It's always like this.

—I always get horny when I least expect it.

One hand looks under my bed

One hand unhooks my pants

The two eyes that are in my head

Assume a most rigid stance

As they eat a bare assed girl

A two dimensional Playboy swirl

Hard as a rock. Feeling no pain. Raquel Welch goes swimming by me. I am buried in her cleavage (My fist! My fist! Pump it harder. Harder!). Then it's Brigitte Bardot. No it's this two dimensional Playmate that I feel and see. Everything's so warm and nice. And then

4

I slow the pace
For I can see *her* face
The one that will bring me
Sweet ecstacy

It's a cheerleader. We're in the shed behind the stadium. Her clothes are falling off her I'm on top of her. She's moaning groaningthisisit THISISIT!!* POW! I catch the shooting sperm in a dirty sock . . . rub a little more . . .

. . . and I'm kind of ashamed. I mean it's kind of gross, jacking off into a dirty old sock. I mean I don't think sex is bad. It's just that I'm ashamed that I still have to masturbate—I'm only 18—Oh come on buddy. You should be getting fucked regularly by now—Oh my day will come. SEX! SEX! SEX! Someday I'll find out what Pussy is like . . . Someday . . .

I didn't put the Playboy magazine into my trunk so that I would have it when I went around the world. I was going to but:

I'm a man
That's the plan
I'm a man
And a man never needs
Pictures
Because a man is man enough
To have the real thing
And he who gets caught with dirty girlie photos
Is a frustrated impotent little boy
And not a man (MEN are sexually competent)

So I didn't put the Playboy into my trunk. Although I wanted to.

—"Adam!" my mother yells at me from downstairs. "Have you finished packing yet?" Nagging. "You know we have to catch our plane in less than six hours."

I know, I know. I hear her. But I don't reply. Why bother. It's
always the same
such a shame
be it shine or rain
there's so much pain
living in the mundane

I don't answer her. Why bother. Spoken words are so useless. Such an effort. Telepathy is so much easier. So much more honest. Telepathy, silent mental telepathy, is the one gift God denied us that we really need. But
Life? Life? Harsh Life? 'Tis still worth the livin'.
Through all the tears and fears, heartache and pain,
'Tis still worth the living. Why there's Beauty
Everywhere if we would but look, if we'd
Only have the courage to see . . . and feel . . .
Why Progress is more than just a fair word,
It can be made, and Opportunity?
The here and now's the stuff of which he's made.

There's plenty of him, more than any man
Can handle. He's standing right next to us,
He isn't off in that distant horizon,
And I say: The world's forever new, never old,
If we would but look, if we would but see,
If, If,
    I'm feeling good. Feeling right. I can't lose and I'm eighteen.

Harriet

Dear God,
    O Lord. Once again I find that you have provided for me. I am so fortunate to have placed myself in your hands (I'm so much safer now than I used to be). As I pack my bags to take this glorious trip around the world I can see your Loving Hand guiding things and Thy Will Be Done (Yes Thy Will Be Done, Thy Will Be Done, at all costs Thy Will Be Done, You must stay here with me and take care of everything Almighty God ((Can't make it on my own oh how I know I can't make it on my own)).
    And Lord? As I pack my bags to take this trip around the world I think of my husband Ozzie and my daughter Dawn (The ungrateful infidels. Refusing Your Love and Peace like they did. How could Ozzie have abandoned me like he did. The spiteful sonuvabitch. And Dawn. My ungrateful daughter Dawn. Thinking she knows what's best for herself). I thank Thee Lord for moving them to take this trip with me. I know that they will find Your Love and Peace while we are on this trip. I just know that You will reveal Yourself to them and that they too will put Christ at the center of their lives as I have done. And then my family will re-unite (You must makes us re-unite. How can I tell people that God is good when by putting Christ at the center of my life I have split apart my family ((You must make us re-unite. Do as I tell You to, Be Who I want You to be, Damn You)). And all will be well.
    And Adam, Lord. My baby Adam. How I hope and pray that he too will see Your Light. He's a fine boy, a good boy, there's not a speck of evil in him, and I know that You will make him a part of Your flock. He has a heart of gold (But some of those ideas of his!!) and not a selfish bone in his body (Well hell, even if he doesn't convert at least he won't abandon me, won't hate me like Ozzie and Dawn do ((Those sonsabitches)). Oh Adam. I do so worry about him though (What if he rejected me ((Fear. Unthinkable. GOD. MOTHER-FUCKING GOD. You wouldn't let that happen. Adam must not reject me (((Or hell. I would reject YOU — Yes YOU GOD ((((But alone, can't cope, can't stand it alone, O God! fall

apart)))). Adam is so smart. So intelligent (He reads too many books). Why Lord, he sometimes talks about You as though You are nothing but myth, legend, psychological necessity, and I just don't understand him. Perhaps he is too smart for his own good but at least he has a generous and wholesome nature and I know that he will always love me (He should convert and be like me ((WATCH OUT HARRIET DON'T PRESSURE THE BOY OR YOU'LL LOSE HIM TOO)) but I hope that he will some day accept You too, Lord.

(My husband Ozzie) Oh Lord. And I hope that Ozzie too will see Your Light. He is a willful man, has some of the Devil in him, but then Your Servant Paul was in grievous error before he found You. And I want so badly for Ozzie and me to have a Christian marriage, want so badly for us to be re-united (Though I try to hide it I know I miss him ((SEX!)). It is not good for men and women to go through this world alone (I'm lonely, even You O Lord do not replace the presence of a fellow human being in the flesh and blood ((SEX. I want to touch him. I want to suck on him. Be full of him (((Harriet! No! No! Sex is BAD! ((((I like it want it (((((BAD!))))). O Lord. Give me Your Peace. I feel troubled (Help me Jesus, Help me Jesus, Help me Jesus ((Sex (((Help me Jesus—I wanna fuck so bad—Help me Jesus—Sex Is bad I just know it is Mother said—A hard penis ((((Help me Jesus! Oh yes Lord there is the Peace You give, You Who know all, You Who are all, I submit ME to You and am feeling much better)))).

Heaven on earth. Here I am packing dirty underwear. I guess I'm feeling rather distracted today. I better hurry up and wash this underwear (Yes clean it, clean all of it. Mustn't let anyone else see the dirt ((Mustn't let anyone think I'm dirty; stained; CLEAN THAT UNDERWEAR)). O Lord. I guess it's the excitement of this upcoming trip that has so confused me. A journey around the world. Imagine that. Why I never even dreamed of such a thing, even when I was a little girl and would spend my time playing makebelieve. All the way around the world. It sounds so exciting (Maybe it will even be a little dangerous at times!! ((Safe. Safe. I must be safe. Excitement's okay but I can't have real danger)). And I am thankful Lord that You saw fit to bestow this opportunity upon me. I know that I am nothing more than a simple religion teacher and how surprised I was when the Semester on the Waves people invited me to join their faculty for the semester (Yes I really was surprised I really don't think I'm good enough (('She'll never amount to much' Daddy says. 'Shhh' says Mommy, thinking (jealously hoping for) the same thing)). I hope I do a good job and that people will find me blameless (What are They thinking! What are They thinking!). Yes I hope I do a good job on this voyage (Oh no. Was it a mistake for me to try to re-unite my family in this way, by having them accompany me on this trip around the world? We will be in the public eye! What if there are incidents! Episodes! Public displays! The gossip could kill me. Have I made a mistake!? ((Help me Jesus, Help me Jesus)).

A noise upstairs. Goodness what is that. It's coming from Adam's bedroom. He certainly is moving around in a peculiar way (Maybe he's touching himself. Maybe he's — ((HARRIET! Red Alert! Don't think about such things!)) My baby boy Adam. Well. He's almost a grown man now (NOWHATAMIGOINGTODOWILL HEUPANDLEAVEME!? ((HELP ME JESUS!)). I hope he's finished packing. He's

7

such a dreamer, such a faraway boy sometimes. And before I know it we are standing in the hallway, getting ready to leave for the airport.

"Ready to go?" Adam asks me.

"Yes dear," I reply (Help me Jesus).

Adam

Fort Wayne, Indiana. Home Sweet Home. Cruising on the By-pass that's clogged with traffic. Wipers slapping
Rapping
Slapping
in the cold February sleet. Glenbrook Mall
I say Glenbrook Mall
Has it all
Your local super-duper
Shopping Mall
Winter Spring
Summer Fall
It has it all
goes sailing on by. It must be ten million sq. ft. It must also be some kind of magnet, judging by all the cars that have been attracted to its parking lot, judging by all the people who scurry about in its confines.

Cruising. Cruising on the By-pass. Mom and me are in the car and life is great—
Yeah life is great
I just can't wait
To go driving in my car
My Twentieth Century Star
We'll all go far
Cause we are free
We can be
Wherever we want to
Whenever we want to
When we're in our cars
Our own private space
Our own private place
the Texacos click on by. I see another Mobil. And there's a Burger Chef. There's a MacDonald's. There's a used car lot. All the square foot frontage is being occupied because we are a solid Mid-Western town and there's no empty space in our city. No

unsightly gaping holes for somebody to fall into. We are filled and thereby fulfilled
(O say can you see!)

The drive to the airport is like the river in my mind. The both of us just keep
rolling along, clicking off the miles and the years, the impressions and the potholes,
the faces and the store-fronts, while the smooth asphalt runs and runs

   runs and runs

      runs like what is inside of me

  —But I am excited about going on this trip—

  —Around the world. My young bones will love every minute of it.

We're Downtown now. Heading south on Clinton. Jefferson and Washington
are standing by. We're looking for the Thruway to the airport but black people line
the streets. There is an angry vacancy in their eyes. I am afraid of them, more afraid
of them than of the white trash that is littering the avenues. I wish we could go faster
and get back to the suburbs where everything is nice:

the lights are green

i am clean

we go sailing through

a computerized route

and we didn't hit any more red lights for a long long time. And we kept looking for
the Baer Field Thruway, the one that's supposed to take you to the airport like
greased lightning, but I'll be damned I never had the patience to find the thing.
So I got off Clinton at Rudisill, right at the Sears store that is kind of old and kind
of fading failing because everyone goes to Glenbrook and Southtown to shop now
. . . because the downtown is overrun by niggers and white trash and *they* are
scary . . .

  —"Where are you going?" my mom asks. "The airport is the other way."

"I know, I know, but we have time, plenty of time, and I want to drive by
Elmhurst."

"What? Why? Your old high school? Well alright, we have the time if you
want to . . ."

  —there's Don Hall's place. Right next to the bowling alley which is turning
into the Rialto, no, no, the Quimby Movie Theatre. The marquee says that Clint
Eastwood is starring in: TRUE MANHOOD. Boy that Eastwood sure is one helluva
guy. I can really identify with him . . . well, I would really *like* to identify with
him . . .

'Beer an' a bottle' he whispers. The bartender hesitates. Eastwood throws him a
withering glance. The beer is served up. Joe Kidd a.k.a. Eastwood a.k.a. the silent
dangerous respected drifter refuses to pay. Cut: To the drifter sitting in a corner; by
himself; drinking

Enter a Mexican. The local tough. Bravado and early death are written all over
him. He spots Eastwood. "Hey look a' wha' da wind blew in amigos," he laughs.

A long pause.

Eastwood i.e. a real man, grimaces.

"You talkin' to me?"

Death is in the air

9

Cause
Machismo's everywhere yeah, yeah, this is what i like, deep down, deep down,
this is what i want SHOOT'EM UP! PROVE YOURSELF! YOU ARE A MAN O
DANGEROUS DRIFTER AND WHILE I WATCH YOU ON THE SCREEN
AND PULL THE TRIGGER I TOO AM A MAN!! for a harmless little while. i
know it's all in fun ". . . there's Elmhurst. You said you wanted to drive by here.
Well?" my mother asks.
    I nod. We had been quiet for a long time.
Elmhust
High School
Alone
Lonely boy
The girls giggle
While I turn
A virginal bright red
-I never went to the football games
-I never smoked much pot
—I never had many friends
—They all thought I was a little Weird
—My teachers thought I was SMART
        and i survived
Elmhurst
High School
        oh hell it's behind me now as the quarry goes flashing by. So what if I had a
miserable high school. At least I didn't peak at seventeen. I have other things to look
forward to. College. Sex. A good job. Fun. Neurosis. Travel. While all the other
adolescent super-stars are twisting bolts in an assembly line, tied to house-payments
and screaming brats and television:
Fort Wayne
So slow so sure
You're always the same
And who needs the heroic?
'Tis better to be stoic
'Tis better to live
In wholesome Fort Wayne
Centered in the plains
        Life begins in Fort Wayne. And Life will end in Fort Wayne. All that is vital is
found in this industrialized city that sits in the middle of the most productive
farmland on earth. Fort Wayne is the balls of the human universe, the stomping
ground of real life and true existence, and if something won't play in Fort Wayne it
won't play anywhere else for very long. Fort Wayne
is
Fort Wayne is
Yes Fort Wayne is
The land of real

The land God has sealed
    —"Can anyone tell me who Lincoln's vice-president was?"
    A pause. Nobody in the class knows. Well that's not true I am a smart guy. I know. But I don't raise my hand.
    "Did *any*one read the assigned material last night?" the U.S. History teacher asks.
    A pause.
    "Do you know who Lincoln's vice-president was, Adam?" the teacher asks me.
    "Andrew Johnson succeeded him, was his second term v.p.," I say. Self-consciously. The center of intellectual attention. A small center, but after all this is Elmhurst High School, Fort Wayne Indiana.
The world is so obvious
People are naturally good
I instinctively trust them
And Evil? Who is he . . .
You see
People sort of like me
And I've not yet seen
The darker side
Not as I ride
A long
With these eighteen year old eyes
That see
Everything as new
Everything as true
Isn't it all true-blue?
    I hit the brakes. It's all the same, driving a car and thinking. I put the right turn signal on since we are entering Baer Field Airport. The plane is waiting for us, waiting to whisk us to Chicago and then to L.A., waiting to whisk us to our grand and glorious trip around the world, and I am excited, and the boat . . . or is it a *ship* . . .that we will be sailing on is called the S.S. Cosmos. The S.S. Cosmos. Well. At least I'll be sailing around on an *important* boat—I mean *ship*. And Mom looks scared as the jet rolls down the run-way and I can hear her praying because she is afraid of flying. . . .

Harriet

    Pressed in my seat I hear the turbines as we roll down the run-way O Help Me Jesus (Jesus Christ I'm afraid of flying ((HELP ME JESUS (((Unnnhhh-Unhhh-Unnhhh))).

Ozzie

"I like to tell it like it is, baby," I replied to the waitress. I had just made a little comment on a certain part of her anatomy and she wanted to know where I was coming from. Well to hell with her. I'll be damned if I leave her a tip. Besides. There's a piece two tables over that's far more interesting. Damn. Just look at her, wearing that skin tight Danskin with the nipples popping through. Nice face too. She has the expression that says she's been around. I'd bet she'd go for it. The cunt. I bet she'd really go for it. And you know what? Even at my age I could still put it to her. Damn right I could. I'm in good shape, haven't lost a step or a hard-on yet, and I don't intend to for some time to come.

The tomato gets up from her table, not so discreetly shakes it, and I almost say something. Then she gives me a look that says I am a little too old and a little too ugly for any of her action and fuck her. She's not as hot as she thinks. If she knew just how I could fuck and just how much money I have she'd come begging for it. The bitch. She really would.

The name's Ozzie. Ozzie Smith. I tell it like it is. Both to myself and to the rest of the sonsabitches who populate this earth. And God? He's a friend of mine. We're both cut from the same piece of cloth, we're both cynics.

The waitress returns with the check. She has the biggest set of boobs that I have ever seen. I pointed it out to her a short time ago and now she no longer likes me. She thinks I'm crude, she with the Dolly Parton face, she with the hoity-toity airs and the dirt underneath her fingernails. Fuck her. I whip out my gold-plated American Express card and when she returns with the charge receipt I pencil in $0.12 where it says tip. I was going to throw in a big fat -0- but I wanted to bring the bill to an even $7.00. Besides. Tipping somebody 12¢ to their face is more humiliating than not tipping them at all.

The waitress looks at the receipt and sees her 12¢ tip. She blushes furiously. But she doesn't have the ovaries to say anything. She walks stiffly away, the fucking cunt. "Anytime baby," I call softly after her, rubbing it in. She pretends like she doesn't hear. I laugh.

"One more, sir?" the bartender asks. I nod and he brings another shot of J.D. on the rocks which I proceed to hammer down. It has a good bite to it, a bite that I appreciate, and I always drink hard liquor. I guess it's because I am a hard man and because everything is a struggle and to drink something like beer or wine would be too easy, too dishonest.

The bartender is a geeky guy. He has a wounded self-conscious look on his face. I wonder if the scumbag has been getting any. He sees me examining him and has to turn away.

I like to examine my fellow human beings. There's nothing more absorbing than perversity and frailty and failure and I like to examine my fellow human beings.

There's no pussy around worth looking at. I wonder if I will have to buy it again tonight. Then I laugh to myself, wondering if maybe Harriet will put out for me. We used to have some very good sex together. She used to really enjoy herself, what with her mind telling her NO! NO! NO! and her body saying YES! YES! YES! until she found the Lord. Then she lost me and there was no more sex.

I hope Jesus satisfies her.

No, no, I don't think Harriet will spread her legs tonight. Well hell, she's probably hornier than a toad, she probably would fuck my lights out if I told her that I *loved* her and that I wanted to get back *together* again and that I thought we could *work* things out. And oh shit. I'm probably horny enough myself to tell her those things.

I wonder if she arranged for us to have separate cabins on this cruise. Ha. I bet *that* presented one helluva problem for her. She's so damn image conscious, she probably wants us to share the same cabin for appearances' sake. On the other hand, after two years of separation, she probably has enough sense to know that our sharing the same small cabin just isn't realistic. That we'd probably end up at each other's throats.

Fuck it. Fuck appearances' sake. I want my own separate cabin goddamn it. Somebody told me that these college cruises are just loaded with pussy, that there's two and a half co-eds for every guy. That means a lot of frustrated snatch running around. Ohhh baby. They might need a fatherly figure like myself to come running to, someone who can give them comfort and advice and a stiff prick. I better tell Harriet that we *have* to have separate cabins. I don't care what she tells everybody. She can say that I fart and snore horrendously. She can say that I tie her to the bedposts and whip her. I don't care. But I want my own cabin.

"Dad?"

I stiffen. Was that voice meant for me? That soft girlish voice? Hell. I turn. My daughter Dawn is standing behind me. Don't know why her being there has so surprised me. After all, this is where my family is supposed to meet, right here in this nameless cocktail lounge in this nameless Hyatt Regency in nameless L.A.

I awkwardly clutch at my drink. My daughter awkwardly stands behind me. We have an awkward relationship. She gives me an awkward peck on the cheek.

Fuck it. You'd think a man could be on more comfortable terms with his own daughter. You'd think—fuck it.

"Hello," I mumble. "You want a drink?"

"A glass of rose," she says.

"A glass of rose," I call to the bartender. "Bring it to the table in that corner," I add. My daughter and I step away from the bar since it somehow just doesn't feel

13

right, sitting at the bar while drinking with my little girl.

"Well how have you been," she begins.

"Fine," I reply.

We keep in touch. Actually we are fairly close. I try to help but I don't know. These days; these goddamn kids. Who can do a thing with them. "And you?"

"School's okay, I—"

"Could use some more money?" I finish. I keep her on a pretty tight budget. She needs discipline.

"No," she blurts back. Resentfully. "No, no, I was just going to say how I'm looking forward to this trip. I needed to get away . . ."

Oh Jesus. Did I really hear that? My god. I don't understand how she can be so neurotic. A *normal* twenty-two year old would be thrilled at the chance to see the world, the whole fucking world, but not my Dawn. She's thinking in terms of 'getting away from it all' and not in terms of what a good opportunity this is for her. 'Getting away from it all.' Hell. As if her life is all that tough. The spoiled brat of a bitch. Shit. I don't know. These women are so *sensitive*—maybe they just *act* that way. It must make it easier to take advantage of other people when you always act like you've been wounded. Like the world owes you something. "You need to get away from it all?" I ask quizzically.

"Never mind," she returns. With bitterness. Like I wouldn't understand. But I understand all too well. She's so self-centered. No wonder she thinks she has so many problems.

I don't know what this girl expects out of Life . . . oh yes I do. Her problem is that she expects way too much out of this world of ours. She hasn't yet learned that a human being's level of unhappiness is directly related to just how much he or she expects out of life. These kids. Spoiled rotten to the core. They've had it too easy. So easy that they just don't know that everyone and everything falls short in the end. So they get unhappy and depressed when things turn out the half-assed way that they always do, the way they always have done and the way they always will. "How's Tony?" I ask her. Tony's her boyfriend. From the way she's moping around they've probably broken up or something.

"Tony?! Uh, well, we're starting to date around . . .I guess . . ." she stumbles.

"Forget about him," I advise, looking her in the eye. Trying to get her to be realistic. "There'll be others."

And she's in a brand new funk. I almost feel like slapping her to bring her out of it. I can't stand her when she gets like this.

We drink quietly.

"What do you think of Mom's big plans?" she finally asks, breaking the silence.

"Your mother's daydreaming. Again," I reply. "I just can't imagine that this trip around the world will bring us back together again."

"She refuses to divorce you."

"The only reasons I'm taking this trip around the world are to spend time with you and Adam and to do some sightseeing," I say. "I mean it. Your mother and I will never work things out. We're never gonna be one big happy family. Never," I add. Hell. And it's not that I don't want things to work out. It's just that it's not going to happen.

"Over here," Dawn calls out, waving. I turn around and see that Harriet and Adam have entered the bar.

I grit my teeth.

Dawn

Well la-de-da. Here we are, all together as we sing our song (Joyfully!). One big happy family. Mom and Dad and Brother and Sis'. It really is funny (But I *do* wish we were on better terms ((Sometimes I get so lonely and afraid that I wish I had a family to turn to, to lean on (((To make decisions for me))).

Mom is throwing hate dart glances at me. She's infuriated with me because I sleep with men and because I don't have the fear of God within me. And because she resents all the freedom I have, freedom that she never had as a girl or even now as an adult (Well fuck her too).

I don't know. It's all so boring. I light a cigarette and Mom turns red with anger and green with envy.

"Dawn?" Adam begins questioningly. "How have you been?" he asks (With his heart of gold. I love him I do). I ponder my reply.

—Oh How, How, How have I been?!

Down, Down, Down in Bloomington!

I say How, How, How have I been?!

Down, Down, Down, in Bloomington!

"Okay (Neither here nor there)," I return. "Excited about the trip?"

My little brother gives me a bug eyed nod. He's so cute. He has nice eyes, all big and brown, with dark full brows running and growing all over them. He has a healthy complexion and a thick head of brown wavy hair (Yes, yes, he certainly is looking good ((But he has looked good before, at other times, and that didn't keep him from getting sick, yes sick, yes Adam has always been sickly, in and out of beds and hospitals (((Brown wavy hair; healthy complexion; dark full brows; Tony? Tony? You know I love to look at your face. Tony? Tony? My honey Tony? Where have you gone, my Sir Galahad, my Mr. Wonderful, my Everything. I want you back, I didn't mean

GOOD-BYE

Never guessed that I would

CRY and cry))).

"How's Tony?" Adam asks. I tense up. Damn him. Why does everybody have

15

to ask me about Tony! It infuriates me, I wish I could put Tony and me and what we had behind me but everybody keeps bringing him up. They ask about him like they are concerned, like they care, like they hope we work things out but shit. What are people really thinking?! I dropped *him*, he didn't leave *me* (But I made a mistake I wish I had him back) and what are people really thinking!? That I'm too ugly and undesirable to keep a man like Tony (Maybe they're right sister!), that I'm too fat, that my complexion is not quite right, that my teeth are a little too green (Well I use tooth polish!).

"Tony and I aren't seeing each other very often," I tell Adam.

"Oh," he says, not knowing what to say. I shrug my shoulders. We leave the matter formless; ambiguous; dramatic contemporary;

"We better get *separate* cabins," Ozzie says emphatically to Harriet.

"Adjoining cabins would be better," Harriet insists.

"Better for what!? For who!? Appearances' sake?" Ozzie demands. They've been together a total of three minutes and they're already fighting; again (I can barely hear them though. It's all so drearily mundane

((ME! ME!

ALL I SEE

ALL I BE

it's all ME!

—Tony where are you

—feeling horny

—Dark heat

—Brilliant fear

—Once upon a time we did it from the rear

(((Lover; school; job; money; phone bill; am I; ugly;))).

"We need—"

"Who says."

"Now Ozzie—"

"Yes *dear*."

"Don't get sarcastic—"

"Be realistic. We're getting separate cabins."

"Adjoining!"

"I don't care what it looks like. Besides. There's going to be all those *girls* on board."

"Ozzie!! Not in front—"

"Of the children? That's a laugh. Everything you've ever even dreamed of doing they've already done."

"Lord!"

"Yes God, where are You?"

"Ozzie. You're being blasphemous—"

And so it goes. People are staring at them. The tone of their voices is rising and I believe I've seen this scene played somewhere before.

Ozzie twists at a napkin. It looks like the big tough ex-cop turned real estate tycoon would like to belt his ex right across the mouth. I think Mom would prob-

ably like to do the same thing (My body flinches, 'Don't hit me mommy I didn't-meanto'—'Clean up your room next time'—'But mommy'—'Don't give me any back talk' Crack! I get it right in the puss. Hard; mean; out of control; crying; my body is; hurting trembling ((Donhitmeplease))
We are a violent family.

Adam

See Mommy yell. See Daddy scream.
They are decorated
In American Obscene
So I will run
Yes I will hide
It's the only way
I'll stay alive
Since speaking up
Means drinking the cup
Of violence, terror,
Bruising aggression
And so I live
In suppressed repression
With myself as my only
Company

Dawn

```
      F
   L     O
   R     M
    S   S
      E
```

Harriet

"Yes God, where are You?" Ozzie sniggers. I wish I could stop up my ears, O Lord, it so hurts me to hear such blasphemy (But these infidels will pay, yes they will pay, won't they, Lord? Are not the evil ones to be sent to Hell and we Your servants to be rewarded with Heaven? Lord? ((The contemptible s.o.b. Contemptuous of me and my beliefs. Like so many others are. And he has the nerve to be contemptuous to my face. The prick. I should tell him what I really think of him (((Use foul language? In front of the children? Sin? Sin? Am I not better than the rest? Oh yes I am, Help me Jesus, Help me Jesus, Help me Jesus))).

"Ozzie. You're being blasphemous," I evenly reply. I am in control of myself. And it is such a strain on me, having the whole family gathered around together for the first time in years. Why this is the way it should be, as we are all united in Christ so should we all be united in this our family and I know the Lord wants to see us together again (Yes I know He does ((Lord: You want to see us together again. Period. (((Sex, I miss Ozzie, I hate being alone, Doesn't look right for my family to be split up))).

And Ozzie. He is being so difficult. And Dawn. My daughter is probably enjoying this, seeing us fight like this. That girl must mend her ways, how she carries on with men (Don't even want to think of it), how she carries herself in public and the language that she uses (Don't even want to admit that she is my daughter). And poor Adam. He is such a fine boy but look at what he has to put up with. He is such a sweet young man, if only he would let the Lord into his heart (He's got to accept You, Lord ((I CAN'T LOSE HIM TOO (((Help me Jesus))).

Lord. The trials that we must overcome before we see You. Lord.

Ozzie

"Shheeiittt," I reply. "I'm not at all blasphemous. God and I are very close."
Harriet looks like her ovaries are set to explode at any second. I have to laugh
just a little bit. "Separate cabins?" I ask, trying to get back to the fuse that ignited
this latest skirmish.

"Whatever you say dear," she replies, giving in because we're in front of Dawn
and Adam. But she'll give me hell about it later. She always puts on an act in public
but when we get behind closed doors I usually have to duck to avoid the flak. And
that's just the way she is. An angel when she's in the front pew, a demon when she's
in the alley.

Dawn and Adam exchange glances. They know that their old lady is ready to
blow up. They know that she'd like to reach across the table and seize me by the
throat. They know that she's putting on an act to fool both the public and herself.
Hell, when Dawn and Adam were younger Harriet used to beat the shit out of them
for no reason at all. She'd always do it in private and she'd really let go.
—I don't like to think about it. It was scary. There were a couple of times I had
pull her off of them.
—Not only was it scary. It was also ugly. Very ugly.

Hell, I go ahead and order another blast of J.D. to try to unwind. I'm trying to
think of something to say to Adam, something like 'How's it going,' but the words
get stuck in my mouth. I guess it's because I don't really know how to talk to him,
guess it's because somewhere along the line I might have failed him—oh fuck it. A
man should never look back if he wants to keep moving ahead. Conscience and
self-recrimination are for losers.

A piece of tuna fish comes swimming on by. It has two arms, two legs, an ass
that doesn't quit and it appears to be unescorted. As in alone. As in available.
Something's in the air and I'm starting to drool but I can feel the disapproval of
Harriet, Adam and Dawn. It's been a while since I was a 'family man' and I'd
forgotten that family men are supposed to keep their pants on when their loved ones
are near. It's not kosher to let it all hang out when the wife and children are around
so I try to channel my aggressive energies in another direction, away from S-E-X. I
think of something safe and wholesome, something where everyone will let it all
hang out on, something called M-O-N-E-Y.

Money. Money, money, money. It's what makes this world of ours go round. I
am a realtor and I deal with alot of people day in and day out and I can honestly tell
you that I still haven't met the man who wouldn't sell his own mother down the
tubes if the price was right. And who can blame human beings for being like this.
Nothing's for free. You have to eat to live, money is the bottom line necessity and
besides: Making money can be fun. Exciting. Thrilling. Nothing gives me more
pleasure than to make a good killing on the open market, nothing makes me happier
than to squeeze that extra 2% out of even the smallest of deals. Making money,

19

drinking blood, fucking a virgin, it's all the same, it's all the kind of thing that makes life worth the living. And I know what I'm talking about. I used to be a cop. I used to taste the pleasure of nailing a punk on the open streets and slapping him around. I used to taste the pleasure of putting a maggot in his garbage can. What I do now as a realtor can be just as enjoyable. Finding that certain builder or developer whose credit is bad and who needs cash in a hurry. Arranging a loan for him and making the bastard put up his house, his wife and his kids, as collateral. Foreclosing on the geek like a merciless demon of vengeance when he can't make the payments on time. Yes, yes, I *like* it, goddamnit, the basest things are the truest things, the lowest desires are the purest desires, and gimme. Gimme, gimme. Then gimme some more motherfucker.

"Ozzie?" Harriet nags.

"What!" I snarl, slamming down the J .D.

Harriet and Ozzie

"Ozzie?" (Fuck him he never listens to me he always ignores me) Nagging again there she goes nagging again.

"What!" Reflex response (Oh Help us Jesus) Some things never change. Like people. They may put on a new shirt or a new skirt but they never change. I thank the Lord for renewing me and giving me a re-birth (But you're still the same old asshole; keep smiling Harriet everyone knows it's fake. Always in front of the children you are so crude. You hypocritical childbeater. I am Forgiven! I am Saved! God *loves* me! (Don't you Lord? ((Say that You do please show me a sign, You *could* be a little more obvious)).

Look at that twat cruising by. Uh-oh Harriet's seen the look I gave. You base ignoble horny sinner. How disgusting, a man your age and with a family oh fuck off why shouldn't I get a little now and then you enjoy sex even more than I do (Help me Jesus) we are separated I can do as I please we are not divorced (Jesus will You not give a re-birth to our family ((JESUS! Listen to ME!)) Here we go again . . .

Dawn

There's nothing else to do (Ho-hum ((Tension))). I might as well read this brochure about the trip:

"The Semester on the Waves program was founded in 1960 by a group of concerned private citizens. They wanted to be able to provide the youth of this country with a chance to both travel and learn at the same time blah-blah-blah-blah-blah-blah-blah and the faculty for these trips around the world are carefully selected. They come from all parts of the United States with impeccable credentials and the highest qualifications. Courses are offered in almost every area of study (Economics, Political Science, Art, History, Marine Biology, Business, Sociology, Psychology, Anthropology, Literature) and the college credits that are received while on the voyage are applicable at almost any universblah-blah-blah- turn the page. Op-cit. Cit-op?

"The S.S. Cosmos is the ship that the program has used on all its voyages for the last ten years. It is owned by Big—Blah—Banana—Blah, a Hong Kong shipping magnate and philanthropist, and blah-blah-blah. Blah-blah-blah the ports that the Spring Voyage will dock in are as follows: Honolulu, Hawaii; Pusan, S. Korea; Keelung, Taiwan; Hong Kong; Singapore; Madras, India; Columbo, Sri Lanka; Port Safaga, Egypt; Alexandria, Egypt; Iraklion, Crete; Pireus, Greece; Malaga, Spain; Casablanca, Morocco, and Baltimore U.S.A. The blah-blah-blah-blah-blah-blah swimming pool, volleyball and basketball court, blah-blah. Blah-blah and prices are quite reasonable. They begin at $4750 for an inside cabin with double occupancy and escalate as follows:

Blah-blah — Blah-Blah
Blah-blah — Blah-Blah
Turn the page.

and I think I've had enough. So this is it. Here I am, standing on one of the outer decks of the S.S. Cosmos as we go sailing out of Laguna Beach. The shore is packed with people saying 'so-long' and 'bye-bye,' and I feel sort of sad (TONY! Where are you I am so empty without you will there be another ((Alone; scared; depressed)).

i feel small. listless. i don't wanna eat. i don't know. its just something. i don't know. there are so many people on board this ship. it already seems small. at least my family is with me. i don't know. it's a curse and a blessing. it's nice to have them to lean onto (But What If I Want To Get Fucked?!).

i feel small. it's a chilly sunset. i drank too much during the bon voyage.
bon voyage.
bon voyage.

Adam

Sometimes I lie awake at night and wonder
As the spirit is torn asunder
And eternally renewed
In Fort Wayne
In agony-ecstasy
In bliss and in pain
I hear the semis
With their late night cry
Rolling down
Sweet 69
Towards Naptown
Interstate 69
And the niggers are far away
And in the suburbs you can play
Softly safely
Yes the people are fat
In outdated hats
But they are real
They can feel
What's really there
Long hairs and short hairs
the night air is warm. Something's stirring. The sheets are cool. I can feel them
touching me. The heat quickly rises. Shhhh. No so loud. I'm not back in Fort Wayne
in my own private room where I can do what I want. I have a roommate now. We
are packed together
Be it fair or foul weather
In this 5' x 7' room
In this inner cabin
This inner doom
This inky black womb
In the bowels of the S.S. Cosmos,
B-deck, cabin no. 735.
And he's not a bad guy
My roomie's . . . a regular guy

. . . but I don't want him to hear me beating off. Masturbating's not masculine. It's kid's stuff (I'll do it later when nobody's around in the bathroom. I'll make it quick, a lightning fast shot into the toilet).

My first night at sea. It's pretty exciting. The great trip has begun. I'm off to see the world.

Had dinner with Mom and Dad and Dawn tonight. Was the first time the family had a meal together in something like two years. The food was plain, hardly a luxury liner feast, but at the prices we're paying who can complain. There was some kind of chicken a'la' Delight and peas and corn and a very plain salad and bread and butter and fruit for dessert . . .

It was pretty quiet while we ate. Nobody knew what
to do or say
do or say
ain't no way
nobody knows
what to do or say
these days
but then again things didn't
go too badly
too madly
there weren't any big fights or anything. Nobody yelled or screamed at each other and that was good because I hate aggression. I hate excessive displays of violent emotion. It's frightening and embarrassing and I like it when everything's nice and quiet. Inside and out. Like a big river making its way through the plains.

Harriet

Dear God:
    O Lord:
    I have finished unpacking and everything is as it should be. I am content, sitting alone in this cabin with You, Being as One with You, and Ozzie is across the hall in his own cabin according to Thy Will (I don't know; appearances; what are people thinking about my husband and me being in different cabins; rather queer ((This whole thing is a bad idea, I am afraid and Help me Jesus (((I must re-unite my family, the nest must protect its integrity, as it falls apart I fall apart))).

    Classes start tomorrow. I will be teaching nine hours. I am looking forward to it and I ask Your Blessing so that I will do well. There are so many different kinds of people on board this ship (Californians. Everywhere I look there are Californians and they are sinful. They do not have the fear of God within them ((The hang loose blonde infidels will be tough to manage, these kids are rich and spoiled and lazy and downright wicked, this will not be like teaching Bible class at St. Francis College (((Fear; Help me Jesus, Fear; Help me Jesus; hope to God there are other Jesus Freaks on board this ship it will be much easier Wherever there are two or more of you gathered in My Name I am there with you))).

Now I lay me down to sleep, Angels watching over me My Lord. Pray the Lord my soul to keep, Angels watching over me . . .

Ozzie

Never did I dream that it would be like this. Never in my wildest dreams . . .

I guess I really am a hick from Ft. Wayne Indiana. I never knew that there was a reality like this one. Shit. I been out in the sticks too long.

There's pussy on my left. There's twat on my right. There's Danskins in front of me and nipples to my rear and I can't take it. This is too much excitement for an old buck like me.

They're all young. They're all tan. They're all tight and lean and supple. And I swear I've never seen anything like it in the cornfields of the Tri-State area. I thought they were joking when they said there were two and one-half co-eds for every male student on board ship but. But. But I sure am glad I insisted on having my own cabin.

The parade of pussy continues on this thing they call the Promenade Deck. All the kiddies are lining up to register for their classes and I love it. Damn straight I love it. Hell. You know, I was reading how they started this Semester on the Waves program so that they could expand educational horizons and make the world a better place and all kinds of shit like that but I tell you: It's a conspiracy. Yes sir. This filling up a luxury liner with girls and having it sail around the world is a male conspiracy. "Two girls for every boy." I think I heard that in a song somewhere long ago.

Uh-oh. I better sit down. Better take 'er easy. The old pulse rate is climbing just a little too high from all of this hormonal activity. Goddamn but look at the way the cheeks of her butt are curling ever so slightly at the base of that thing that she has the nerve to call a pair of shorts—

"Hi Dad," my daughter calls out. Catching me. I think I blushed.

Dawn and Ozzie

"Er, um, hello," mumbling, embarrassed tumble out the words. His cheeks are a bright red (I saw him looking at that girl's butt, foaming at the mouth, thinking of how he wanted to cup those cheeks in his hand and fuck her lights out ((Daddy Daddy is that really you I see looking at a girl like that how can you think such a thing—what!? She's nothing—who me!? How can you think such a thing—come off it
she's nothing
compared to me
please look at me
your little girl
oh shit you caught me staring at that young girl like that yes i did catch you you dirty old man what do you have to say about my cheeks are burning a bright red . . .aww hell . . . I'm a man, Yes a Man! Don't give me that look for Christssakes my little girl for all I know you've been in and out of more beds at your young age than I ever have (((You—failed me. Grow up. Grow up? Well maybe))).

The girl with her ass hanging out of her gym shorts is still standing there. We don't know what to do. Or say. It is awkward. It's true that a hand has been caught in the cookie jar but it was a thief who spotted the crime. I get up hurriedly he leaves thank god all in mutual consent.

"See you later," I said.
"So long," I replied.

Dawn

Dad says good-bye and hurriedly vacates his lounge chair. He leaves a tense wake behind him . . . oh I don't know. I think there was too much accusation in my eyes. So what if he was looking at a young pretty girl. It doesn't mean that he's

Roman Polanski or anything . . . I don't know. I'm jealous; after all he is DADDY; MY DADDY (Watch out little girl your Daddy is desirable your Daddy is male and all the other hungry bitches in this world want him badly and are trying to take him away from you ((You'll be left alone
Alone
ALONE — No!!
keep him make him feel guilty the fucker he belongs to me he's mine make him feel guilty that's the way to CONTROL HIM))

Oh I don't know. This jealousy thing about my Dad and other women I really should try to grow up . . .
Other women
Everywhere there are other women
Pretty women
SEXY YOUNG GIRLS
who WILL spread their legs
(gotta beat'em out—you're too fat—gotta beat'em out—you're too ugly—your teeth are green you'll never get the attention you need ((The fucking cunts; I hate 'em; women can be so mean; so petty; so disgusting; I hate THEM; I, I despise myself)).

The same old scene. College U.S.A. Once again I'm standing in a line. Waiting to sign up for the classes that I will be taking on this trip around the world. It's a cloudy day and the swaying of the ship is making me feel nauseous because this is my first time on the ocean and the line is long and I'm in a bad mood. Shit fuck . But at last it's my turn and I confront the registrar.

"You're a senior?" she asks.

"Yes. I need Marketing 350 for my major," I say (Need. NEED. I need Marketing 350 for my major I *have* to have it. I can't graduate without it ((Subject: Dawn Smith; Age 22; Born and raised in Ft. Wayne Indiana of Upper Middle Class calibre; Attending Indiana University, Bloomington, Indiana.

—Recommended Program for Subject: Completion of Business Degree, Bachelor's Level, with Minor in Fine Arts, as a Business Degree is needed for a job and material comfort and as a Fine Arts Degree is needed for self-esteem, grooviness considerations, etc. etc. Also. Subject must do a fair amount of sleeping around, must attain a certain level of cool, must party aggressively and have a good time, must be an independent sophisticated female, must have serious relationship(s), must lose weight, must know something about foreign films, must know how to roll a joint, must be willing to do cocaine, must fight desire and inclination to have and raise children until a career is started, must, must must ABOVE EVERYTHING ELSE AT ALL COSTS THE SUBJECT (me) *MUST* FOLLOW *THE PROGRAM!!*
((((i
just
wanna be
i just *wanna be*
me
free
me

26

free
can hardly fake it anymore but the program; must; must; THE PROGRAM!!))).
"I think we can squeeze you into the second section," the Registrar announces.
"Since you're a Senior."
"Thanks, I appreciate it," I reply happily. I *needed* Marketing 350.

Harriet

". . . and although the Bible was written by many different authors, Christians everywhere still believe that each section was *divinely* inspired," I say in introduction to my World Religion Class 260. I am giving them an overview of the great spiritual works that mankind has produced.

Somebody yawns (The impolite smart-ass prick. I swear this ship is filled with rich spoiled brats). I pretend not to hear and I continue with my presentation but I sense a lack of interest in my class. It is something I find hard to believe, O Lord, since my religion is my life, since my spiritual convictions are more important to me than the air I breathe, but yes Dear God I feel a certain ambivalence hanging about this room like a deep grey curtain.

I shudder; some of these young people are like the walking dead.

The class ends as it was begun and continued. It just sort of peters out with everyone drifting away in a monotone and I am discouraged. I had expected the S.S. Cosmos to be a beehive of intellectual discovery and academic excitement but now, after just one class, I have my doubts (The spoiled brats from California and Arizona and Boulder, Colorado. Everyone of them born with a silver spoon in their mouth. Everyone of them lazy, arrogant and insufferable. Everyone of them taking this trip around the world for granted, as though it was a right that belonged to them instead of a privilege that had been granted ((They think I'm a hick. I heard them snigger when I told them that I normally taught at St. Francis College in Ft. Wayne Indiana (((Fuck 'em they aren't as clever as they think but Help me Jesus . . . Help-me-Jesus, the rocking of this boat is causing butterflies in my stomach and I think I'm going to throw up. Help me Jesus Where are You Lord!)))

Feeling better as I sit back down to rest for a moment. Thank You God, I am glad You prevented me from throwing up. You are most kind in addition to being Almighty. I am still afflicted with a weakness of spirit though and I think I know what it is. I read to the class from Genesis as a part of my presentation (The Lord God then built up the rib, which he had taken out of the man, into a woman. He brought her to the man . . . "Bone from my bones, flesh from my" . . . why a man leaves his father and mother and is united to his wife and the two become one . . .

27

and Ozzie; he is not here with me. We have been torn apart ((Come together I am lonely my family is shattered: 'Harriet?' 'Yes Mom.' 'Someday you too will have your own family

                                                 I

I

    I've failed (((Why. Why! Why! Why! Jesus! Goddamn You! Sometimes I feel like I've lost everything because of You — "Very well, Harriet. If you wish I the Lord God Almighty personified in Jesus Christ will leave you and you may live alone once again" — No don't leave I, well, Catch-22))).
    I must bring my family closer together. Yes indeed I must.

Adam

    We're running in place. The boat has turned around and is headed back to L.A. away from Hawaii.
    I told everyone but nobody believes me. It almost makes me doubt myself . . . but I believe myself. I saw it.
Whirring, Whirring, Whirring
The helicopter blades
Are Whirring
For a heart attack case
And we're running in place
and we really did turn around and head back towards L.A. because some old person got sick the night we left Laguna Beach. And so we had to turn around
Around and around
For a helicopter to meet the ship
and rush the sick man
Back to the mainland
Where he died
           anyway.
Though someone said
"At least they tried . . ."

    —some kid about my age asked me where i was from. i said ft. wayne. the kid—i think he was from l.a.—laughed; made a big deal out of it; said he'd never met anyone from ft. wayne.
    —i wonder if he really has the nerve to think he's better than me just because i come from ft. wayne. i mean alot of people come from ft wayne. i mean ft. wayne is real, maybe realer than l.a. i mean just where the hell is l.a. huh? where the hell is it? ft. wayne is in the heartland but where is l.a. where?

—that kid was a prick. he may have been from l.a. but he's still a prick.

Knock. Knock. Knock.
I got embarrassed
Cause I was warming up my rocks
Thinkin' about Raquel—Brigitte—Ann Margaret—
But I heard the knock. Knock. Knock.
That spilled my fantasy cup
That caused me to zip her up
        "Adam?" It's my mother's voice. Uh-oh. The last person in the world I want to
see.
Caught in the act
Will she put me on the rack?
        "Dinner," she says, standing in my cabin now. I roll over on my bunk bed to
hide my crotch from her. "I came to see if you wanted to go to dinner."
Girls, Girls, Girls, Girls.
Everywhere on board this ship
There are girls
Oh shit I'm only eighteen I wish I knew
What to do
I'm blowing this chance
For unlimited romance
If only I was older
If only I was bolder
My virginity would be hence
If I but had some experience
And hold: These hot red hots that I carry
Do color me a frustrated grey-blue.
I would and I would — and I would again!
But for the chastity belt that chokes me.
Chastity belt? Aye. Chastity belt! 'Tis
Shameful but true that I, a fighting young
Cock, am kept away from the hens by a
Most mysterious harness, by, by, by,
What!? Conscience!? Inexperience!? Hate!? Fear!?
Neurosis . . . And who has afflicted these
Unseen chains upon me. My Mother, *dear*?
My father? A sister? My spinster aunt!?
A childhood mem'ry vaguely powerful?
God: I would and I would, I would *again*,
If I but could. And yet. I keep the hens
Waiting; I keep myself; waiting; I think;
I think I do it — for nothing; for — O
Heavy youthful load! I would be unleashed!

"Adam? You're picking at your food," my mother nags. "What are you thinking about?"

"Grump, er, ummm," I reply to my mother. And I try to look her in the eye. But right behind her there is the curve of a breast—

"Adam?" she says again.

"What!" I reply, wolfing down a piece of bread. She looks hurt at my tone. I don't know. I try to be patient but sometimes she can be

Such a nag

Such a rag

Mom's a nag-rag

(Shh—it's not nice to think such things)

"How do you think your father is?" Mom begins.

"Fine."

"What about your sister?"

"Fine."

"I—"

"Look Mom. I know you're trying to bring the family together again and I think it's a good thing, but—" I stop. I've said too much.

"But what!?" she demands.

With honesty and sincerity. "Don't push so hard," I advise.

She doesn't take it well. She doesn't like to think of herself as the bossy meddling type. She only does it 'for our own good' she tells me, with a very sour look. I try to focus in on my mother but all I can see is the curve of that breast.

Harriet and Adam

there was a blank sheet of paper
an empty consciousness wafer
you can have all the rest
just give me that curve of breast
        (And I'm bustin' down your
door. look at me—
but all i can see
is a titty
        ((My titty, my titty, it's the only titty you should have eyes for. It suckled
you—I know, I know must you constantly remind—Come here my baby—In guilt I
obey—MOTHERHOOD
we are swimming together

30

through time's endless maze
of changing weather
forever and forever
in our within
in our hidden parts within
we are swimming together

"I want us to be together again," there she goes again. All she can ever think about is family. All she pursues is some ideal that can never be reached . . . and the pursuit of that ideal drives us her loved ones even farther away.

"I know Mom," he replies. My baby Adam. I've never seen a sweeter boy (He won't end up hating me like Dawn and Ozzie. He's too sweet).

"I'm sure your father and I can work things out,"
she's dreaming
living,
a 'seeming'
my poor mommy
my poor screaming mommy
i feel her coming closer
bearing down
she wants me
always around
she is a blanket
smothering me
a blanket that will never
set me free
cause a blanket needs something to cover
if a blanket it will be

"I hope so," (Damn him. He's being evasive. He doesn't really think that Ozzie and I will work things out. Sometimes I wish he'd be more blunt ((Oh no I don't; I can't stand the rain of Truth; Help me Jesus)).

help me jesus
won't ya please us
please help us jesus
cause she-i can't make it (HELP ME JESUS)
she-i will break
why she-i must lean on YOU
to she-i You must be true
cause who will be there
don't think i-he will be there
in a pinch
in the clinch
and everything will be easier; for all concerned
if You will just continue to please her (Me!)

. . . because who else will assume responsibility for her (Jesus I need You!)

". . . and I want to get closer to Dawn."
"I'm sure you will Mom."

Ozzie

"I'm from Dallas," the fellow drawls. He has a fat face with big fleshy jowls. Red blistering skin is plastered all about his puckered nose. He is a Texan and he is proud of it. "My Daddy made a little money in oil and we done right well with it ever since," he brags. "And what is your name, suh?"

"Smith. Ozzie Smith. Ft. Wayne Indiana. I own a real estate agency. We turned over fifteen million dollars worth of property last year."

"Fifteen million? I say fifteen million? I say not a baaaddd piece of change, suh. I say we are involved in a little real estate ourselves. Jed Hendricks is the name and we are building a five hundred unit condominium development in Ft. Worth. I say perhaaps you could give me a little advice on how to market this property."

"Is it dreg?" I demand, eye-balling the Texan.

"Low-income housing but of the finest quality I might add."

"No one has ever gone bankrupt by underestimating the public's taste," I return and I map out a little promo campaign for the Texan. He is impressed. Dollar signs light up both of his eyes and maybe we will do some business. The thought of the incredible amount of money I might make off of this Texan gives me a warm feeling all over. Another killing!

"I say what do you think of this trip around the world?" Jed asks me when we finish our discussion on how to rape the public while getting thanked for it.

"Wonderful idea," I reply.

"Your missus is a teacher on this cruise is she not?" he questions.

"Yes."

"Fine lady, fine lady. I must say you two are some of the highest quality people that we have in the Adult part of the ship."

"Why thank you," I return, wondering how much butt sucking will be required on my part to sell his condominiums for him.

"Yes, yes, it's an interesting little deal they have here," the Texan continues. He is one of the adults that accidentally heard about the trip and decided to shell out his five grand to take the cruise. The program has about thirty people like him on board ship, older folks who are not in college but who wanted to see the world for the bargain price of five g's.

The program takes on such people because it wants the money. The program is like everything and everyone else in this world of ours. "I say there are quite a few young fillies on board this ship," the Texan drawls, giving me a wink. "I say I wish I was a little younger," he rambles on. "I say I wish my wife was not on this trip with me."

"I saaayyy yes suh," I reply, mimicking his drawl, as a young co-ed goes prancing by. We laugh.

"Ohhh. Ummhhhh. Ummmm," she moans. I see stars exploding. This is what living is all about.

I have never picked an easier cherry. Well hell, she certainly isn't any cherry, but who the hell cares.

I can't believe how lucky I am. I can't believe how easy this was. She was just sitting there in a lounge, a little tight after a few drinks, and nice guy that I am I asked her if something was wrong. If I could help.

After all, I am the fatherly type.

"I miss my boyfriend," she burst out.

"Let's go talk about it in my cabin," I offer sympathetically. And did I ever comfort her. The horny little bitch. I don't think she's a day over nineteen.

It was easy. I held her when she started crying. I held her tighter. I stroked her thighs. Oh man was it good. She protested for a while but that made it even better and once I got her shorts off she saw that it was hopeless and she gave in. Oh man was it good. I'm riding her like I used to do it twenty years ago—

The cabin door creaks open. Harriet walks in. Oh shit. Shiieettt. Harriet takes one look and storms out. The co-ed freaks. She throws on her panties and shorts and runs away. And there I am, semen dripping off my rod, the cabin door wide open and a hellacious grin upon my face.

Shiieettt. It was a little premature but it was still worth it.

And Harriet? Shieettt.

Harriet

Lord forgive Ozzie for his grievous transgression (You prick; you motherfucking prick; in bed with some slut of a girl the second night we are at sea. No wonder you wanted your own cabin you asshole ((And who was taking advantage of who in that cozy little scene I know she's a drunken little slut and she got what's coming to her but did you have to push her just a little (((You motherfucking prick; ungrateful sonuvabitch; this is all the thanks I get you selfish bastard always thinking of yourself, never me or the children, the family, the FAMILY))). Lord forgive Ozzie. Though he is a sinner he needs Your Help as much as I

33

Your Righteous Servant do (You prick ((You motherfucking prick I'll get you for this you'll pay I'll find a way to make you feel guilty someway (((Help me Jesus, the motherfucking prick, and I am righteous))).

Dawn

A new day. Or so it seems. At least I think so. But who can tell. Everything is so dark. There's no natural light in this inner cabin (Dark; dark; my body warm; alone ((I need; someone; to touch; to touch)).

I snap on a cold fluorescent light. I crawl out of the sack and stare at myself in a mirror (Ugly; fat ass; dried; crooked nose. And the weight,
the weight
I hate
having so much weight
cause you know
you just don't rate
lonely nausea's your fate
when you have too much weight
((And the boys won't like you and they are everything)).

My roommate's already up and at 'em. There's no way she'd be caught in bed at this ten o'clock hour (Dragging
Ragging
Dragging
i feel like i'm paralyzed. had a baby was a honey of a guy he left me after I told him to get out. don't know why but today i'm ragging
dragging
ragging
again). I don't know. It just goes on and on. I never find shelter, there is no relief (When I was a little girl all young and starry-eyed I could hardly wait to grow up. There would be Prince Charming and there would be continual fireworks. But now I don't know ((Fuck me life fuck me do it to me I wanna just lay back and have it done to me all of it it's so much easier that way (((
))).

My roommate's talking about me behind my back. That's just the way she is. And I think this girl that I share this tiny cabin with is my friend, we spend alot of time talking together and sharing things (But she's talking behind my back. She doesn't like me today, she's changed her mind about our friendship ((Fuck her. She'll come around. The girl is crazy; weak; neurotic. She needs me more than I need her,

34

she'll see. Today she's riding on top because her hormones are giving her a boost but tomorrow she'll be down. She'll need me. And I'll make her pay (((A friend; need a friend; feeling lonely; must find another lonely female; to talk to))).

Oh hell. Just another day. And I know I'm taking a trip around the world and I know I should be excited—but it's just another day (And the American Dream? And the excitement of being young and alive? ((Heavy; feeling heavy. Slow. Dragging. Heavvvy))).

Adam

"They're just begging for it," the ship's doctor tells
me
knowledgeably.
the girls
those choice little pearls
want it bad
are horny mad
and I *should* be getting fucked. Yessir.
SEX! SEX! SEX!
has thrown its obsessive hex
all around
defenseless me
me and my aching
cherry
—Shhh! I didn't say that. Don't try to imply anything about my masculinity. After all I'm only 18 and a fellow needs a little time to sort things out . . .

Hell who cares. I pop open a beer that someone has offered me. And I am thrilled. I mean here I am, drinking a beer in the middle of the afternoon, having a good time like I've never had a good time before, and golly. Golly gee. Can you beat that? I'm growing up and it's great and I love it.

I never before got to drink a beer in the middle of the day. Hell I seldom get to drink beer at all. Yet here I am
Feeling my oats
Wearing
This grown-up coat
Gaining self-respect
Pursuing my quest
To be something grand

To be known to all
  as a man . . .
  Yessir. Life is great. The clear blue sky. The pounding of the waves. The rise
and fall of the ship as she plows on. This vitality in my bones. Far-off lands waiting
to be explored and conquered. Yessir life is great and I better go for it. I better grab
some gusto. You only go round once in life and yeah, I had another Schlitz. And it
was my *second* one *in* the *afternoon.*

Ozzie

  ". . . and we will see, on this trip, that an over-bearing American presence will
no longer be tolerated in many parts of the world," some geeky poli sci teacher
pontificates. "The days of colonialism and imperialism are coming to an end as the
earth's peoples become more and more educated—"
  —"Bullshit," I whisper. I can't believe the nonsense this self appointed know-
it-all is telling these kids. I'm sitting in on one of his classes because I got bored just
laying around out on Promenade Deck and Bullshit. Bullshit, Bullshit, Bullshit.
  "Did somebody say something?" the bespectacled whimp demands. Wondering
who had the balls to call him out.
  "It was me—I don't quite agree with some of the things you've said," I replied,
eyeballing him. Everybody in the room turns to look at me.
  "You're welcome to express your opinions," the fellow smoothly returns. He
is about thirty, probably owns a Ph.D. from the Ivy League. There is a certain
emotionalism in his face that tells me he's a radical from the 60's. I don't think he
ever had the balls to take it to the streets though and now he is a privileged part of
the system that he so angrily repudiates. Fuck him. "I like it when you members
from the adult community speak up," the boy continues, twisting the word 'adult'
ever so slightly. "It's refreshing to get a non-student, non-academic opinion now and
then—"
  "Believe it or not I pulled a Masters in Sociology," I interrupted.
  "I'm sorry I didn't mean to imply anything—"
  "Before I decided it was so much bullshit," I smoothly continued, implying
something, "and I think you got it all wrong. For the last half-hour I've heard you
tear apart U.S. foreign policy in a typical left-wing way. To hear you tell it we
Americans are the biggest sonsabitches who ever walked the earth, guilty of every-
thing and with a need to apologize to everybody, and I say that's all a pile of crap."
  "At least you're getting to the point—'
  "Somebody's got to tell it like it is," I ramble on, trying to get up a full head of

steam. "I don't agree with this loser's philosophy that's in vogue these days, the one that you preach, by the way. I was brought up to be a winner and I think we ought to pursue a winning foreign policy. To hell with caving in to each and every demand that any two bit hood has the nerve to make. I say send in the Marines before you send in Foreign Aid."

"That type of attitude has produced the tinderbox world that we now live in," the boy interrupts, getting a little hot.

"Wrong, wrong, wrong," I shoot back. "The reason we're having so much trouble these days is that we've lost people's *respect*. People wouldn't try to push us around if they knew we'd make 'em pay for it," I say, giving him a lesson in basic human nature.

"We've tried before to impose our will on other people by using force and it just hasn't worked. In Vietnam—"

"We never should have lost that war."

"The Vietnam problem—"

"The only reason Vietnam is a problem is because we lost it," I snap. "If we had won that war of yesterday you wouldn't hear the people of today calling it a 'dilemma,' a 'problem'."

"There was no way we were going to win in Vietnam—"

"That's just the kind of 'loser's' attitude that I'm talking about," I say, taking the offensive. "We could have won that war if the politicians had had the nerve to take it straight to Hanoi. Hell I don't know, maybe we should have stayed home in the first place, but once we were in it we never should have lost it—"

"The world of today," the boy blurts out, his voice shaking, "is simply too complex to be dealt with your, your, your nineteenth century reactionism, your Wild-West approach to problem solving—"

"I'm from Ft. Wayne Indiana and proud of it," I snap. "If you want to step outside I'll show you just where it is I come from—"

And so it went. I guess I got a little too aggressive there at the end but nobody got hurt. And all the kids got quite a bit of entertainment out of it but hell. Fuck 'em. Fuck all of 'em. I meant what I said. Even if it fell on ambivalent gutless ears.

There's that pain again. A sharp tingling in my left shoulder.—
—It's nothing. I'm in great shape. Never felt better.

Oh shit. Here come Harriet. Haven't seen her since she caught me last night, porking that luscious young thing . . .
Oh shit.

Ozzie and Harriet

"Hello Harriet."

Silence (You loathsome prick).

Finally. "Good afternoon Ozzie." Oh that's it. We are so high and mighty today. We are so much better than the rest of the scum that decorates this dusty earth (Asshole; fucking a young girl like that ((I am going to make you pay for it, I'll use every trick in the book so Help me God—and You too Jesus ((('Men!' 'Yes Mother?' 'They hold the world in their grubby little hands A woman has to have one at all costs To be exclusively her own Don't ask me why that's the way it is but you listen to your mother and *remember* what I said'))).

"Nice day." We look each other over. There is love and hate, revenge and vengeance . . .

'Nice day.' It's simple. A complete thought harmless yet true. But whose is it. Is it his? Is it hers? Is it ours? Is it divinely inspired? Is it a product of Consciousness—with a capital C? Is it Humanity communicating? Is it an easy way to continue a conversation? Is it an easy way to avoid the naked truth? Is it?

Why did you do it

Oh Hell I was only

I know, I know, just another piece of ass but you could have thought of the children

Oh shit the children are grown they could care less about their old man getting a little

What about me

I don't owe you a thing

You prick

You're the one who split us apart

If you would only accept Him

Forget the whole thing

I can't forget

What you need is a good lay

Give it to me (No! No! yes! yes! you are my husband but there must be more than physical need there must be love

Shit you need a good lay

You cynical sickly sonuvabitch you think Sex and Power and Money is all there is

You said it

There is righteousness

Remember when

There were some good times

Your body next to mine

How can I forget

Still
Still Still
Yet (You loathsome prick)
"Yes it is a nice day," nodding good-bye.

Harriet

Direction. Dear God I need direction. A sense of purpose. Why I don't know if being on this ship has anything to do with it but I feel as though I am drifting . . . . floundering . . . .
. . . . and my husband has sinned most grievously. Taking advantage of that poor young girl (Oh shit. Even at his age Ozzie is still desirable. He's wealthy too and some pretty young thing with a fresh face and a willing body could come right along and pick him off. Where would I be then . . . deep black fear ((Help me Jesus. Am I getting old!?—Of course you are. Am I losing my desirability?!—Just look in the mirror sister—Younger women: Always prettier and always sexier than their mothers and older sisters. And Nature? He's a male chauvinist pig. He has conspired with men to permit the male of the species to retain their desirability as they grow older while we women wilt and sag: Victims of Time (((Alone. ALONE! I am doomed to age by myself—Help me Jesus Help me Jesus, HELP ME JESUS YOU PROMISED TO RESTORE OZZIE TO ME AS A REWARD FOR MY RIGHTEOUSNESS— If you wish I your Shepherd will leave you—NO!NO!NOT THAT! NOTTHAT!!))).
Dear God: Please give me the strength to carry on. I am feeling weak, perhaps it is the travelling that is wearing on me, but with Your Goodness I will carry on. I, I, I do need a sense of direction though, I do not feel my family coming together on this trip as I had hoped, and Lord Help Us. Let us stand as a Christian family before Your altar, let us (That fucking prick Ozzie).
Dinner. I will gather us together for lunch. It has been so long since my family has broken bread together and I just know that this is the first step we his servants should take.

Ozzie, Harriet, Dawn
and Adam

Mother said grace. It was a farce (Help us Jesus I am sincere, Bless our family and pull us closer together) but mother said grace.

Sis kept the conversation moving for a while by telling everyone about her classes. It was light easy, avoided anything delicate or sensitive, and we all listened to it. Father was quite jovial. Word of his conquest had spread throughout the ship and he was feeling like a young stud. He ate heartily and told several jokes that were very good. Everyone laughed except for Mother but even she managed a smile.

Baby Brother was the glue that held us all together. He is the only one in the family who is on good terms with everybody else. Whenever War breaks out he is the only one who can travel between the opposing camps unharmed. Everyone knows that he has such a good heart. And me? I am the Smith Family. Welcome to our Happy Home.

I am the basic unit of existence. I bring human beings into the world and I develop them. I am a man and a woman, making and raising babies, and you can see me in your own home town.

I am Ozzie and Harriet. I am Dawn and Adam. I am all of them together in a very fundamental way.

Am I real? Do I have my own independent existence? I don't know. I don't have the answers to any of these questions.

But don't sit there looking so smug. Don't worry about who I might be. Just go ahead and try to find out who you yourself are. Are *you* real? Do *you* have your own independent existence? Are *you* a figment of something else's imagination?

What is Personality?

Time is Memory. Memory is Human. We are slaves to ourselves.

"Pass the gravy," Ozzie demands. I have the night shift and I gotta get going. I hope the niggers are quiet tonight. I don't like patrolling Downtown Ft. Wayne on a hot August night. But when you're a cop—fuck it you're a cop.

"Yes Dad," Adam replies excitedly.

spilling
it's so thrilling
i spilled the gravy
i made some waves(y)
dad gets mad
he's so big and bad
but mommy protects me

never rejects me
—though she HITS me now and then

"I'm going to the movies tonight," Dawn announces. And then I can smoke some pot. Mom nods like the silly thing she is. She doesn't know what kids are up to these days. But the old man (Daddy don't be angry with me—Why don't you pay more attention to ME!) knows what we do at the drive-ins (I wish he'd make me stay at home tonight. Sometimes; I; I? Yes I don't like what I do at the drive-ins ((Daddy! Daddy! I'm here LOOK AT ME)).

"Fine dear," Harriet says, giving the okay. She's only thirteen. I don't know. Maybe I should exercise closer supervision over Dawn (she doesn't even know how to get into real trouble yet ((Does she?!))

Ozzie looks mad. Well I (Maybe we should have made love earlier but with the kids around (('Never in front of the children' Mother silently told me)).

"Time to get to work," Ozzie says slurping down some coffee. A big event. Our breadwinner is going out to do battle and bring home the bacon. We all watch him. Adam runs over to give his hero a hug. Harriet gives her husband and honey an affectionate smooch. Dawn keeps her nose in her pudding, angry that Father has been ignoring her lately. And the big tough cop walks out the door while everyone does his or her best to keep on playing the roles that support me.

And how I am doing. Oh on the surface very well but Ozzie is getting restless now that everybody is talking about SEX. And Harriet is having trouble coping and she's taken to reading the Bible again, using it as a source of comfort and escape just like her fundamentalist parents did, and Ozzie can't stand Religion. Could be big trouble on the horizon and Dawn will not be an easy teen-ager to handle. She is now a young rebel and there is all kinds of trouble she can find in this '69-'70 climate. And Adam will just go along with it all and my foundations are c . . . r . . . u . . . m . . . b . . . l . . . i . . . n . . . g . . .

. . . and here I am at another dinner. And they are trying to pump some new life into me. Harriet is the one who is really trying to push me into the forefront, who is trying to put meaning into 'The Smith Family' again, but I think that they'd all like to see me healthy and whole. But who cares. I mean I'm always there, kicking around in the backwaters of their minds, even if there is a divorce or a separation or a what have you.

I am the Smith Family. That's who I am I say. And I guess I'll never die. I'll just fade away into other people's lives and then they'll put new names on me and then and then and then again and again . . .

"Ketchup, please," Adam demands. We all look at him.

I gave him the ketchup; something fierce in the air between Mom and Dad; those two have been at each other's throats since I can remember (You loathsome prick ((I'll get you for fucking that girl. With His Help I'll get you)). Self righteous hypocrite. So I got myself a little piece of ass. And why not. A man's entitled to ketchup
red gooey
ketchup

41

for my fries
keeps me alive
heads up
thank god for
ketchup
it can cover
everything
it will make your taste buds
truly sing
ketchup!
 . . . there's so many pretty girls on board this ship (So much competition!). I
feel (Wanna be home; where is Tony; my old beau; if I could;
i really would
feel his naked body next to mine
 "Perhaps we should have an outing together in Hawaii," Harriet hopefully
suggests . . . No, No, *Mother* hopefully suggests.
 Silence.
 Gloom.
 Unenthusiastic response.
 Oh shit she should know by now that everyone
wants to do their own thing. Her trying to make
us one big happy family together is:
a nice idea
a nice idea
but not indicative
of very clear
thinking
but Mom has been hurt
so much
always been left
in the clutch
i love her
(and my love has an element of guilt)
Hell Yes I freely Admit it
 . . . shiieettt. The kids don't want to be with us old fogies when we're in port.
She's being ridiculous again; no, no, she's being *pushy* again, the dictatorial bitch—
 —Tony? (Maybe I should sleep with that guy on C deck. He seems awfully
nice—he's cute as hell ((Don't do it; I don't know; it might make me feel better
about myself)).
 'Maybe not,' the rest of the group silently obviously replies to Harriet's pro-
posed outing.
 "Well I think a picnic would be nice," Mother adds for the record.
 I smile.

Ozzie and Dawn

I am a relationship between this Father and that Daughter. I am currently absorbed by Father's sleeping with a co-ed who is younger than Daughter.

Dawn is jealous; frustrated; angry; resentful; hurt; almost willing to forgive; trying to accept Ozzie, her Father, as a sexual being in his own right.

Ozzie is embarrassed; ashamed; telling himself that he had every right; anxious that his little girl come around.

I am the looks they give each other over the dinner table. I am the unspoken things they keep to themselves. I am their love and desire for each other. I am the hidden quirks that haunt them when the other is not around. I am changing . . . while staying the same . . .

After dinner it was tense; thick; hard to breathe.

Perspective didn't seem to make any difference. We were both uptight. The thing, the thing, the SEX was bigger than both of us. Bigger than Personality. Bigger than Thought. As big as Consciousness.

So for now we just let the whole thing slide. We avoided a 'confrontation.' For how long we just don't know though.

Sitting in our cabins on opposite sides of the ship we are still thinking of each other. Because
he—I did something. Because
you are a sonuvabitch
Chorus:
you are a sonuvabitch
oh I don't know maybe
you are entitled to get a
little now and then
    —You're damn right I am little girl
    —but you're still (a sonuvabitch. you belong to me)
    —You sleep around alot more than I do little girl

Adam

I gotta get laid. I mean really. I gotta get laid.
to show i'm a stud
not gay
i gotta get
laid
period.
   . . . and the beers I had in the afternoon are getting to me. Hiccup. Burp. Hiccup. I feel SICK. Like I want to, wanna, like I wanna THROW UP. And puke down into some toilet bowl. I mean
   —it hasn't been a bad trip around the world so far. I'm feeling more GROWN-UP
everyday
as i prepare
TO THROW UP
   Bleeccchh. . .

Harriet

It is 3 o'clock in the morning. I can't close my eyes (Tense). I am thinking . . . of my life (As the sheets touch me, oh touch me again). I have had a husband, I have made babies (So why do I feel so empty), I have done my best to serve You (God Where Are You? I FEEL SO alone. I need ((Damn You God I Need! Are You Listening!? (((You Omnipotent Motherfucker))).

Dear God: (And just where has my faith gotten me. What has it accomplished. I have renounced sin. I have renounced sex. I have renounced *pleasure* and for *what*!? A reward in the hereafter? A finer place in heaven? A gold star from The Man Himself? And what if when we die we just *die*. Think of all the things (SEX!) I have missed out on just because of being faithful to You ((It's so confusing. It has always been confusing, and ever so frightening, but You My Lord have given me dignity, purpose and direction. You gave me the Way when I was afraid and lost (((I want a cigarette. I want a drink. I want to laugh. I want to sleep with a stranger and I want))).

It is 3:30 in the morning. I still can't close my eyes. God?

Dawn

"Come on I'll show you the engine room," he says, leading me down a flight of stairs.

I follow.

"This is the engine room," he yells, above the racket of the boilers. "Let's climb up this ladder to the smokestack."

I climb.

"Let's go back to my cabin," he invites after his late night tour is over.

I go.

"Would you like a drink," he offers a bit nervously.

I drink.

"Dawn," he whispers, breathing in my ear, nibbling on my lips.

I pucker.

"Unnhhh. Unnhhh. Unnhhh," he groans, on top of me, thrashing about spasmodically.

I sleep.

Ozzie

"You cover the front. I'll circle around from the rear," I told Meyers. I pulled the Magnum out of its holster.

It was a hot muggy night in July. It was so humid that your clothes stuck to you like wet rags. My footsteps echoed like firecrackers in a cave. I pulled off my shoes and kept on moving.

The smell of raw garbage was everywhere. It was pungent; deep; powerful. I moved so quietly that I surprised a tomcat. He shrieked. I nearly pulled the trigger. My hands were moist.

Getting closer now. I bit my lip. Time to put this one away. The fluorescent street lights painted their ghostly picture and I waited. Something moved.

"Freeze," I snarled, dropping into a crouch. There was an orange flame and a deep report and the sound of something whistling but I wasn't listening. I let go with the Magnum once; twice; a third time and a fourth and the shadow crumpled. I felt a sweet tingling.

That was how I used to set 'em down when I was younger, on the force, when I was younger than that, fighting in Korea. And I'm as sharp as ever—damn that pain in the shoulder. It keeps waking me up in the middle of the night.

Adam

New Morning:
And I'm *ALIVE!*

and I am content. The night is gone. The fear and anxiety have been melted away. The demons are cast down, Life is again a choir that never stops singing, and the best things? They carry no price.

Why we are who we are. No one needs to be anything but himself. And the need for justification? He is the son of Doubt and we have murdered that foul monster.

New Morning
Such a New Morning!
And the girls are by the swimming pool
Slyly swaying with bikinied cool
As a painted toe is daintily raised
Male heartbeats beat-Beat! Beat! Ablaze!
Causing me to be enchanted
By what the narrow-weary-minded take as granted
By the show of Love in all his splendor
His matchless thrilling brilliant splendor
That beguiles this young and eager fool
Who bug-eyed sits at the swimming pool
Watching . . . Hoping . . . DREAMING . . .

"Morning Adam," Ozzie says, coming up to greet me

Adam and Ozzie

"Hi Dad." Friendly. Yet perfunctorily (Somewhat resentfully?)

We are Father and Son. We are so-so close. Father left home several years ago. The Son understood. But still . . .

Bathing beauties are everywhere. They litter the decks of the S.S. Cosmos like sand on a California beach. There is wantonness. Fresh young wantonness. Co-ed style.

And the Father is in his twi-light.

And the son is just beginning.

Sex? Perhaps they are both pre-occupied with it. Perhaps everyone is pre-occupied with it.

The girls. Everywhere the girls. Moving about on Faulknerian levers, those levers that move the world. Everything and everyone is sacrificed to those levers. The Father. The Son. The Father and the Son together. And it all begins and ends with those levers because they are the ultimate object of Desire, of Lust, of Motion and Activity, of—

I bet the kid hasn't popped his cherry yet. Oh he's good enough looking, with his big brown eyes and that wavy hair, but he's a little shy. Just a little. And a man has to be aggressive with the ladies, has to make the first move and show them that he can take care of himself—

Daddy

Da-da-Daddy

Dad.

So big and strong

So big and mad

My Dad.

A real he-man

—Someone to look up to

—Someone to live up to

—Someone, someone, and yes my Dad is the most special and most powerful person on this planet, the most everything . . . at least he used to *seem* that way when I was a child. Now that I'm grown up . . . I don't know . . . I look at Dad

a little more realistically

Feasiblistically

Categorically

    speaking

My Dad's

    not all that bad

BUT HE IS HUMAN

although deep down i sometimes like to think

                that he is kinda like god

—My boy's not a bad kid. A little different but he's smart. Got alot of brains. I bet he goes far someday. But he's funny to watch these days. Jumping out of his pants the way that he is.

"Lotta girls out today," Adam remarks. Yes, yes, pussy is everywhere, hot smoking pussy, oh by the way I heard you scored last night and I'm awful excited about it and more than a little jealous though you shouldn't have done that to Mom

A man's a man and besides she's an old bitch

Don't *say* that about *my mother*—though I sometimes think the same way

Hell it's nothing it was just a one-nighter

I . . . I AM

I know, I know, don't get excited. Don't mistake me for your Mother. You can be around me

Sure I know. I know I can be around you. The fact is you don't give a good goddamn do you. Always thinking about yourself. Always remembering just who No. 1 is. You are a perfidious s.o.b.

A what

i don't care

everyone fightin'

for their share

when all i wanna be

is peaceful easy free

And the Father and the Son were joined by the Daughter. And though it was comfortable the complexion was slightly changed. For she was a *girl*!! And though they maybe thought she was inferior, and though they maybe tried to ignore her, well: She did change the complexion of things.

Adam and Ozzie and Dawn

Nerves. A bad case of

N-E-E-R-R-R-V-V-E-S

Don't know why I feel like I wanna cryin' die

and i am the Daughter. i am small today. The Father and the Son are in very high spirits, they are as high as an erected ten inch prick and as intimidating as the Washington Monument

—Why look who's here

—It's our Family member, our beloved sister and daughter, our Dawn

—Uh-oh. The boys have been looking at all the pussy around the pool. Caught red handed. You think our possessive related female here is angry about it

—Hell who cares I don't

—Dawn are you alright you're looking rather pale and the Son is concerned

48

—Hell she's a baby always down in the dumps as if it's all so tough on her she
should straighten up and be like us
Will we ever be
One big happy
Family?

The Father did not understand the Daughter. Though he loved her he did.
Occasionally the Son got fed up with the Daughter. She was so neurotic. And the
Daughter was fed up with everything and unhappy with herself and unhappy with
the world.

And the three of them formed a triangle of little significance. Because the most
important corner was not there, the one that would have made them a square.
-F-
  -R-
    -A-
      G-
        -M-
          -E-
            -N-
              -T-
                -E-
                  -D-
they were:
    engulfed by alienation
    swamped by the vacuum
    unable to
    . . . but they all wanted to laugh, they really did, they really did.

"Well hi there," Harriet exclaimed, spotting the three of them together. And
Harriet wanted to be: 'A Mother: With Her Happy Family,' so she hurried on over
in a maternal state, so maternal that not once did she think (Help me Jesus!).

Adam and Ozzie and Dawn and Harriet

Is there no Beauty?
Is there only tawdry SEX!?
Or is *SEX* beautiful, is it we who need to re-arrange our eyes instead of trying to
make our hands re-arrange the world?

The Family was now One. Well sort of. I mean we were together, all of us
standing there, but perhaps we stood apart.

Beauty
The idealistic cutie
That the Son can see
But never quite reach
From the swamp
Of Sexuality
But perhaps he should
Himself accept
As is
And not reject
Truth for Fantasy
Just because Fantasy
Seems better . . .

And God was with us I just know He was. I just know he wants us to be a *Christian* family

Look at the piece of young firm butt go waddling on by (Daddy! Ozzie! We your females see you seeing other females ((You degenerate lustful dirty old cocksucker. Take care of *us, Your Girls*, Love and respect what you already have))

Many are the times we wish we were at Peace

Oh many are the times we wish we were at Peace!!!

—There's that pain again. A fiber of agony running through my shoulder. Then down into my chest. As I stand here with what you would call my family. Ah fuck it. It's nothing (Oh yeah? Oh Yeah!? Listen here Ozzie Smith. That pain in the shoulder, that pain in the chest, it's bad news my man. Face up to it.

TIME IS RUNNING OUT MOTHERFUCKER
the days are getting shorter
your bones a little colder
and even you you s.o.b.
must know and see
that Death has
its own kind of poetry

"Unnhhh," Ozzie mumbled, stiffening. We turned to see what was wrong with the Father.

"I'm fine nothing," he growled.

But he had lost a little color. And there was something in his eyes, something we'd never seen before. We all noticed it and we are all afraid of it because what we saw in his eyes was FEAR. With a capital F. And FEAR is the one thing that everybody notices because that's when you're most alive. When you're afraid. And Ozzie was afraid and it was a new experience. For everybody.

"I'm fine don't worry leave me alone," he growled again.

I grew up in the dustbowl. We didn't have a fucking thing. It was the Depression and it was a hard time to be alive . . .

So the boy grew up a hard man. He asked for little and gave little. He was tough on everyone and everything and when he became the Father he made it hard on the Family. The Smith Family that is. I am the Smith Family

50

"Dear are you sure you're alright?" Harriet asked. Concerned.

"Fine, fine."

"How do you like your classes?" Adam asked Dawn.

"Boring." —Do they know about last night? With that boy? I wasn't very discreet (Shame; Embarrassment; Confusion)

The ocean breeze is strong. The ocean breeze is fresh. For a moment I believe that I have a chance. For a moment I believe that nausea and alienation, that fear and confusion, that it all can be swept away. That a re-birth is possible. It would be like taking a long hot shower after a hard grimy day when everything is sticky and small and mean.

And i am swaying
With the ship
My mind playing
With the swells and rips
Of the ocean

Hard. Ashes to ashes, dust to dust. Nobody gives you a fucking thing. You gotta take it.

My family together (I love it maybe we could work things out and then everything would be nice ((And then I would have a show-home of a family, my very own show-home family (((But these assholes have to do exactly as I tell them, oh righteous me, oh with Your Help Dear Lord I shall benevolently manipulate them))).

tony? your'se so far away. and i need (because i bleed because i am a young woman and i am bleeding).

We speak but who can hear us in the deafening vacuum.

Adam

'SIN!!!
try it you'll like it
And though it seems like a crime
That very first time
It'll get easier
As you grow sleazier'

. . . she says indirectly. She is married, over-weight and not very pretty. She has me in her cabin but I don't know how she got me here.

"POT!!" she demands, pulling out a pipe. I'm scared. Drugs are *not* allowed on board the S.S. Cosmos, they throw you off the ship at the nearest port if they catch you with them. And *they*, the *Gestapo*, are everywhere, at all times. And I've never really smoked pot and I'm freaking out about it.

I take a puff. And another. After all I'm a man. I have to at least *pretend* that I know how to handle myself.

51

"You're so cute," she says,
Patting me on the thigh
And I wanna die
I wanna cry
    OUT
With what's inside of me
But I'm
    Nervous! Nervous! Nervous!
Theatrically frantic!
About what this lady has on her mind
Does she want to do
The do-do!?
And just how is the do-do done?!
    —shhh? I'm supposed to know how—I am the man—even though I've never
done it. Though I've thought about it alot. I mean I've looked in all the books and
I've memorized every picture, but intangible ideas will not help one deal with the
concrete fact of soft flesh.
    —feeling f-u-n-n-y. F-a-r-a-w-a-y yetParanoid.
    She pats me on the thigh again. I jump up. "I GOTTA GO," I say, running out
of the cabin. I think she sighed but I was moving too fast to hear her.

    I should have done it. My big chance. My opportunity at bliss. My young
man's dream totally fulfilled. Who knows. She might have put out for me for the
whole voyage.

    Goddamnit. I should have. I could have. I would have only if: I was really a
man.
    Boy. How soon will I get another chance at SIN in the afternoon!!

Harriet and Dawn

    "And of course there are navigational tools to determine proper course," the
First Officer says with a heavy accent. He is taking me on a tour of the bridge along
with several other passengers.
    The Way. The Way. The Daughter is nudged by the Mother. 'You see that?!'
There are tools with which one can determine The Way. There is A Path (So Help
Us God. Listen to me child. Be good. Be holy. Do not make me ashamed of who and
what you are ((Goddamnit do what I tell you to. Jesus won't You make her listen to
Me))
tired; confused; small

heading for a fall
i would
if i could
but it's so wearying
so fucking wearying

"Dawn?"

"Yes Mom."

"Clean up your room."

"But I want to go out to—"

"Clean up your room."

"I want to—"

"CLEAN UP YOUR ROOM!" hysterically.

"I, I,"

"And another thing. When did you get home last night," (You slut what were you doing)

"About 11," (You don't trust me)

"Oh you did did you," (What were you doing not THAT I hope ((kids are so spoiled these days they get to do anything and everything (((They won't do the right thing like Mother taught me, Dearest Mother, a fine lady who never let herself go)))

Silence. Stony silence.

". . . and we use automatic pilot by day," the Chinaman says. "At night we find our way by the stars."

"How much longer till we reach Hawaii?" someone asks

"About 40 hrs if we hold present speed."

The S.S. Cosmos glides along.

"That was a nice tour of the bridge," the Mother says at its conclusion.

"Wasn't it," the Daughter bites off.

And I am tense; irritable; like a taut live wire ready to unravel. The pressure is unbearable. As Mother and Daughter I am as permanent as the stars, as fixed as the rotation of the planets, and it makes no difference if the Mother and Daughter are physically together. They are always with each other no matter how far apart they may seem to be . . . though when they are far apart I am murky; clouded; swirling like the currents in a turbulent pool. But since they are close together today, since they are standing right next to each other and trying to live through all that is and all that has been and all that will never quite be I am tense; irritable; like a taut live wire ready to unravel.

"Yes it was a very nice tour."

Dawn

Integration.

That's where it's at.

To be groovy these days you've got to have an *integrated* personality. You've got to be 'together' man if people are going to dig on you and I think the reason that being 'together' is so highly valued these days is because everything and everyone seems to be falling apart.

Like me.

sometimes i think i'm falling apart

other times i think i'm typical

but sometimes i think i'm falling apart

like last night. when i slept with that guy. i guess i enjoyed it but who knows why i did it. i mean i guess i need direction. purpose. a goal. i need to put my life into a straight ———————— so that I can follow it and reach a ★ (One that's preferably gold plated) but instead everything is

like that you know what i mean (Although sometimes, deep down when I just let myself go and feel, everything becomes smooth and dark and wavy ((I mean I am a woman and there is a beauty to being female))

Ozzie

It just goes on and on. Anybody in their right mind could tell you that one.

Dawn

Ozzie

"Politics?"

"Yes Politics," the Texan began.

"Well I'm a Reagan man myself," I say.

"Good for you."

"I think '80 will be his year. I think he'll turn this country around—with a little help."

"Yes he will. Yes he will."

"Cigar?"

"Why thank you."

"About that condominium development of yours. If it's to be marketed properly we'll have to get together with some banks so that it can be financed properly, so a fellow who wants to buy one can come in with a small down payment and get a decent interest rate for his mortgage."

"I say my brother-in-law is chairman of the board of the Dallas-Fort Worth First National Bank."

"Good, good," I say rubbing my hands together. This is going to be like taking candy from a baby.

"I say have a pleasant day, suh," the Texan drawls, continuing his stroll around Promenade Deck, and I let Moneybags move on by.

Well hell. Been a good trip so far. I've made an incredibly good business contact and I've managed to bang a sweet young thing—

Uh-oh. Here she comes. That girl I nailed. She sees me and blushes. The old heartbeat picks up a tad and I start to make my way towards her. God she's a hot little number and I better see if she wants to come up to my cabin again. For some fatherly advice but damn. She's scared and embarrassed and turns away from me, heads off in the opposite direction.

Shiieettt. Even though she doesn't want to see me I sure would like to see her again. Damn. I don't know what she's so embarrassed about. All we did was have a little fun. Ahhh fuck it. She's embarrassed and ashamed because she's young; inexperienced; still holding on to some idealistic notions of dignity and pride. But you wait and see. She'll learn. As she gets older she'll quickly understand that anytime you get the chance you better take it, whatever it might happen to be, cause nobody gives you anything for free. Not a damn thing. And some old fart with a hard on isn't all that much, I admit it, but at least it's something. She'll learn.

Damn. If I had just five minutes with her I'm sure I could convince her to see it my way. But to hell with it. Another that got away and only a fool spends his time looking back.

Nothing else to do so I ambled on over to the news print out. Every day the 'big' news comes in over the wireless and they post it in a hallway where the passengers can read it. Let's see here—now don't you think my eyes aren't as sharp as ever—there's more fighting in Southern Africa; more terrorist attacks in the Middle East; the Vietnamese are fighting somebody in Indochina; another summit ends with no agreements and alot of praise; Carter is having a fight with the unions; the Democrats want to raise Social Security Benefits; a who's who has died; oh hell; there's nothing new in the news today. It's the same old story—

"I've been looking for you!" Harriet exclaims, grabbing me by the arm and pulling me along.

"What—"

"Come on. Adam is very sick and he's down in the infirmary."

Adam

What am I doin' in this place
Why does the doctor
Have no face
I feel—like a deadened drone
Like a crippled Rolling Stone
     "His roommate found him passed out on their cabin floor. He's passed a lot of blood. We don't know yet . . ."
Men in white
Through bright hot lights
Out of time
Like mimes
They roll me
Through the doors
     "Oh Adam my baby!"
     "Shhhh!"

"We're running every test we can think of but the facilities on board ship are rather limited."

"My baby—"

Cold sweat oozing down my forehead. Where am I. In the hospital again?

"Get Dr. Nolan here immediately. The little boy is in big trouble."

"I can't find him."

"Who's on duty?"

"How old is he?"

"He's seven. His mother, the one over there in the corner, just brought him in."

"What's his name?"

Hands moving on my body.

"Where does it hurt son?"

Everywhere.

"He's such a cute kid. Has he started school yet?"

"Second grade."

The smell of alcohol. Of Lysol. Of antiseptic cleanliness. It's always been like this. And I hate hospitals. I've been in and out of them for as long as I can

Remember

The various

Dismemberments

That I have tasted

That have been wasted

Upon my body

A nurse touches me. Her hand is cool. And though the moment of compassion is fleeting the moment is real—I think—

—"How do you feel?" I'm asked.

Again.

"Hot. Pain in the stomach."

"Eaten anything you shouldn't have?"

"Umm-uhhh."

I see my father. He's in a haze. He's always been that way. Mother? Don't mother me!

Alone

On your own

Is the way

Pain does play

Upon the soul

Yet the people who care

Say they'd like to share

But hah! 'Tis folly. True agony cannot be cheapened. It is known alone, with no one else there, for agony is a friend who demands intimacy. Who demands one's full attention. Who demands and demands and takes everything and then leaves one empty and cold. Just like that. But he does give a certain authenticity to one's existence and perhaps he is worth his price.

57

Harriet and Ozzie

. . . and we looked at him lying there. As we had done so many times before. Our son. The bearer of the family name. Sick again. Running a 105° temperature and passing pools of blood through his bowels.

We almost didn't have him. We weren't sure if we wanted a second child, we weren't getting along, hell we had never planned on Dawn, or on even getting married, and there was a man who said he could take care of our problem for us, but there he is. Our son.

(My God, My God, Why Have You Forsaken Me)

Should we be holding hands. Should we be coming closer together in this time of crisis? I-she would have it so but I-he stands off. And some tears can never be repaired it would seem (But He has promised the Resurrection! ((Goddamn You God!))

The Father is nervous; upset. Thinking of the Past and of all the times he was not there. Has he failed his boy? He knows it is so, knows that he has let down his son, but still the Father is hard. He can not bend. He will break before he gives in. And the Mother? She thinks she is well-intentioned but she is selfish; self-righteous; hiding much of herself from the world and from her very own being.

Tough break for the kid. I've always been as healthy as a horse, have never had the health problems that Adam has had, and it's too bad. Yes it's too damn bad. And what the hell else is there to say about it. A guy is put on this world and then left on his own and he has to get along as best he can and it doesn't make any difference if we don't like it because that's the way it is. For better and or probably worse. Like marriage. Like Harriet and me. Like everybody else on the block. And some people try to slip along quietly and feel nothing and pretend, they are the ones with the flabby smiles and the weak voices, but I was born to face the Truth. I am Ozzie Smith. Adam is my son. He is sick and he is alone and he probably resents me but fuck him. I can't do anything for him, no one can do anything for another, one must do on his own, and though that means failure is the bottom line because one can never quite do on his own you can't blame me for it. Fuck it.

My poor baby. I've never understood why you were born to be sick (It must be Punishment Damn You Lord. And have I, the boy's Mother, not been Faithful? Have I not been Righteous?)

A pile of crap Dear Wife

It's all your fault

It always has been
If you had been there
We would have strangled each other
Selfish prick
Look — who's thinking
Always ME! ME! ME
Aren't we the martyr
Leaving me, abandoning me
You drove me away. You drive everybody away
((Mother never said it would be like this. At least she kept her man with her till
the end and though they didn't have much they had something))
Your mother was a frustrated old bitch
She was not! (She was)
Cold as ice, hard as nails
We stood there watching our son not touching for sickness is a spectator sport.
"Unnnhhh!" he groaned in pain.
"Maybe it's something like hepatitis, his color, his white count, his—"
The doctors have never known what the problem is.
They never do.
They are helpless.
We are helpless.

Dawn

He's sick," a somebody told me.
I clutched up. Felt kinda
Queasy
Sleazy
    inside.
Again? Again and again? He's always doing things like this. The poor little guy
(How I love him so) is always getting trampled on by one disease or another. And
another.
Hurrying; down a hallway; lump in throat; heart in hand; head in confusion.
And I wish pain and tragedy did not have to exist. But they do and I really don't
know why and so far no one has explained it to me (But you know dear why there is
pain and tragedy. Heartache and suffering. It is because you think and feel. Because I
am as I am ((Crying, crying, in one way or another I always seem to end up crying)).
Tiptoeing into the infirmary. Slithering like a snake who would not be seen.
Can anyone see me? I hope not (I don't deserve to be seen or noticed ((I am inferior I

just know it)).

"He's in here," a nurse says, sharing a secret with me. Hospitals and infirmaries are blank walls as we all know but so much goes on behind them that is never told. Like my baby brother Adam. Just what are they doing to him.

Creeping
Peeping
Through the slit
Of an image
Paying homage
To timid curiosity
Trying to sort
Through a cacophony
Of silent shifting
Perspectives
   . . . he was in a dark little room, stretched out on a bunk bed. He smelled of sweat and nausea and fever. He recognized me.

Adam and Dawn

Punctuation.

There is none to describe what happens between us as there are no pauses or exclamation points just a steady flow of feelings and I-she would like to help but we both know that there is nothing to be done as Nature Himself has seized control and put the fever-hepatitis-intestinal disorder-sickness within me-he and we were young together once and very close until we sort of drifted apart but the Sister still loves the Brother and the Brother the Sister as there is something always familiar between us and I am he and I am she and I am we and I am the two of us as we are together.

Fever: An intruder. Coming between us. Blanketing everything with a blasted haze. And that is a shame. Because there is no contest of will between us, no need to prove somebody wrong and somebody right. The Brother and Sister simply blend together.

Yes together
As they are tethered
By an intangible chain
No hands of stone can sever
And exposition?
Posturing for position?
As we are one creation

There is no 'situation'
To speak of
 "Adam?"
 "Hi Dawn."
 Laughter.
 "Flat on your back—"
 "Again."
 "Mom and Dad?"
 "Concerned and confused. As usual."
 "I—"
 "Shhh. I know the Doctor's a quack."
The Brother's forehead is stroked. Calmly and coolly.
 "UnnhHH!"
 "Nurse!!"
 "It's just a cramp—there it's better."
 "Easy there. Why don't you lay back and rest."
 "I better go."
 "No I'm fine please stay."
Drifting. The room is dark except for the light that comes thru an open doorway. A person (ality) can shift here and there, there and here, when it's twi-light lit like it is. The boat creaks softly but there is no Poseidon Adventure disaster type scene in view. I have let go of Apprehension and the swaying darkness is a comfort, a soft comfort. I let it be for sometime before the Sister finally gets up to leave the quietly resting Brother.

Harriet

 We had dinner in silence. There was a certain tenseness at our table, but then again, Dear Lord, I also felt as though we were drawing together. It was a time of need, a time of crisis, and of course I felt Your Presence.
 My daughter, Dawn, could only pick at her food (It's just as well she could lose a little weight) as she was obviously concerned about Adam. And it made me feel good to see that she was concerned, that she still had within her the capacity to care about something, and even Ozzie appeared to be a little anxious (I know he cares about his only son Adam Does he I just know it Does he He is such a hard man, arrogant and unforgiving ((I used to love it when he would walk all over me because then I could respect him and his strength and feel like I would be protected while knowing all the while that he would be a lively challenge that had to be reformed

(((Bad men are the best men Sex Ozzie hold me Ozzie fuck me Ozzie)))

"Ketchup," Ozzie grunts.

"Do you have to smear that stuff on your corn?" Dawn demands, baiting him.

"You take your poison your way and I'll swallow mine my way—"

Help us Jesus. Here we are with one of our loved ones seriously ill yet we must have another insignificant squabble (And Ozzie can be a crude s.o.b. but you can't teach an old dog new tricks ((Attention; male attention; threatening me the woman-child-daughter wants him all for herself must protect my interests the selfish little bitch))

"Dawn dear let's not nag at your father tonight of all nights," I say quickly. Ozzie nods his warm approval while Dawn grumbles.

And there is a righteous pause.

"Hell I hope the kid pulls out of it but you know he's always had these health problems and you know he always will," Ozzie blurts out over his coffee all in a rush. I freeze up at his brutal frankness (You know it's true what Ozzie just said NO! NO! My baby boy's a healthy boy So Help us God ((GOD!? You know it's true what Ozzie just said Adam, Adam, my sweet little baby (((But if my child should stay sick, weak and dependent then Thy Will Be Done Dear Lord and I Your Handmaiden will care for him and protect him and love him and mother him ((((And you know if he stayed sick it might be a good thing sort of he would become dependent on me and could never leave me and then I would not know the aloneness of frightening ALONE))))

God?

I say GOD?

'where are you'

The quiet rocking of the ship. Outside the porthole the wind does blow when and where it will but I am trapped in here. Jesus? Come to me. Sweet Jesus? Why do I feel like You are not here. Jesus (And Ozzie is across the hall in his own cabin and his own space and I could cross the threshold and offer myself up to him ((And get fucked)) but I don't know perhaps that would be wrong if only my Sweet Jesus were here to see me through the night ((Another cold empty night?! And how does the spirit of the Lord touch you think of how Ozzie will touch you one warm body next to the other and Ozzie will be inside of me in a way that the Lord never could be (((Evil! Evil!! Ozzie is Evil!! And Mother said and I could sleep with him tonight but that would not guarantee Tomorrow I would get fucked over in the end again but Tonight I *need* him ((((it)))) tonight and Jesus is Just. And God is Holy. And I can see them far away in the long-run of the future when I will need them but I need my s.o.b. of a husband Tonight. Right Now. Can't bear the weight of Denial any longer)))

. . . and I arose because Jesus had told me to do so, had told me to go and see Ozzie so that we could discuss Adam (Dark and warm. Had to have it no holding back. I slipped out of my cabin across the hallway ((To Hell with: God; Jesus; Spirit; Righteousness; Denial; The Future; The Long-Run; his cabin door is open and I creep in and I am jumping out of my nightgown and I will lay down naked next to him and I will take him in my mouth like I used to do and we will fuck the night away and hold each other BUT))

Ozzie was not in his cabin. He was probably out drinking and carousing (Trying to fuck still another young co-ed that evil sonuvabitch) and I returned alone to my cabin (And to You O God. And You know that I was only going to see Ozzie so that we could discuss our Adam. I am Your Handmaiden ((Don't leave me now O Jesus. I say DON'T LEAVE ME ALONE NOW DO AS I TELL YOU)) and there is no sin within me ((alone (((GOD YOU *ARE* HERE ((((alone, suicidally terribly alone and i am the scum of the earth (((((GOD YOU ARE HERE AND I AM RIGHTEOUS. I HOLD YOU IN THE HIGHEST ESTEEM YOU ARE THE ALMIGHTY SHINING IN THE DISTANT GOLDEN GLASS ENCASED FUTURE THAT WE CAN NEVER QUITE TOUCH BUT UPON WHICH WE CAN ALWAYS RELY SINCE IT IS TOO GLORIOUSLY INACCESSIBLE AND RIGHETOUSLY UNREALISTIC TO EVER FAIL US GOD YOU ARE HERE AND I AM RIGHTEOUS ((((((alone; horny; sinner; i am a lonely sinner; i need flesh and blood and a hot cock; i'll never get through tonight no not ever; jesus? i say jesus?))))))

(((((((and you know I would have fucked Ozzie if he had been in his cabin because i was exhausted after the inner struggle and once you're exhausted you always do the easy thing, take the immediate pleasure and fuck the pain that Tomorrow will bring you because of the Sin you did tonight and hell; got to have it; i'll try to wait up for Ozzie and then i'll go fuck his brains out)))))))

And yes Dear Lord I will wait up for that sinful Ozzie so that we may talk about our Adam in his time of need . . .

Adam

Home
is America
the *Mid-West*
Ft. Wayne! Ft. Wayne!
through joy and health
through sadness and pain
the landscape of eternal Indiana
is the landscape of my mind
of all our minds
and though
      Performance (Discovery)

is my obsession
my current young man's obsession
—gotta prove myself
—gotta be able to hold my liquor
—gotta get laid
—gotta accumulate more Experience(s)
—gotta do this
—gotta do that
—gotta
Well you know after all the current immediates
HOME
is
the fundamental
thing . . .

"His temperature is 105°."

"Well shit. Wrap some more cold towels around him; we have to break that fever . . ."

Ozzie

It was a dark night. Perfectly suited to our purposes. Me and three other guys . . . ouch! Just cut my hand on a rock. It bleeds. I go ahead and suck on it but it's still bleeding. Fuck it. And fuck this hill we're climbing. I don't know why we have to take it. All I know is that the lieutenant wanted us to take it and in the Army orders is orders.

Creeping. Almost slipped but I kept my balance. Moving like I am a directed wind, silent but purposeful. Not thinking about fair-play. Not even thinking about glory. I just want to get it over with. And I hope I don't get my ass blown away but there is nothing else to do but keep on climbing inch by inch with my stomach in my mouth.

On the very top of the hill now, goddamn we made it, and Intelligence was right. Coming up the back door like we did is gonna make this a cakewalk. We start to set up on the bluff that is overlooking their camp . . .

Daybreak. And then there is a little more light and then they start to wake up. The anticipation is itching and then they are mustered, all lined up for us.

—I opened up on them with the machine gun. I must have dropped a baker's dozen of them right away. Now they are running, scattering, looking for their guns and for a way out that just isn't there, but they are meaningless silhouettes that crumple beneath my fire. Shadows without substance that I easily annihilate with my gun. One blank geek face after another that fall to the Korean Wayside. The bombers come roaring in

—"Have another," the fellow says, offering me one more bourbon.

"Sure why not," I agree, listening to the hum of the S.S. Cosmos, watching the bar roll from side to side.

Tomorrow we arrive in Hawaii. Tomorrow we really start this trip around the world. Hell. I guess a guy ought to do something like this once in his life. Even if it can't really make a difference

Goddamnit there's that pain again. It's sharper than ever—oh shit it's nothing (That's right you old motherfucker just keep on ignoring me but we both know that you do it because you're scared. You sonuvabitch. You're afraid and deep down you damn well know that you should be. You know damn well that you're getting older and that your ticker has just about come to an end—Never)

. . . so I dragged it on back to my cabin. Feeling kind of low (old) tonight but I really don't know why. There's a mean boozy edginess in my gut and my hands, my mouth and my chest, but what's this?! Something warm and pleading

—Hell I don't protest. She is my wife. There were some good times. She must be lonely as hell and there's this urgency. I think of saying something like there can be no promises but why spoil it for her. Or for me. Naked and willing is how she does it and I let her go. There really were some good times, back when we were younger. Harriet was awful pretty then and I remember clearly now. All those nights. They weren't bad. Better than it had been with anybody else. She puts her head on my chest when it's all over, her face wet with tears, but who am I. . . to say anything . . . drifting off to sleep . . .

Dawn

It was one of my Contemporary Nonsense classes. Stumbled into it; dragged through it; something about a novel; trying to look forward to docking in Hawaii later today;

"What do you people believe in?" the teacher (groovy) suddenly irrelevantly asked.

Nobody made a move. Nobody said a thing. It was weirdly embarrassing (Discomfiture: Having to face up to me, myself, things, the world ((Hell who knows

65

but I do feel I need something))
    Class dismissed.
    . . . and I buzzed on out of there (Nausea). With my books in my arm (and my co-ed cunt in my body) I trudge on down Promeande Deck. And
Why look who's here
Look with anger aggression
Love hate jealousy fear
It's my Mother
My Mother Dear
    "Good morning Dawn," she says. Looking refreshed. Looking nervously pleased. Looking like (Has she gotten laid? Daddy!?)
    "Good morning."
    "Beautiful day."
    "Yes . . .yeah it is."
    "Have you seen your father around?"
    "No."
    "Well. He certainly should be up by now. I thought the three of us might have an early lunch together and then go visit Adam in the infirmary."
    "I'll go see if Dad's in his cabin," I say. Wanting to get away from her.
    "Okay dear," she calls but I am gone. Whirling up the stairs to the adult section where all the teachers and faculty and staff and old farts have their cabins (Did the two of them? Nahhh. Yes?)
    Knocking on Daddy's door (Again ((The man has never quite answered his door the way I want him to))
    Anybody home?
    Knocking on Daddy's door.
    so I was about to leave but I don't know. The door wasn't locked so I turn the knob and enter
    Late morning greyness cause the curtains are drawn. Silent. Quiet silence. Don't think he's here and I turn to leave but wait. I just barely see a lump in the bed he must be asleep (Funny Daddy is an early riser ((Uh-oh Big Trouble (((NERVOUS)))
    I creep up to the bed calling softly, "Daddy? Daddy?"
    No reply. And I'm suddenly thinking of all the things, the *unfinished* things, that I wish had been finished
    "Daddy? Daddy?"
    I touch him he's icy cold. I suddenly realize (Conclusively)
CONCLUSIVELY!
what? why? how? is this it?
I scream!!! "Daddy!!"

66

Adam

Oh boy
Another nurse
That adds
To the mad—
ness
Burning in my
Churning brain
    R-r-r-o-l-l-l-inng
    "Wheel him in here for now," a voice says. "Shhh! Somebody next door is sick, has a fever."
    "What about—"
    "Yeah. Cover him up for Chrissakes. Here let's drape this sheet over him."
    "Too bad—"
    "Yeah. Right. An ambulance will meet us at the docks in Honolulu to take him to the morgue."
    FOOTsteps going away.
    But wait and see
They'll come again another day
    . . . and I have an urge to pee. I'm still feverish but I can move around so I get up. Wobbily speaking. The bathroom is through the next room and down a hallway—
    What's this!
    . . . and a body is stretched out on the operating table. And he is covered with a sheet. Presumably dead I presume. None of my business not really. Still I wonder who it could be. It looks like a male of about six feet—an accident of some sort? Still it's none of my business
    —But no one is around
Curiosity
The need to see
Is upon me
So I circle
A timeless circle
Around the corpse
The passive corpse
The peaceful passive corpse
Who no longer says
Just who he is
Or who he pretends
To be

Since pretenseless Death
Unforgiving Death
Is now his master
Forevermore, Foreverafter
With anticipation I unmask him
And remove the shroud; but; Father; Father!
O revelation unbearable! I—
Father? Father? Can this really be you?
What has my curiosity shown me:
Cold death? Unfeeling lifelessness? Truest
Permanence? I— I do not understand,
My seedling eyes refuse to recognize
The ultimate appointed destiny
That this their own root has found . . . A loss, A
Loss. Nature's final comment on human
Expectation and hope. And this silence?
This void that wraps around me? Unnhhh! 'Tis the
Awful Unsaid, the heavy cloak of the
Emptily Unfulfilled . . . I would have done
More; would have said something; would have; would have;
If I had but known; if I had been told;
If; if; but where is the 'if' in Death. Where's
The conditional in Eternity!
        —Look at his face.
The lips. The nose. The wrinkles of time that
Curved his mouth, that bracketed his eyes, that made
His very ears grow larger and deeper,
More prone to deafness and disease, wisdom
And weariness, and please. Cover him up.
The Truth is not meant to be gazed upon,
Not by this poor fool who stands here, who's lived
His life as though it were a dream. Why I
Had thought, had believed, had imagined and
Fantasized that he would not leave until
I was ready, until I permitted it,
Until . . . How awful. It has taken Death
Himself to show me the difference between
'What is' and 'what seems to be . . .'

Adam and Ozzie

'dad?'

i say 'dad?'
But the Father did not speak. And the Son knew why. There was only the
memory, and though the memory was a living thing that the Son would carry with
him, was a living thing that helped make the Son what he was and what he would
become, it was still only a memory. Subject to fading and alteration, to joy and
sadness, to a creeping decomposition that would feed something new . . .
    i can't
           say
    what it is that
    i don't know what should be said
    'dad?'

    'dad?'

And the Son drifted away in a vacant haze that was not all there. Tears were in
his eyes.

Harriet

"Mrs. Smith?"
It was one of the nurses. I trembled (Help me Jesus). Had Adam taken a turn
for the worse? "Yes?"
Nervously. "The doctor would like to see you," and her nervousness became
my nervousness (Help me Jesus!) "He's downstairs on Promenade Deck in the
Dean's office."
"I know where it is."
"I'll go with you," she offers. We start walking.
"Is something wrong?" I ask, almost reflexively (Mommy, I am a Mommy, it
is my job and duty and pleasure and burden to worry).
"Please come with me," the nurse evasively replies and when we enter the
office (Help me Jesus ((HELP ME JESUS!! I don't like the feel of this as I have been

here before, like the day they told me my father had died, GOD!))

The first thing I see when I enter the office is my daughter Dawn. Her eyes are red and her face is drenched with tears (Oh no. It is tragedy, it has to be tragedy, where is my Rock of the Ages). "Adam," I gasp.

"Sit down please."

"No I won't—"

"Sit down—"

"Mom it's Dad!" Dawn blurts out

"Sit down."

"Your Father?" I ask, surprised.

"Mr. Smith is dead," comes the judgment in a cold tired voice that is as lifeless as the news it gives (Ozzie? You're alive. I say last night you were alive and when I slipped out of your room early this morning ((Oh Lord I may have sinned last night, Lord I know I will need your help, Lord did I sin last night O Lord forgive me—DEAD—Help me Jesus—DEAD—Help me Jesus—DEAD—I need You now O Rock of the Ages—DEAD—Thy Will Be Done—DEAD—(((ALONE—DEAD—NOW I AM ALONE—DEAD—JESUS)))

"His body has been placed in the infirmary. An ambulance will meet the ship when we dock in Honolulu four hours from now."

"What? How?" I croaked out.

"Heart-attack. I believe he died at around seven this morning—I'm sorry . . ."

(Help me Jesus O You Who are Just ((So Meaninglessly Fuckingly Just and all our dreams You so thoughtlessly shatter in all Your Omnipotent Glory))

"Mrs. Smith?"

"I-uh-umm—"

"Nurse go get me my bag."

"Take it easy Mom."

Take it easy Takeiteasy

"Mom?"

"WAHHHH!!"

Dawn is holding me but I wish Ozzie was holding me I have always wished (And what will become of my Desire, a lifeless tomb? Help me Motherfucking Jesus ((Then again perhaps a blessing in disguise he *is* Gone (((Maybe there can be *others* sweet sister at least you are now free to look again for a man but I am alone—free—alone—FREE—alone—FREE—a-l-o-n-e—)))

"Here's a handkerchief. Feeling better?" the Doctor has his bag (silencer) now I try to get a grip on myself because those bags can be a help (Or a killer).

"Adam?" I sob.

"He hasn't been told yet," Dawn sniffles (Poor girl what will she do now without a father ((Oh hell he never was much of a father to her. Maybe she'll be better off for if he had kept on living he would have brought each of us more heartache and disappointment (((Though his touch was warm))) heartache and disappointment))

"WAHHH!!" (Hysterical outburst designed for public consumption and also truly felt ((But am I happy he's gone(((Now that the big cat's away his mouse can

70

play-O Help me Jesus through this tragedy ((((Am I still desirable enough to attract someone else—Turn on the inhibitor these feelings are sinful camouflage them— Ozzie?—DEAD—Ozzie?—DEAD—GONE—YES HE IS—but I sort of feel him here (((((O JESUS HELP ME NOW I'M REALLY ALONE LIKE I'VE NEVER BEEN. But then again. I'm also free of Ozzie. Perhaps I can find another cock in total freedom from my conscience. It probably won't be as hard as Ozzie's but it will probably be a little easier to manage ((((((And I can pretend that Ozzie and I were getting back together again and that my family was as ideal as it has to be (((((((After all when someone is gone you can remember them and what they did any way you want to but HELP ME JESUS I can't make it without You though I'll try to survive him THY WILL BE DONE OZZIE!!)))))))

The doctor is moving around like he's going to poke something into me. "I'll be alright," I re-assure him, sobbing, and the physician (Vulture) puts the bag (Silencer) down. "Adam must be told," I squeak out, giving Dawn a hug.

Adam

Tragedy?
The stuff of existence
—For those who would but feel
Idealism?
The stuff of youthful naivete
—For those who must try
Knowledge?
The stuff of joyful searching and painful openness
—For those who are foolish
The Self?
The stuff of I know and I don't know
—For those who are

Harriet and Adam

"Are you feeling any better?"
Shrug. "A little."
"The doctors say no more travelling for you."
"I admit I really don't feel up to it."
"We'll have the funeral in Ft. Wayne."
A nod.
"Adam I—"
"At least he went quickly and without pain."

God I really am sick
Don't worry I will take care of you my baby
Don't 'baby' me as soon as I'm up and around again
You'll owe me
Damn you I have to be myself don't smother me
But it's so hard to be alone (Help me Jesus)
Mother!
I know what's best (O Jesus I do)
You're risking
I know what's best (As Jesus is my Savior)
Damn you do you want to totally alienate me by insisting
I'm your Mother (I love you—you owe me—I love you—you owe me)
For Pete's sake the old girl is really losing her grip could be hysterical Trouble in
the future WATCH OUT

Dawn

the funeral
was final
kinda
        daddy i wished we had talked some more cause there were a few
things . . . maybe more than a few things not complet—
        there was old friends and old faces all very familiar in ft. wayne familiar though
the setting was new (old) for me

72

and then they all drifted away and i drifted with them though my body stayed put for a while (dreams must be demolished and that is the way it must be ((d-r-i-f-t-i-n-g here and a-there (((weak-tears-weak-tears ((((now; which way; fear; doubt; crying, crying, crying))))

"Do you think you'll re-join the trip in Korea?" Adam quietly asks. The S.S. Cosmos is now somewhere in the Pacific. "There's no point in you hanging around, you could catch a plane and . . .

"I don't know," I honestly wearily say.

ARTHUR

ONE

1.

"Who's there!?" McNulty cried out. A figure dark and uncertain was moving towards him.

McNulty peered into the mist of the night. The wind screamed and the rain lashed. The only thing visible was the foul black clouds of the horizon.

"Who's there!?" McNulty cried out, again. There was no answer. Nothing but the rocking of the ship, as she made her way through the storm sickened waters.

The figure drew close. A silent silhouette, brooding and fathomless. A mirage that was nowhere when you looked for it, everywhere when you tried to flee it.

McNulty was speechless. He wanted no part of it. He longed to run and to hide. To retreat and to escape. To scream with terror and to ignore in bliss.

The figure was upon him. Frightened, McNulty jumped away. But it didn't matter. The figure gave him no heed since the figure lived for nothing but its own heedless pursuits.

"Introspective sonuvabitch," McNulty muttered, when the figure had disappeared from view. The silent shadow had been Arthur, watching yet another storm from the crows nest of the S.S. Cosmos.

"The boy's a story that won't be told," McNulty thought, after he regained his composure. "He's a picture that won't be framed, a symphony of mystery that the maestro is always re-arranging.

"An' he reeks of danger," mused the plain McNulty. "He's best when avoided."

2.

"Have you seen Arthur?" Sally asked, the next morning. Sally was Arthur's mother.

75

"No, no," Donald, the boy's father, replied.

The parents put their heads together over their wayward child.

"He's certainly been quite gloomy these past few days," Sally lamented. She wrung a pair of beautiful hands, hands that were attached to a beautiful body.

"I've noticed that he's been down in the dumps," Donald returned. "I wonder what's bothering him."

"Still upset over his brother's death," Sally said. "That's the most obvious reason and why bother to look any farther than the obvious. Isn't the obvious brother to 'the truth'?"

"Bull. David has been dead for five months now. You think Arthur still weeps for him?"

"Why not. There are times I still do," the mother replied.

"Well it's unmanly. Arthur should snap out of it. David is dead. Dead, dead, dead. Arthur can't bring him back by becoming a martyr to mourning. David's gone, gone forever. One such as he shall sleep and sleep no matter what the living do. Makes no difference to one who's gone if we laugh or cry, make war or peace, wear black robes or flowers in our hair. Those who've left never return to see what we, the living, have done. Arthur should realize that. The loss of one life never deserves the wastage of another!"

Sally nodded distractedly. Donald was quite a talker.

"I bet it's that *girl* who's got him so blue," Donald continued knowingly. "Only one thing turns a young heart inside out, and that's another young heart."

"Who? Julia?! Sally demanded, snapping to attention. "Is she making life miserable for our Arthur?"

"Shhh. Control yourself. Look, here he comes! Don't let on that we've been talking about him!"

Donald re-opened a year old copy of the Wall Street Journal. Sally threw her eyes upon a paperback novel. And Arthur, their son Arthur, came shuffling down Promenade Deck.

His back was bent and stooped as he walked along. His eyebrows were screwed tight with obsessive concentration as he glanced from side to side, looks he gave without seeing. And distraction, moody distraction, dribbled from his lips whenever he spoke.

Donald and Sally stiffened in their lounge chairs when he reached them.

"Nice day," Donald began.

"Huh? Oh. I guess so," Arthur replied. His pale blue eyes had never been paler.

"How do you feel, dear?" Sally asked.

"Uh, well, uh, well, okay," Arthur mumbled.

"Something eating you?" Donald demanded.

"If so, I wish it would finish the meal," Arthur murmured.

"Now Arthur. You've got to snap out of this, this, er *depression* that you're in," Donald said angrily. His son's gloomy act was beginning to get to him. Whenever Arthur felt blue, his mother Sally felt blue. And when Sally was blue, life was not sweet for her poor husband Donald. Sally, woman she was, saw to that much.

"You should quit being such a baby," Donald exasperated, at Arthur. "Life's tough, but you've got to be strong and—"

"Don't be so hard on Arthur," Sally interrupted. "Arthur dear. Why do you carry on so? What's wrong? Still trying to adjust to David's death?"

"Well, um, I, I, er . . ." Arthur's voice trailed off. He just didn't know how to explain himself.

"Your girl giving you problems?" Donald brusquely asked. "Well. Don't let her get you down, don't let her run your life. You're a man, and a man doesn't play the chameleon to a woman's whim. He's a weak womanish fool if he does. Now it's true that a fellow must tolerate a shift in the wind, but need he bend so easily to suit a woman's mood? No, no, a thousand times no. Stand up, stand tall, stand hard and fast and firm. Be certain that she won't respect you until you respect yourself."

"Umm, ahhh, perhaps. Maybe."

"Arthur. *Please.* We want to help you," his mother implored.

"I don't know what's wrong," Arthur returned indifferently. He shrugged his shoulders and drifted away without another word. Donald nearly exploded at his son's rudeness and disrespect.

"Why that little—"

"Oh be quiet," Sally ordered. "Arthur? Don't forget to try out for the play," she called after him. There was to be a play performed on the S.S. Cosmos and Arthur's parents were hoping that he would become involved in it, that the acquisition of an outside interest would still his inner turmoil.

"You're much too easy on the boy," Donald complained, after Arthur disappeared from sight, without showing the courtesy that he had heard his mother. "You shouldn't put up with his bullshit," her husband fumed. "You give the child too free a reign. You don't break a wild horse by loosening the halter. Why in *my* day, if I had ever treated my parents the way he just treated us, I'd have been clobbered a good one!"

"Don't you dare lift a hand against Arthur!"

"Uh I won't, I won't—"

"And another thing. You better accustom yourself to putting up with Arthur's moods, with what you call his bullshit. In a few days he'll have his eighteenth birthday. Don't try to tell me you've forgotten; the exact terms of the will must be made known to Arthur when he turns 18! I'm sure you've given it plenty of thought!" Sally hissed.

Surprisingly, the talkative Donald had no answer.

3.

"Arthur, Arthur, Arthur. I just don't know what to do about him," Julia swooned. Julia was a small, a pretty thing, touched with the beauty of youthful innocence.

77

"He's certainly a character," Gwen Richards agreed. Gwen was in her late fifties and she was taking this trip around the world by herself. She was a badly abused matron from the American Mid West, a neurotic female dinosaur on the verge of extinction. Gwen had led a hard life and she gave lots of advice to the young co-eds who were on board the S.S. Cosmos.

"I just can't figure Arthur out," Julia griped. "We've been going steady for over a month now and yet there are times I feel like I'm talking to a total stranger."

"A month? You complain about failing to know Arthur after seeing him for only a month? Hah. There are plenty of times when my *husband* is a total stranger," Gwen lamented.

"How long have you been married?" Julia asked.

"Almost thirty years."

"Huh. I see that these males who play the part of the stranger are a common problem. But Lord. *Men.* Just what are they trying to hide from us girls?" Julia wondered. "What's the big terrible secret they can't reveal to us?"

"Who knows. I doubt *they* do. Must be a part of the male psyche that they're afraid to face up to. Maybe it's the fact that we females aren't the only ones who have periods," Gwen giggled.

"Maybe. I guess," the girl sighed, staring off into space.

"Is Arthur your first real love?" Gwen asked. She knew the symptoms that Julia was exhibiting.

"Yes, I guess, well, *yes he is*," Julia admitted.

"There's no need to be ashamed about it. Arthur's a fine boy. Handsome. Sensitive. Comes from a nice family that seems to have plenty of money. Is he good in bed?" she asked.

Julia turned a bright red. Arthur *was* good in bed, or at least she thought he was. She really didn't have enough experience to know and so she blushed. Besides, Julia was terribly embarrassed that a woman of Gwen's age had asked her such a question.

"You're the color of a cherry," Gwen teased. "Surprised that an old woman like me could ask such a question, could think such a thing? Hah. I don't know why youngsters always imagine that they invented the art of fooling around. It's silly, the way children just naturally assume that they play harder than their parents once did. "*We* had our *own* good times," Gwen smirked.

"I'm sure you did," Julia said, smiling.

"From your look I bet that Arthur is just fine in the sack. Well good. You should be grateful. In troubled times a girl needs someting hard and fast to hold onto and believe me: Every time I've ever know has always been troubled. But come, we're joking too much about fooling around, fallen into the usual trap of doing more talking than fooling. To the point, to the point. Your problem is Arthur. You love and cherish him, yet you're often left wondering if he holds you nearly so dear. You give and you give, without beginning or end, but it seems as though you walk a one way street that never returns. And more than anything else, for him you're always there, be it foul or fair, while he's permitted to hide himself away in his private nowhere. He has the u......ng of your having to do the guessing, and come. Have we hit the lover's thorn on its head?"

"Yes, yes I think you have. Arthur's starting to take me for—"

"Granted." Gwen finished. "Well. What a typical male. Hmmm. A common problem, and common problems call for common solutions. Let me see. Ho. Hmmmm. Well. My advice . . ." Gwen hesitated here, collecting her thoughts.

"Out with it. What's your advice?" Arthur asked. He had snuck up on Gwen and Julia while they were chatting away in the lounge.

"Mercy," Gwen ejaculated. Among other things, Arthur had scared her by coming upon them so quietly.

"How are you doing?" Julia asked. She had the look of the guilty hand in the forbidden cookie jar.

"I'm just fine," Arthur replied. "The question is, how are *you* doing. I believe Gwen was about to give you some advice."

"Oh, it was nothing, nothing. Just the silly talk of hens," Gwen said, rising from her seat. "I'll go ahead and leave you two alone," she finished, beating a hasty retreat out of the lounge.

Arthur was amazed to see her fat old body move so quickly. "Who would believe it," he muttered. "I guess it's true. When frightened, old fools run like young deer."

"Did you say something?" Julia asked.

"Wasn't a thought worth a penny. What were you and Gwen talking about?" Arthur suddenly demanded. "Me?" he correctly guessed. "I seem to be open season these days," he growled. "Everybody's taking a shot at me."

"You know how I feel about you," she whispered, throwing her arms around his neck. She kissed him hard, long and wet. She was waxing lonely today, a feeling that she often had.

"*Do* I know how you feel about me??" he asked, pushing her away.

"What do you mean?" she whimpered, hurt at how he had slighted her.

"You say you love me," he said. "But come. Is it really *me* you love? Or do you *love being in love*. And you tell me, over and over, that you *need* me. But is it really *me* you need? Or will a *somebody* do.

"As soon as this trip around the world is over, as soon as we get back to the States, you'll forget about me. When you get back to your family and friends, your beaus and your good times, I'll be nothing more than the photos you took while on this trip!"

"Arthur! That's not true! Why are you saying these things?" Julia pleaded. "What's wrong?"

"Nothing. Everything. No one. Everybody. Oh you're a fine one. Discussing me, dissecting me, with that old fool Gwen Richards. Sounding out a dinosaur for advice on how to survive in the present. One fool fooling with another. So tell me, what kind of gas did she pass in your direction," Arthur sniggered.

"Quit making fun of Gwen," Julia returned angrily. "She knows alot. She's been through all sorts of things. There's truth in the counsel she gives."

79

"Oh hogwash. She's nothing more than talk and words. You know that talk's cheaper than the air that carries it, that words are emptier than the voids they fill. Why do you listen to the old bat?" he chided.

"I tell you there's truth in her advice!" Julia exclaimed.

"Baloney. Her life's been a disaster. Here she is, an inept neurotic mad woman, a living failure who only succeeds at dying slowly. She's a female Edsel, a cripple who crawls on downers and hysteria. Can somebody like her know the truth?" Arthur asked. "No way," he continued. "Don't be foolish. The truth is more than words, more than advice or talk or idle chatter. The truth is a thing; don't make the mistake of confusing truth's wholesome substance with the empty words used to describe it.

"Truth? Truth? He who has it lives it, he does not speak it. These elderly counsellors, giving so freely of their exceptional advice, should all have their tongues cut out without exception. They are failures, every last one of them, and beware: Only failures ask a failure how to succeed!"

"Arthur," Julia moaned, at his outburst. "What's gotten into you? Why are you so bitter and cynical? What's—"

"Wrong?! God, I can't take this anymore. *Leave me alone!*" Arthur spat out.

Hurt, badly hurt, Julia walked away. Arthur failed to see that she was crying.

Without further ado, Arthur sat down in a corner by himself. He immediately commenced to brooding. It was what he most wanted to do these days. He thought: "What's wrong? What's wrong? What's wrong?!

"God. Why is that the only question I hear these days! My friends, my parents, why even my lover now asks it. 'What's wrong?' everyone whimpers. 'What could possibly be bothering you?' they demand. 'Don't you have *everything?*' the small minds implore. Christ Almighty. The shit that people deal in. It's as plain as day the whole fucking mess stinks. Yet we smile and wink, grin and nod, pretend that all is well when Hell itself could be no worse. God forgive, but people hate me just because I have the courage and sensitivity to show the world what a dumb show it really is.

"Well nuts! To smile is to lie, to laugh is to ignore. I'll do none of these. The color black may not be pretty but the color black is true. I'll wear it though it kills me.

"Fools. Every last one of them fools. They grope and stumble, fall and rejoice, laugh and die, all for the entertainment of the even bigger Fool who made them. And God? Who is *He!* Should I crook my knee to the Malignant Being who has given me a life of crucifixion? Hah. To Hell with Him!

"I don't know what's wrong. I don't know why I feel like flinging myself off this ship late at night, when no one else is there. I don't know, I don't know, I don't know . . ."

80

4.

"The play's the thing—Wherein I'll catch the conscience of the King!"

"Excellent! Excellent!" the Director cried out. "And you say you've worked in summer stock since junior high?"

"Yes," Arthur replied.

"Wonderful. You were superb. You shall be our Hamlet," the Director exclaimed. "What do you say? I'm sure you'll do the part and the play great justice."

"I'll play any part be it just or great," Arthur returned.

"A fine reply!" the Director exulted. "It shows you're a real professional, a true actor."

The Director then gave Arthur the once over. He noted Arthur's curly blond hair and his ruddy complexion. He saw the pale blue eyes and the sensitive mouth and he thought: "Here's a young man, not quite steady but quite quite ready. This is metal indeed for our Hamlet. I bet he'll be a hot poker with the ladies in the audience!"

"We have about a week to rehearse?" Arthur asked. "I have a week to become Hamlet?"

"Yes, give or take a day or two."

"Well. Shouldn't be any problem. Know it alls know all about a man in their singular knowing moments, so a fool like me, given a week's eternity, can surely hide 'neath Hamlet's disguise, 'neath the cloak of a singular fellow such as he."

"Hah. Not bad. Almost there. Do you write verse?" the Director asked.

"No, no. But now and then things occur to me. Can't always seem to hold them back," Arthur murmured.

"Ho-ho. Today's undisciplined youth—"

"Should learn from yesterday's undisciplined youth. But then youth wouldn't be youth, and we'd all be old and senile."

The Director laughed. "I see you're very quick," he said.

"Hmm, Hmm, Hmm," Arthur returned, growing moody again.

"Well anyway, I want to discuss the play with you," the Director continued. "You're going to have the play's big part and I want to know how you feel about Hamlet in general and the play as a whole."

"This roundabout fag of a Director," Arthur muttered. "A holy general indeed!"

"What? What?" the Director asked. "Tell me, what do you think about the play?"

"It's neither obvious nor hidden, neither plain nor obscure," Arthur replied. "But then again, I really don't know. After all, I'm an average guy, a misguided creep creeping creepily in the somewhere between heaven and earth. Who am I to know a thing about Hamlet?"

"Oh, I'm sure you can do better than that," the Director babbled. "I'm sure you have some fine ideas concerning the work. I myself think that Hamlet is the greatest play ever written, the greatest documentation of the human condition ever penned. Don't you agree?"

"That's one way of putting it," Arthur returned.

"Yes, yes. Well, I must be off, we'll talk more later. See you at tomorrow's rehearsal, same time same place. We'll be rogues and peasant slaves when we meet again!" the Director cried out, as he left the ship's theater.

"Certainly, certainly," Arthur mumbled, watching him go with relief. He'd had enough of the insufferable fool. But something gnibbled at him after the man had departed.

"Can everyone and everything be as they seem?" he grimly wondered, alone in the empty theater. "Is this all there is?"

5.

"So lately, the world's been a cage, cornering the moody beast within me at every turn," Arthur admitted, to his roommate Dan. Dan was solid and reliable, a good listener and a true friend.

"Things are that bad?" Dan asked, concerned. "There's nothing in the world that gives you joy or pleasure?"

"Only the occasions that affirm my cynicism."

"That's a great attitude," Dan muttered, unable to understand his roommate's sudden distaste for living. "Don't you have any idea what's bothering you?"

"I'm beaten by an invisible whip."

"Your family, your lover, the sun setting and the moon rising. Don't any of these things make you happy?" Dan asked. Hopefully.

"All's a plague, a plague on all."

"Jesus H. Christ," Dan murmured. He and Arthur were speaking in the dark, lying in their bunk beds and trying to sleep. Dan squeamed and squirmed as his roommate spoke for when it came to preparing a night's sleep, the bitter musings were a poor seasoning.

"I saw my older brother last night," Arthur quietly said.

"What?! When?! Where?! How?! Your brother's—"

"Dead. I know. But he came to me."

"In a dream?" Dan demanded.

"I guess *you* could call it that, but *I* won't. My brother was in pain when I saw him and he was crying. I think he was trying to tell me that something was *wrong*," Arthur whispered.

"Now Arthur, it was *just* a dream—"

"And isn't this *just* a life? It's only our minds that say, '*this* is waking,' '*that* is sleeping.' Why believe them? Haven't our minds been wrong enough before?"

"Arthur Arthur, quit this, this brooding. Why are you so bent on torturing yourself?" Dan asked, almost pleading. "Why do you so willingly mount the rack?"

"For a better view of the world. Pain is the most potent illuminator."

"Jeeminy Christopher—"

"I *heard* my brother last night," Arthur whispered.

"Huh?"

"I say I heard my brother last night," Arthur repeated. "It was after I woke from dreaming about him. In the still of the night, I heard him call my name. 'Arthur! Arthur! Arthur!' his voice whispered."

"Come on. You're joking," Dan nervously complained. Dan certainly hadn't heard anything last night.

"I tell you, I hear my brother call my name!" Arthur exclaimed. Dan cringed when he saw that Arthur was serious. "If you would only listen, maybe there'll come a night when you too shall hear him," he promised.

Dan reserved judgment on the matter.

Arthur stood alone on the Sun Deck of the S.S. Cosmos, unable to sleep. It was three o'clock in the morning.

Arthur felt something as he watched the bow of the ship bobbing up and down, surging through the waves. He thought: "To know! To know! To know! Must I remain forever ignorant of this hidden cancer that feeds upon me? God, all knowing God, You know that there is nothing worse than to be eaten away by an unseen disease. It's a torture that the Devil himself would not inflict. Why give me pain, calamity, brimstone, heartbreak, hunger and sickness, give me Hell, punishment, damnation, the seven plagues and Death herself, but at least permit me the sight of what destroys me! Am I not a man? Do I not deserve as much? Lack I the dignity to be endowed with the sight of my oppressors? I suffer forever in blindness!! God Damn God, but He curses men with myopia while He murders them with glee! He pricks us with thorns that we can not reach or see and is it good sport? God? Why don't You answer!

"To know! To know! To know! I bleed from an unrevealed wound. I rot with hidden contagion. And for what. For what?! Why do I bleed? Why are my assailants always unknown? Where come these demons that thrust daggers into my heart? Who owns these heavy hands that weigh me down? Why am I given the *dream* of omniscience, the *reality* of crawling in foulest darkness? I yearn to feed on knowledge, yet ignorance remains my meal. I long to be free and knowing, but always I play the puppet-fool. And through it all, one question torments me: Is the Creator a Sadist?

"I wish I could sleep. I wish I could laugh, eat, drink, talk and play. I wish I could be like all the rest. Will deliverance ever arrive? Or will I only find a desperate courage that draws my own curtain."

Sleepless, Arthur returned to his cabin, seeking a sleep that he would not find.

TWO

1.

They were the most admired of the admired at the Captain's Dinner. They sat at the center table with the Captain on their one side and the Dean on the other. They sat, and sat and sat and sat at the center table, with the approval of all the eyes of the world. And everyone, everyone just loved the gorgeous couple that sat. And sat.

Donald was a fine looking man, large, broad and handsome. He had a flashing smile, a bluff manner. He was always quick to voice the common opinion, the currently popular position and the *right ideas*, so as a matter of course, Donald was very well liked.

His wife Sally was a beautiful woman. What more needs be said? As a matter of *nature* all the world hurried to grovel at her feet. Seeking a smile or a nod of approval. And Sally could be soft and sympathetic, sweet and gay. She could control the female impulses within her that wanted to nag and rag, to be angry and depressed, so people (Particularly men) loved to be around her.

Taken together, Donald and Sally were the ideal couple, the pride of the community. Taken separately, they were all that one could ask for. Taken truthfully, they were to be watched and distrusted.

"Divorce. D-I-V-O-R-C-E. That's how you spell it, you prick."

"Now Sally—"

"Don't you 'Now Sally' me. You're not my patron. You're not my father. You're not my boss."

"Now Sally—"

"Goddamnit. Have you forgotten yourself? You exist at *my* pleasure. If we split up you're out in the street without a penny to your name. I've talked to my lawyers about this."

"Okay, Okay—"

"We're going to do what *I* want to in Egypt. We'll eat, shit, sleep and breathe when and where I say so. Got it?"

"Okay, Okay."

"And what about the will?" Sally demanded. "Have you decided how you're going to explain things to Arthur? For your sake you better come up with one helluva line."

"The will isn't just *my* problem. It's *our* problem," Donald shot back. "I've noticed the style of living that you've become accustomed to. You can't possibly afford it on your own. Once the will is read you'll need Arthur as much as I do."

"I'm his mother," Sally returned angrily. "He'll never do a thing to hurt me!"

"And I'm the boy's father!" Donald exclaimed. "So what? In times such as these what difference does blood make? When Abel's hour came, did the bond of blood cause his brother to hesitate? You're overconfident. Maybe your hold on the boy isn't as strong as you think. Maybe the boy will side with *me*. At the very least, you'll need my help when it comes to swaying him."

"Keep talking Donald. That's the *only* thing *you've* ever been able to do."

"What kind of cheap shot is that?" Donald demanded.

"As cheap as I care to make it," Sally said evenly.

Donald faltered.

"God you're a joke," she spat out. "Everyone look here and laugh, at a man weaker than his woman, at a master the slaves defy. A bowl of jell-o has more stomach than you do. Oh you're a fine one. You're a lion when the audience is watching, a weasel when the stage hand says 'boo,' a dangerous looking man till danger arrives, a coward who cowers 'neath the guise of a warrior.

"You may fool the world. But I, your wife, know you for who and what you are!"

"Where are you going" Donald asked bitterly. Sally was now standing at the door.

"To do as I please," his wife replied.

"What's his name this time?" the husband asked.

"I don't keep track. Why should you," Sally hissed, slamming the door.

Donald bit his tongue until it bled.

2.

"Again. Again," the Director coaxed. "Remember, you're trying to fool Claudius and the Court. You're playing the part of a man who is himself playing another part. Deceit is everywhere. Remember that as you play Hamlet. Again."

"Again," the Director encouraged.

Arthur recited the lines.

"Now be careful," the Director warned. "The scene has switched from blank verse to prose. The pronunciations and inflections will be quite different. Careful."

Arthur repeated the lines. With a considerable degree of success.

"Good, good," the Director applauded. "You're making excellent progress in your portrayal of Hamlet."

"It's nothing difficult," Arthur replied. "When a deceiver spends his easy time acting, an actor's deceit comes easily. With practice, the once impossible becomes the only possibility."

"Ahh yes," the Director affirmed. He wasn't sure what Arthur meant, but it certainly sounded good.

"And why not," Arthur continued. "When it comes to a man, there's neither good nor evil, right nor wrong. There's only a 'this' which we do, a 'that' which we don't, and only Habit says that is 'this,' this is 'that.' Why Habit's the most powerful liquor in the world. Once drowned in her intoxications, a soul will see even the Holocaust as being trivial."

"Well put, well put," the Director agreed.

"But Habit is also a whore," Arthur whispered. "Her fidelity will serve her lust. Her integrity is slave to her desire. The momentary whim thoughtlessly breaks the practice of a lifetime. Caprice is custom's capital capital. When the exotic beast of fancy turns the corner in our minds, the bitch Habit will find her excuse to make love to the fresh new face. If she's not too old, lazy, ignorant and unimaginative (If she's not too *much* the whore!), Habit will forget her old self in the hot pursuit of the new.

"So. How does this strike you?" Arthur asked.

"It's most confusing," the dull witted Director stumbled in reply.

"So's the truth," Arthur muttered.

"Well. I must be off to talk with the lighting men," the Director said, not hearing Arthur. "It was a good rehearsal but keep working on that bedroom scene!" he encouraged, as he departed.

"I will, I will, but I think that scene works on me," Arthur called after him.

"Ha-ha, Ha-ha. Here's hoping we'll all be Kings and Queens when we meet again," the Director said.

"Idiots and queers, idoits and queers," Arthur agreed quietly. "God!" he then exclaimed. "Must the wasp sting his nose before he can even sniff him?! Heaven should cry out in protest! Another directionless dope, another dope who's a director!"

"Telegram for you sir," a steward said, handing Arthur a note and departing.

"What's this?" Arthur murmured, at having his musings so suddenly interrupted. "When I am half way 'round the world who calls my name?"

Curiously, Arthur tore at the message. It read: "Stop. Your older brother's death no accident. Stop. Will cable more details when S.S. Cosmos reaches Egypt. Stop. Breathe not a word of this to your parents. Stop. As they may be involved. Stop. A friend. Stop."

Arthur looked to see that no one was looking. Then he tore the telegram into little pieces. Then he went and threw the pieces overboard. And then the full impact of the message hit him.

"And what was that?" Arthur thought, watching the torn up telegram as the ocean swept it away. "What the hell did that mean?! My brother's death no accident? Why he died of a heart attack. And don't tell my parents anything? Who can I tell if I can't tell my parents. And what's this about their being involved? *Involved*?! What could that mean? And who's 'a friend'?

"Blast this message. Burn it to make me healthy. It's a collector's collection of mystery, a museum that's stuffed with rumor and half truth. More a communicable disease than a communication, it warps my healthy clear day into sick chaotic night. My older brother's death no accident? Say nothing to my parents? Why doesn't 'my friend' simply simplify, say that nothing's sacred, nothing's sure!?

"Damn. Fresh uncertainties, certain to further corrode my already uncertain mind. What else can happen? Away! Away! On this and more my thoughts must play!"

3.

"No, no, you mustn't let yourself become his doormat," Gwen Richards said to Julia. "A girl's got to stand up for her rights now and then, most especially now since Chivalry's long been dead."

"You mean there are no more knights in white shining armour?" Julia asked.

"The only knights who remain sleep in the unreachable night, in the dreams of naive little girls," Gwen returned.

"Perhaps that's the way I've been for far too long," Julia moaned.

"I think it's a case of your turning the cheek once too often," Gwen said. "With every turn of the cheek he grows cheekier by the turn—"

"A vile phrase—"

"Is needed to describe a vile case. At any rate, you need to assert your independence," Gwen continued. "The woman's a shortsighted fool who becomes too dependent on a man. They're Hitlers, every last one of them. Give them an inch and they'll take the nation. Why men are murdering rapists, dominating fascists, slave driving tyrants—"

"(Would it were so)," Julia thought dreamily. "(How thrilling)."

"And ohhh. I burn when I think of how they have burned us. All they care about is a full plate and a warm bed. All they want is a willing field in which to sow their oats. The bastards. And I've never met the man who was up to being a man, who was willing to face his responsibilities. The big pussies. None of 'em can handle a real woman. All they long for is a toy, a little girl who's a marshmallow of a female, who'll let them play the role of 'Daddy.' Trouble is, none of these men can ever fill the shoes of 'Daddy.' They're all all too small, so a woman's got to lie and deceive, pump up their puny egos on every occasion if she ever wants an occasional puny pump.

"I tell you. The only solution is for us girls to quit being so dependent on these men," Gwen said.

"Is such a thing possible?" Julia asked.

"It has to be. There's no other choice these days."

"Well . . ."

"So you've got to show Arthur that you mean business. You'll be a clown unless you put your foot down, a pipe he'll leisurely play when and where and how it suits him. And would you be nothing more than his leisure suit? Hah. Enough's enough, a girl must be hard and tough less she loves the love life bitter and rough!" Gwen advised.

87

"Okay, I guess," the young Julia said quietly. She wasn't quite sure. Was Gwen talking about love? Or war?! Julia didn't know and playing the game that Gwen advised went against her better instincts, her youthful naivete. She wished that her father or older brother were around and that she could talk things over with them. But Dad and Big Brother were far away, and Julia didn't have many friends on board the S.S. Cosmos. Since that was the case and since Gwen's advice was the freest and most available around . . .

"So I've made my *own* travelling plans for Egypt," Julia said to Arthur. Though *she* had wanted to see him, she had managed to arrange it so that *he* had to come looking for *her*.

"Huh?" Arthur dumbly asked. He and Julia had always travelled together.

"I'm doing my own thing in Egypt," Julia announced.

"What? Why?" Arthur asked, confused. "Don't you have a good time when we travel together?"

"Yes, but that's not the point."

"The point? What's that mean. The only point that I can see or feel is the one that's hurting me," Arthur moaned. "A week ago, no a day ago, you wanted to be with me as much as possible. Now you're making your own travelling plans!"

"I need to be my own person," Julia blithely continued. "We're getting much too dependent on each other. I'm not sure that I want as entangling a realtionship as we now have."

"Oh. What?!"

"Can't think first of we, got to first think of me!"

"Oh. *Ohhhh*."

"Well."

"Well, well. Well what?" Arthur demanded. This was all very unexpected.

"Have a good time in Egypt," Julia said, trying to sound as casual as possible. Arthur looked very hurt. Suddenly she doubted that she was doing the right thing. Her spirit whirled.

"Julia," Arthur groaned. "Can't we *talk* about this?"

"What's there to say," she murmured. Her impulse now was to run away from Arthur. This lover's kitchen was growing far too warm. Things were starting to boil and her tender young hands were finding the pot of first love too hot to handle.

"I *need*—" Arthur began.

"I *need* too!" Julia exclaimed. She then thought of all the times that Arthur had been an inconsiderate prick, of all the times that he had thought of himself first, her second. *Well fuck him*, she felt, the buried resentment within her springing to angry life. The bullet already wore her teeth marks; let him taste its cold steel.

"See ya later," Julia next called, girlishly, childishly skipping away. Stunned, Arthur dropped into a chair. People moved on by him but he saw nothing. He turbulently thought: "My lover: She was to be the last to leave; yet here she is, the first to go. God. Am I a sinking ship? Will I soon find that even the rats scurry to keep away from me? What a neurotic confusing mess. She says she needs to be her own person. She makes her own travel plans. She announces her declaration of independence, and yet, and yet, is she only playing hard to get?! Or does she even know what she wants . . .

"Desperate times. My whole world seems ready to collapse. My moody mood; a mysterious telegram; and now my love withdrawing her love. I grow ill. My stomach sits as unsettled as my surroundings. My hands shake. People stare. Time waxes and wanes without reason. Rampaging disorder in disorderly rampage. Is it daytime, nighttime or nether time? My crazy times father a time that's crazed. Can I be found?? I'm here, there, everywhere, lying in bed unable to sleep as my thoughts lie elsewhere. They rest with her, my lover, with the careless young girl who no longer seems to care. And oh. Is this the fatal error? Can it be? I assign my heart to one who's heartless, I sign my death warrant with my own hand.

"Hah. This melodrama grows tedious. It's a sham, a fake, a soapy sloppy soap opera. And yet, the *pain* is *real*. I would laugh but it hurts too much to breathe.

"Up, tired body, up. Now you vomit, having drunk a bitter love's cup. And where to next? Hmmm. A woman has made me sick, t'will take another to make me well. Yes, yes, there's more than one place in this world that's safe and secure, dark and warm. I must rise and find it."

4.

"Who's that?!" Donald cried out in alarm. It was late at night. He and Sally had been sleeping soundly

"Mom! Mom!" Arthur howled, beating on the door of his parents' cabin.

"Arthur!?" Sally exclaimed.

"Why that little," Donald muttered. "What the hell is wrong with him, waking us up like this. It's four in the morning!"

"Mom! Mom!" Arthur repeated. Sally got up and opened the door. When she saw how pitiable her son looked she paled.

"You poor baby come in," she gushed, embracing Arthur.

"Now Arthur," Donald began, snapping on the light. "We all have problems, problems will always have us. You've got to learn to live life like a man. Just because trouble's got you on the run doesn't mean that you can come running to us. You should—"

"I'll always be there," Sally said sharply. "You speak for yourself," she said to her husband. "Get out of here while I talk to Arthur."

"What?!" Donald demanded. "It's four in the morning. A father shouldn't lose a warm bed because his son has cold feet! That's Freudian garbage. I'm your husband—"

"And Arthur's my child. A man may be king of his castle but a woman's queen of her bedroom. I serve you notice that there'll be hell to pay if she's not served there. Go on. You get out of here," Sally said evenly.

Sulkily, Donald put on his bathrobe and went for a walk in the cold night air. Sally then led Arthur to a bed and laid him down. She rubbed gently at his temples.

"My little humming bird," she cooed. "Why has your song gone so sour?"

"Well Julia and I—"

"That little bitch I knew it," his mother interrupted. "What did she say? What did she do?"

"Well it's not so much anything she said or did," Arthur replied. "All she *said* was that she needed more space. All she *did* was make her own travel plans for Egypt. It's just, well, her change of *attitude* that has so upset me.

"Two days ago she wanted to be closer than close. Now she wants to back off, cool things down a bit. I just don't understand," the young man blubbered. "I feel like I've been—"

"Rejected?! Baloney. Don't be foolish. That's ridiculous," Sally exclaimed. "I'm your mother and I know that it's impossible for that girl to have rejected you. How could she have rejected you?! After all, you can't be rejected by someone who isn't good enough for you!"

"You're sweet," Arthur sniveled. Sally hugged him. Arthur kept sniveling.

"I don't know," he moaned. "One night she's holding me tight, the next night she's kicking me out of bed. I just can't take it."

"And there's no reason you should," Sally said. "She'll blossom, ripen and die before your best years even begin to bloom and I tell you. I know all about these young females. Just you listen to your mother. I'm aware of how these budding bitches operate, of how fresh lilies bear hidden thorns. Hah. As she turns your young man's spirit smaller and smaller, her young girl's head turns bigger and bigger. Young lasses get their kicks by kicking young lads, I know all about it.

"But don't you worry, poor baby. You're worth a thousand of her. She'll quickly regret what she's done. She'll soon come crawling back. Then you give her tit for tat. Those who make others sing the blues must someday pay their own harsh dues. Why that wanton little whore—"

"Here's text for the textbooks," Arthur muttered. "My mother seems to be taking my rejection more personally than I do."

"That slutty slut. That poisonous little girl. *We*'ll show her who's boss!" Sally raged, holding Arthur tight.

"We will, we will," he murmured.

"You look pale," Sally said sympathetically. "Are you having trouble sleeping?"

"And eating," Arthur finished.

"That's no good—"

"But I think the worst has passed," he said, rising. "I feel much better now. Why look. Here I am, myself once again. This lover's agony was but a passing thing. I see how I now feel fine. Having died for love I find the resurrection redeemingly sweet. I think I'll be alright when morning comes."

"Good for you!"

"Thanks for listening," Arthur said to his mother from the door. She blew him a kiss as he departed.

Arthur returned to his cabin. He took a long hot bath to calm his nerves. He was certain that the worst was over with Julia. He was glad that his mother had proved to be reliable and true and he was certain that the mysterious telegram would prove to be phony and false.

His spirits rose. He had much to learn.

THREE

1.

The S.S. Cosmos was now docked in Port Safaga, Egypt. She would be there only for a day, just long enough so that the shipboard community could travel by bus to Luxor and back.

Luxor was a town filled with the mysterious ruins of Ancient Egypt. It was there, amidst the crumbling columns and the weathered statues of the Temple of Carnack, that Arthur and his father went looking for each other.

The Temple of Carnack is a huge place. It takes lots of time to go through its acres and acres of ruins, so it wasn't surprising that it took Donald and Arthur a very long time to find each other.

"He must be around here somewhere," Arthur thought, peeping in and out of the shadows of this and that. He had been looking everywhere for Donald. He was very anxious, wanted to question him about the mysterious telegram that he had received the day before.

Arthur wasn't planning on mentioning the existence of the telegram to Donald. He merely wanted to feel his father out, to see if his father had been totally up front with him concerning the circumstances of his brother's death. "When I meet Dad I'll be round about with him," Arthur *unconsciously* decided. "I'll confront him from the rear, never touching on the matter at hand directly, always lighting upon it indirectly. True knowledge is never found by our reaching for it," he mused. "We reach Truth by letting Truth reach us and so: I'll question the man without asking him a question."

"I must lie while telling the truth," Donald thought, while looking for Arthur. "I must tell him all about it, but not what it's all about. The will. The will. THE WILL! How can a scrap of paper be so important!? How can a piece of parchment rule men's lives!?

"The boy's grandfather, my wife's father, oh he was a fine one. The old curmudgeon. He never liked me, his only son-in-law. He never even liked his only child, my wife Sally, for she was much too strong and independent. The old coot. Out of a perverse hatred, he penned a document to pen us in! Only a willful codger such as he could have written such a will! AHHH! It ages me, in the sweet and mellow years of my autumn, to have as my bequeathal Grandfather's bitter winter of senility and resentment. To have been deeded such a deed!! God! Is the word Justice just another word!?

"It all started with him. The jealousy. The fighting. Sally's wild ways and that which engulfed David. Grandfather never trusted Sally after she ran off, and he always hated me, his younger rival, for stealing away his little girl. So he set down his hatred and mistrust in black and white, on a piece of permanent paper that would survive the fading and aging of time. He made sure that his spite would live on though he had to die.

"I better handle it better than I did the last time," Donald worried. "The police, the lawyers, the trustees and the high and the mighty, they were all suspicious concerning how David died. They all wanted to know if the will had been properly explained to him, if he had been made aware of his rights.

"David. David. My oldest son. Dead and gone. A runaway child, lost wild. I cannot bear to face myself, whenever I remember that last look upon his face . . ."

"Ho-ho."

"Why hello."

"Funny meeting you here."

"Great day, isn't it?"

"Yes, wonderful, wonderful, not a cloud in the sky."

"Everybody seems to be having a good time, poking around these ruins."

"They're very interesting. The architecture. The building materials. The religious meanings."

"Yes. It's amazing what these Egyptians were able to accomplish."

"Certainly. They were a people's people."

Father and Son stood beneath an obelisk that was four thousand years old. It's enormous shadow engulfed the both of them.

"Arthur," Donald said. "We have a few things to talk about."

"Oh. Of course. Fine. I'm all ears," Arthur mumbled.

"Good. Errr, you look rather pale. Is everything all right?" Donald asked.

"Oh fine, fine. I was just . . . thinking about David, wishing that he were here to see all of this."

"It's terrible that he's not with us," his father quietly agreed. "But that's life—"

"And death," Arthur murmured. "It's amazing, an outrageous twist of fate, that his appendix could have simply burst open like it did."

"Your brother died of a heart attack," Donald gently corrected.

"Oh yes, oh yes, I'm sorry, it was a heart attack in Queens—"

"No, he died in the Bronx," Donald interrupted.

"Oh. I'm sorry, yes of course that's right. I'm sorry. Oh. Excuse me," Arthur said. "You said you wanted to talk to me about something? That there was a thing of substance on your mind?"

"Yes," Donald began. "As you know, you'll have your eighteenth birthday four days from now."

"I'm not so far gone as to have forgotten that one," Arthur muttered quietly.

"As you also know," Donald continued, "almost all of our family's wealth is tied up in the company that your grandfather started."

"What sort of bush is he beating around?" Arthur wondered silently. "He avoids it like the plague . . ."

"And, er, ummm, there are certain, well, shall we say, yes, we'll say provisions, in the will, that are to be made known to you on your eighteenth birthday," Donald stumbled. "They're just unimportant details, a few papers that you'll have to sign, nothing serious," he blubbered.

"Is this not my very own father?" Arthur thought. "Why does he hem and haw, haw and hem, with *me*, his only son. Why does the cat strangle his tongue. Does my own flesh become stranger to me?"

"The papers are nothing but paper," Donald said in a rush. "They'll simply give me power of attorney over your stock in the company while you're attending college. Just a mere technicality. You did say you were thinking of Law School, didn't you?" Donald hopefully asked. "I hope so. It's a wonderful career. It takes a long time to get started as a lawyer but it's a wonderful career."

"What's this!!" Arthur mused. "The way he makes it sound, it's law that I should go to Law School. Am I not eighteen? It will turn me blue, being given a blueprint for life when life's just beginning. Have I not just emerged from the womb? No wonder we are dragged screaming into this world! Is this what being a man is all about? Meekly going from one prison to another?"

"And since it takes a while for a young fellow to get a law career started," Donald ran on, running off at the mouth, "perhaps we'd better draw up the power of attorney papers for until you reach *thirty*," he hurriedly suggested. "After all, young people have enough problems managing their own lives without having to worry about Management Problems."

"Thirty? Management Problems? Papers to sign? Power of Attorney? Company Stocks?" Arthur silently asked himself. "What have we here! Hmmm. Ho. Now that we talk business, he gives me the business!

"A strange case. This is my father. This is the man I thought I knew better than any other man. He's always been so open and honest, so straightforward and to the point. Why is he now hiding, closing, backtracking and mealymouthing? Why doesn't he just tell me the truth?! I am his son. I am first in his affections. Yet he now treats me like an opponent, an adversary, a stranger, and why does he play this game with me?! What game is worth the playing when the affections of loved ones are at stake? The prize must be great for a father to risk his only son's love, and—

"Money. The child of human greed, the father of human chaos. Money! Money! Money! It's plain to see, what with his talk of wills, company stocks, management and powers of attorney, just how plain my father is, how he puts the worship of the golden calf ahead of love for his son. He turns a foul green over the basest of green and I'm not so green that I should miss it. O heavy vision, to see my father fallen so low, to know that he who I thought I always knew has never been known at all . . ."

"Well what do you say, what do you think about all this?" Donald asked worriedly. "As soon as you turn eighteen we should get those power of attorney papers signed. It's a big company, a lot of responsibility. Decisions have to be made quickly and correctly," he urged, wiping his brow, "and your mother and I want you to be able to concentrate on your studies and not have to worry about business.

"Well what do you say?!?" Donald demanded, repeating himself. So far, Arthur had said nothing. His only reply had been reticent hesitancy, his only commitment had been to noncommittal.

Arthur continued to say nothing.

"Do you feel alright? What's wrong? Why aren't you saying *anything*?!" Donald demanded, nervously gasping for breath.

"Why speak, when speech leaves the soul speechless," Arthur wondered, noting his father's exhaustion at having talked forever while saying nothing. "But I must answer him," Arthur realized. "My silence is a disturbance, disturbs his state of noisy quiet. Shall I tell him the truth, that I doubt the man I never doubted before, that I think he deceives with legalese?

"No. Fight fire with fire, deceive deceit with deception. I'll *pretend* that my silence and distraction is lovesickness over Julia, is unrelated to my new distrust of him and these murky provisions of the will.

"At least I know myself, myself I know. This being the case I'll case my being, reveal the parts of me that serve my purpose, purpose to conceal the parts of me that do not serve."

"I'm sorry, I'm so sorry, I'm sorry," Arthur mumbled. "I'm sure that it's all just as you said. Excuse me, but I was thinking, dreaming, thinking of Julia. Of Julia. Of Julia."

"Oh. So your girl has got you off balance," Donald replied, mollified. "Well. We'll talk more about this later, on your eighteenth birthday when you can sign the papers," he said, relieved.

"Surely, surely," Arthur murmured despondently, doing his best to appear despondent. "He seems to be buying my act," he then thought, eagerly. "Good. His buying my act buys me the time to think his act through.

"Hmmm. I had wanted to find out more from him concerning my brother's death before this business about the will came up. Ha. An idea peeps at my creeping imagination. An innocent way to know damning knowledge."

"Yes, we'll talk more about the will," Arthur said to Donald. "You can fully explain its provisions to me, what papers you think I should sign.

"Too bad my brother David is no longer here to advise us," he slipped in, without missing a beat or raising a threatening eyebrow. "Surely the will touched on him. What was done then, how did you and David handle it when David turned eighteen?" Arthur casually asked.

Stunned, Donald could not reply. Guilt and past troubles crossed his face as an immobilizing iciness clutched at his body. Arthur saw the reaction. He thought: "A hot question freezes him up! The telegram must tell a tale of truth! I'll have to find out more."

"Are you okay?" Arthur asked. Concerned.

"Ummm, uhh, eerrr," Donald had not been expecting the unexpected.

Father and Son sat down to rest, underneath the obelisk where they had been standing.

2.

Late that afternoon, the shipboard community left Luxor and returned by bus to Port Safaga.

Arthur had a long time to think things over while riding on the bus. He went over the mysterious telegram and what his father had told him about the will. He went over how things stood between him and Julia and of how his father had reacted when he mentioned David in connection with the will. He went over and over and over . . .

The only conclusion Arthur came to was that almost everything was uncertain. He needed badly to be re-assured.

Arthur stalked the hallways of the S.S. Cosmos, looking for someone trustworthy, for someone he could talk to. His mother could not be found, was not in her cabin, so Arthur decided to go talk to his Art Teacher, to a man he was on good terms with.

Arthur was disturbed. Unsettled. He didn't even bother to knock on the door to his professor's cabin. He simply walked right in.

There were sighs. Groanings. A familiar squishy sound. A body. Female. On top. Two bodies. Moving. Making. Moving making love. The heated scent of desire. With the lights on.

Arthur looked. Looked again. A third time to be sure. Then he knew. "How naked is the naked truth!" he gasped, running out of the room. He had no idea, had never expected to find—

"What was that??" Arthur's Art Teacher asked.

"Oh Arthur, *Arthur*," Sally groaned. "Ohhh. What a wayward way for my boy to become a man!" Arthur's mother lamented. She tried to think, but there was no place to begin.

"Young chicks never dream of what the old hens have been up to," Arthur raved, pacing back and forth in his 5' by 7' cabin. His roommate Dan looked on with concern. He had never seen Arthur in such a state.

"Woman, thy name remain unnamed," Arthur ranted. "It would burn fairer ears to hear it!"

"Uhhh, Arthur—" Dan tried to say.

"They smile and they coo as they call black white, white black, lies truth, truth lies. Honeyed on the outside, bloodied within! And they perfume themselves to mask their foul odors, wear fine lace over their most malignant tumors. Their skipping, dancing, fluttering, whirling and prancing, their jigging the distracting jig, why it's all done to hide their baser movements. They act out the sham of the care free whim as a cover for their heavy desires and I tell you: Women play the fool to make idiots out of men!"

"He loses faith, he loses control," Dan murmured.

"Hah. *Motherhood!*" Arthur sniggered. "*Fatherhood. Brotherhood* and *Sisterhood*," he spat out. "Garbage, garbage, grouped together garbage. They're all nothing more than hoods that we use to hide our real selves under. Why not be fair and honest, why not tell the truth, why not say when it comes to the group known as Mankind, speak of *Whorehood* before you speak of any other hooded grouping!"

"Arthur—"

"Trust no one. Trust nothing. Speak not to the seamy shadow that lurks in darkest corner, speak not to the seeming maiden who lurks in broadest daylight. They're all one and the same, the same as always. Keep to yourself if your self you'd keep," Arthur stormed, flying out of the cabin.

"He's desperate, I'd better follow him," Dan thought, following.

3.

"He's a Hamlet's Hamlet," the Director exclaimed, observing Arthur at rehearsal. "Such distraction. Such depression. Such a pale complexion. Why he outmoodies the moodiest character of all moody time!" the Director chortled, pleased with Arthur's performance.

"I see his unseeing eyes," an actor agreed. "Here's a man who freely acts his actor's part. Here's a man who'll cry for Hecuba! The audience shall gleefully clamor at this rousing performance—"

"While the performer silently weeps," an actress muttered. "Sounds to me as if he almost means it," she continued, as Arthur went through the motions of, "To be, or not to be."

"To die, to sleep—No more—" Arthur rasped— "and by a sleep to say we end/The heartache, and the thousand natural shocks/That flesh is heir to; 'tis a consummation Devoutly to be wished./To die, to sleep To sleep—"

"That's enough, you're doing it just fine," the Director called out. "You don't need to run through it one more time."

"Perchance to dream:" Arthur continued. "ay, there's the rub./For in that sleep of death what dreams may come/When we have shuffled off this mortal coil,/Must give us pause."

"I say," the Director said, loudly, distinctly. "Enough's enough. You've revealed that you have the part, the part reveals that it has you. You've shown us your show, let someone else have the stage," the Director directed. The rest of the crew silently watched.

"For who would bear the whips and scorns of time,/Th' oppressor's wrong, the proud man's contumely/The pangs of despised love," Arthur groaningly continued.

"Arthur—" the Director exclaimed.

"I heard he hasn't eaten in three days," an actress whispered.

"His roommate says he sleeps no more," a stagehand muttered.

"Poor bastard. I think Julia dumped on him," an actor gossiped.

"I saw him late last night, stumbling around Promenade Deck," someone said. "He looked like a wild man. His clothes were undone, his hair blown about. His eyes gleamed, his hands trembled, and I could have sworn that he was talking to himself!"

"Arthur, get a grip on yourself, stop—" the Director begged.

"Thus conscience does make cowards of us all," Arthur exclaimed.

"And thus the native hue of resolution," he continued. "Is sicklied o'er with the pale cast—"

Stunned, the entire crew looked on at the spectacle.

"He's just not himself today," someone finally remarked.

The Director found Arthur's father on top of the Sun Deck of the S.S. Cosmos, watching disinterestedly as the big ship made her quiet slow way through the Suez Canal. "Hello there," the Director called out. "Hello there."

"Hello, hello," Donald replied. "How's the play coming?" he asked politely. "Fine, fine."

"Has my son properly learned his role?" Donald asked.

"Oh yes, yes. If anything he plays it too well," the Director murmured. "In fact, that's one of the reasons that I've come looking for you."

"Come again? You still haven't found me."

"Your son. I mean he plays the part of Hamlet all too well. He seems awfully moody and depressed lately," the Director confided. "I'm getting quite worried about him."

"Well the boy has love problems," Donald said hastily.

"So I've heard."

"When she smiles again, he'll smile again," Donald continued hopefully. "Lovers are mirrors, mirrored are the lovers."

"Of course, of course. But just the same—" the Director began.

"I know that people have been talking about him," Donald said evenly.

"He has created a scene here, an episode there. The Dean, the faculty and staff, they've all noticed," the Director warned.

"Look, what are you trying to say—"

"I say what needs saying," the Director continued, softly but firmly. "It's been noted that Arthur's notes are noticeably off-key. If people continue to talk, and talk, and talk and talk, if they talk 'the enough' that's too much, the powers that be must eventually take action."

"Can't you give plain speech to your plain thoughts!" Donald demanded.

"Don't take offense at good intentions, don't be a man defensive, taking the world as totally offensive," the Director said. "I'm only trying to help. What I'm trying to say is that the Dean will send Arthur home if he doesn't shape up! It's more serious than you think. They'll send him back to the States if he doesn't get his act together."

"Oh," Donald lamely replied.

"I like Arthur," the Director continued. "The faculty and staff had a meeting today where he was discussed and I was one of the few voices that spoke up for him."

"Thanks. Thanks," Donald said, thoughtfully rubbing his chin. He hadn't realized that Arthur's antics were getting quite so out of hand.

"Do you really think it's love sickness that has him so upset?" the Director asked.

"I can think of nothing else," Donald replied, openly. As he inwardly began to think of what that something else might be.

"Well. If it is something else, it well eventually be revealed," the Director said. "The ceaseless hands of Time, working forever and ever, always strip naked the most hidden hiding place."

"You think so?" Donald asked, worried, his spirit suddenly dwelling upon his own something else.

"Sooner or later a crime must find its own punishment," the Director queerly said.

Donald tensed. *Wasn't that out of context?* He then wondered if the Director knew more than he said, if he knew something else.

4.

"Nothing follows anything," Donald muttered. "The world is all too ass backwards; he who says differently is all too forwards a fool."

"Well what did Arthur say when you confronted him about the will?" Sally asked. "Is he willing to sign the power of attorney papers?"

"No. Yes. Yes. No. Maybe. The boy was all distance and distraction when I tried to pin him down," Donald replied. "Claimed his mind was on that girl Julia."

"And how does she fit in?"

"Last week they were close. Now they have a fight. Tomorrow, tomorrow they shall marry and divorce within the same day, if the future can be read in all our yesteryears," he proclaimed. "Love's only surety is its uncertainty."

"Ohhh Jesus. Bring me meat not garnish, give me truth not cliches. Will he or will he not sign those papers?" Sally demanded, nervously lighting a cigarette.

"You're on such good terms with him you ask him," Donald shot back.

"Hell. Did you suggest that he leave us in control until he turns thirty?" she asked aggressively.

"Yes, yes, but I think we overshot the mark there. Twenty five is far more reasonable. He'll not wait till thirty to call the world his own," Donald said, thoughtfully. "Why the world is his this very moment if he but has the will to so name it."

"No, no, make him leave us in control until he turns thirty," Sally urged. "That leaves us *twelve* years, not the seven we'd get if he signed for his twenty fifth birthday."

"I don't know. A good climber knows when to stop climbing," her husband warned. "The reach for that final rock is often the final reach. Shall we fall off the mountain to gain a foot?"

"Bah. Woman!" Sally spat out, at Donald.

"Hummm. Big words to hide a small heart!?" he silently wondered. "You don't seem as sure of your position with the boy as you once did," Donald said to Sally. "A few days ago, you were certain that he'd do nothing to hurt his mother. Now you want to imprison him for half his life, till he's thirty. Why?" he asked. "Has the son seen his virgin mother blackened?" he sniggered.

"You're a nasty man—"

"With a nasty wife—"

"We should find out what Julia's plans are," Sally said, businesslike. "The mountains bow to the valleys, the moon reveals more than the sun.

"Go to her," his wife ordered. "Find out where she wants to lead our son. Heaven knows I can't talk to her, she *hates* me. Go to her. The foolish young girl loves the attention of the foolish old man," the older woman said knowingly.

"You think she likes me?" Donald asked, surprised.

"Of course. She loves to play father and son against each other," Sally answered. "She may be a young girl but she's still a woman."

"Alright, alright, I'll try to find out how she feels about Arthur," he said.

"Good."

"You know, they're talking about sending Arthur home," Donald began, after a pause. "His antics are getting quite out of hand. Do you think it's the girl that has so removed him from himself?"

"What else," Sally answered. "The only other thing—"

"He *has* been asking lots of questions about David," Donald said meaningfully. "About the circumstances of his death, about how the will concerned him, about—"

"That's a door that's best left closed," Sally replied, cutting him off. "Some books are not meant to be read. Go feel out the girl before her wild ways leave us senseless," she admonished, and Donald went to look for Julia.

Arthur walked about, aimlessly, trying to unravel the knots that had closed around him. He had no destination in particular that he pursued, no logic in general that he followed. He simply let his feet do his walking.

His brooding, after a time, carried him by some portholes that were on an outer deck. For some reason he stopped. Then he realized that Julia's cabin was on this deck, that two portholes down was the window to her cabin.

He crept on. Watching, to see that no one was watching him.

He was at her porthole. The curtains were not completely drawn, so. He looked down through the opening.

He didn't know why he did it. He couldn't explain the unexplainable urge that had grabbed hold of him. He simply did it.

He just had to know.

And there in Julia's cabin was Julia, sitting on her bed. Someone sitting next to her . . .It was *Donald; his father!*

Arthur had to keep on looking.

Laughing. Talking. Laughing. Talking. A hand on a knee. A smile returning a smile.

Arthur looked and looked.

"Of course it all looked very innocent," Arthur thought, pacing about. "He simply talked with her, she simply talked with him, a simple matter, very simple, no need to make it all so complex, it certainly seemed as though there was nothing seamy there . .

"An' he's my father, my father, certainly I can trust him, doesn't the man I honor have honorable intentions? An' she's my girlfriend, my lover, my better half. Why she lives for me—at least I think so—and no, no, to think of her and my father? God. What a monster I would become, thinking thoughts such as these. If my imagination continues to dwell in such foul slothy regions it will surely abase me. We are as we think, the colors of our ideas color our complexions, and no, no, I'll not think on it, to muse upon it would not do my better parts justice!!

"Still . . . Still . . . Still . . . It bears examining. We cannot simply wish or dream evil away. No one has ever exterminated a maggot by closing his eyes and wishing that it would happen. Now, he was with her, my father and my lover, and they talked and, and—"

"Telegram," a steward stated, handing Arthur a message. Arthur lifted an eyebrow at the interruption. Then he tore at the communication. It read: "Stop. Have more knowledge concerning David's death. Stop. Speak of this to no one. Stop. More proof of your parents' (Father's) involvement. Stop. Call me from Cairo for details. Stop. A friend. Stop. 812-732-4784. Stop. USA. Stop."

"Hah. Ho," Arthur muttered. "I need less stops, more starts. Hmmm. Fresh shadows come raining down, further obscuring the dark cloud of my brother's death.

"What should I do now? Confront my parents openly? Throw this message in their face and demand an explanation? Or should I continue to pretend that I am love stricken, that I am blinded by wild passion to the rest of the turbulent world. Is Truth found head-on or do we know her from the rear. Is she common, perverse, or commonly perverse. What shall I do?

"Ha-ha. I speak as if there were rhyme or reason to this world we live in. Who knows if we make decisions or if decisions make us. Hah. I ask 'What shall I do?' Better to wonder what shall be done to me!

"Which way to turn, which way to turn . . .

"Telegram. Will. Second telegram. Julia slighting me. Donald, my father, with Julia. Sally, my mother, untrue. The will. David. David. And the play? Yes the play, I must practice, I must rehearse, I must play my part well . . ."

FOUR

1.

It was a forced confrontation. Neither Mother nor Son wanted to face each other for shame and embarrassment, truths and shattered dreams, now obscured their once clear relationship. Still, the facts had to be faced.

It was Sally who went looking for Arthur. She had not talked to him since that awfully telling moment and she felt like she had to . . . explain. But what could she say?

Arthur had never suspected the truth about his mother. He had always thought she was above THAT. And he had always assumed that she led such a model life, within the model scope of her model marriage with Donald. He had thought and assumed, assumed and thought, never realizing the distance between his assuming thoughts and truth's unassuming reality.

It was a forced confrontation.

"Arthur?" Sally called, knocking on his cabin door.

"What do you want?!" Arthur returned sulkily.

"Let me in. I want to talk to you," Sally said.

"What else is there to say?" Arthur asked.

"Oh grow up and open this door," Sally replied forcefully. This woman was no weak sister.

"Don't tell me what to do!" her son shot back, his teenage need for self flaming forth. He hated it whenever either of his parents told him what to do, who to be.

"Oh Arthur!" Sally cried, sniffling. Sobbing as if wounded. This woman was no one's fool. She was determined to enter that room. And if it took falling tears to fall the resistance of a stubborn man, she would rain her clever weakness upon his conscience until he collapsed.

Guiltily, Arthur opened the door. He wondered, as the hinges swung, why *he* felt guilty, why *he* felt bad, when it was she who had sinned.

Mother and Son gazed at each other. All the well rehearsed lines fell completely apart. Sally immediately knew the full weight of her guilt. And Arthur knew the cold touch of the hard facts of life.

"Arthur," Sally pleaded, "don't turn away from me just because—"

Arthur walked out of the room, hating the known and the unknown for what they were, hating himself for having ever believed in anyone or anything.

"Fucking cunts," Arthur muttered, over a beer in the ship's bar. "Every last one of them a false bitch, every last one of them proof of the bitchin' truth. They're all thoughtlessly selfish, selfishly thoughtless. Why the man who gives them the slightest quarter should be quartered and drawn.

"Ten to one it was a pious old woman who invented the crucifix!"

Arthur continued to drink as the night wore on. He thought of his lover Julia. He thought of his mother Sally. He thought and he thought till his thoughts made him sick, till he got to the point where he lashed out.

In the bar, there was a girl who was *available*, who was fucking everything and accomplishing nothing. She was pleasing everyone to punish herself and Arthur took her. In an obvious place in an obvious way.

He wanted to be sure that everyone found out.

2.

Julia bit her lip. Julia bit her lip. Julia bit her lip. Julia bit her lip! Till the blood ran. No matter, no matter, no matter. Didn't change a thing. All the blood and the tears, all the tears and the blood, why they all went for naught, were useless waters, cryingly shed in a desert that could care less. And all the bloody tears in the world, all the bloody bloody tears, they were, no matter, no matter, no matter, they didn't change a thing. Fate, past and present and future, paid, pays, and will forever pay, no heed to the pain of women, no heed to the suffering of men, so no matter. The girl would weep and bleed herself into oblivion and who could care.

Julia had a secret. She had just found out she was pregnant. And she was young and scared and she didn't want anyone to know. That she was young and scared and pregnant.

"Something bothering you?" Gwen Richards asked. Gwen had seen Julia staring moodily out to sea. Concerned, the older woman had approached the younger girl.

"Who? Me? No! No! No troubles worth the trouble of telling," Julia lied. "The life I live is no bother, no bothered living for me," she mumbled. She was too ashamed to say that she was pregnant, even though she had read and heard that it was nothing to be ashamed of, that it happened all the time.

"Are you sure?" Gwen questioned.

"Of course, of course."

"You look rather pale."

"Perhaps the trip wears on me," Julia countered.

"And Arthur?"

"He's—he's fine," Julia sputtered. Julia had heard of Arthur's fooling around, had felt his slap in her face. She had almost called him a bastard when Gwen asked about him but since Arthur was a bastard she needed, there'd be no calling the bastard bastard.

102

"That's nice," Gwen replied. "You sure it's nothing more than the weather that has you so blue?"

"Yes I'm sure. Or maybe it's time for that time of month," Julia said, excusing herself. Wishing desperately that it really was that time of month.

"How did Arthur respond to the hard line you showed him?" Gwen demanded suspiciously. She knew that Julia could not be so blue over a momentary grey sky. "How did he react to your refusal to be his doormat?"

"By finding a new place wipe his feet," Julia quietly moaned, to herself.

"How did Arthur react to your refusal to be his doormat?" Gwen patiently repeated, taking into account that young hearts only hear their own sighings.

"Well I think we'll work things out," Julia said quickly, queerly. She had thought that all the world knew how Arthur had made a fool out of her and she was glad that Gwen still slept in the darkness when it came to that. After all, it would not do for the advisor to know how bad her advice had been. It was a thirsty fool who had gone to suckle the old cow's counsel, and none but he should be made to drink the resulting sour milk.

"Was Arthur mad when you told him that you wanted more independence, that you no longer cared to live for him and nothing more?" Gwen questioned.

"Oh no, no," Julia replied, heavily, trying to sound breezy. "He managed to accept my need for space (By finding himself a new space!)"

"Good, good, but are you sure everything is alright? You look rather poorly for a girl who's on top of the world," Gwen remarked.

"If only she knew, if only she knew, how my bottom now carries the world in punishment for having once ridden upon its top," Julia murmured. "Should I tell her? Why keep such a big secret when it will soon be so hugely obvious? Do I know what I'm doing? Why not come clean of the whole foul business? Why does it shame me?"

"Julia," Gwen prodded. "Is everything okay?!"

"It's alright we'll talk tomorrow," Julia responded hurriedly, her body trembling. She wanted to tell somebody, and Gwen, next to Arthur, was the most obvious somebody. Yet here went Julia's feet, sweeping her away. And away, and away, and away . . .

"Yes we'll talk tomorrow," Gwen said, easily, commonly, never realizing uncommon truth, that tomorrow never comes since today is all we have.

A dream, a dream, for Julia it all became a dream.

"Arthur," Julia began, groping for words. She sat in an unfeeling chair, having groped her way to Arthur's cabin without pretense or trickery.

This was no time to be fooling around.

"Arthur," Julia began again.

"That's my name," the boy replied. "Why do you call it now? Why only yesterday you'd forgotten it," the young man snapped. He was angry with her. Angry with her games. Angry with her previous rejection of him. Angry at having seen her with his father, no matter how innocent the meeting had seemed.

103

"You just don't seem to understand—"

"What? Who? You? Oh I understand you. One day I'm to be your master. Tomorrow I'm to be your equal, unless you would have me red, green, yello, blue or purple.

"Well I'll not color myself to match your female moods. I'll not eat caviare one day, potato soup the next. I'll not change my suit to suit your changes of mind!" Arthur spat out. "I'm no puppet for your whim!"

"Why did you hurt me so badly!?" Julia burst out, in tears. "Sleeping with . . . *fucking . . . that* girl! Everybody on board the ship knows—"

"You said you wanted your freedom. You said you didn't want to be so dependent upon one person. You said and you said and you said so I took you at your word," Arthur replied. "What's wrong now?! Having tasted freedom, does the slave long for his chains?"

"I said we needed more time apart," she returned. "That didn't mean you had the right to go out and plug any hole that was parted."

"Rights? Rights? Hah. You're a fine one. You only speak of rights when you've been wronged," he shot back. "God, but is there no judge to give the self righteous their rights?! When you wanted your space, your freedom, you had no concern for my rights, for my feelings, for how I had been wronged! You only thought of yourself, and now that being footloose and fancy free no longer strikes your fancy, you want me to step to a different tune."

"You hurt me, you hurt me, you—"

"You asked for it!" he interrupted. "Maybe we were too happy together, too happy for a girl bent on punishing herself."

"Oh boy. Here we go. You expel your psychological crap to cleanse the shit you pass," she accused. "An asshole, coming and going."

"Baloney," he returned. "We got hotly close, so closely hot that you developed cold feet. And you tried to push me away, to put me off, but now you cry because I strayed too far. That's the truth, that's what happened, but don't expect to reel me back in because you're lonely, don't imagine that I'm your dog on a leash!"

"Arthur I'm pregnant," Julia gasped, groaning and moaning, heaving, cradling her breasts within her arms.

A pause.

"Tethered with child, the woman seeks to tether a man," Arthur finally murmured.

"You don't have to ask if it's yours," she said. "There's been no one else. Ever."

"I'm sorry I got you into such a mess—"

"We! We! We! Don't say 'I', don't say 'you'. This is *our* problem!" Julia exclaimed. "We! We! We! Not I-you-me. We!"

"I'm not ready to be a father—"

"Nor I a mother!"

"You could have an abortion—"

"Hang it with a hanger? No! No! That's not for me. I just don't believe in that," Julia said emphatically. Her voice was shaking. Rising.

"Julia. Calm down."

"When I feel like throwing up?!"

"Julia, Julia, I, I, I'm not ready to get married. I'm not ready to have a child . . .

"An abortion would be *so simple*," the boy urged. "So easy."

"Easy? Easy for who? You? You've had it far too easy far too long."

"Honey—"

"Don't 'honey' me, don't 'sweetie' me, don't hide sour motives with candied words!" she bitterly admonished. "It's a damned angel who crosses over Hell by glossing his way with sugar and sweets. You'll roast in a sticky web if you use that bridge," Julia warned. "Fine words for false deeds is phony restitution."

"But baby—"

"Our baby—"

"If you don't have an abortion, what are you going to do?" Arthur asked pointedly.

"You make it sound like it's all *my* burden!" Julia returned.

"You could put it up for adoption—"

"*We* could *keep* it," she pleaded. "I wouldn't be ashamed to have your baby!"

"But, but,"

"How many times did you swear that you loved me! That you could imagine no one better to spend your life with. Arthur! Don't you care?" Julia asked, frightened. "You should never say forever if you don't mean it."

"Oh back off," he lashed out, angry and afraid. "Like any woman, you exaggerate. You wrap a summer's fling into an eternal cocoon for your own nesting purposes. You hypocrite. You were not to be relied upon when I was in need. Was I to keep myself for you after you kept me waiting? Why you disgust me. I'm galled by your gall. A rich man turned beggar, able to conveniently forget how he once turned the beggars away out of convenience—Where are you going, *I'm not through with you yet*," Arthur thoughtlessly yelled, but Julia had run out of the cabin.

Too proud to follow, he foolishly let her go.

Julia locked herself in her room, avoiding everyone. In one way or another, over a passage of time, she thought: ". . . Well, well, here's to Hell, the only place for a maiden who's been made—a fool. Having had me he no longer wants me, hors d'oeurve hors d'oeurves, human appetite hungers for hors d'oeurves, the single plate, no matter how substantial, never satisfies inhuman craving—They have you one way, then it must be done another, and another and another, as they go through you, one after the other, one after the other. Love's not constant, Love's no conscience, there's only love conscientiously inconstant.

"There's a stranger in my bed. I know him not. He's slept there since I can remember, but I know him not. He's kissed me and held me, sworn never to sell me, but I know him not, as he steals himself away into the silent night. And Arthur? Arthur? Arthur's the name of a dream I never quite knew, of the book I never quite finished. Intimate, intimate, yes we were intimate locked in hot embrace, wrapped in two in our quilt weaved for one, telling everything, everything we knew, yes, yes,

yes, we were intimate, intimately intimate, until the cold hands of the stranger pried us apart.

"What's kind of life after love's bitter death?

"A baby, a baby, I cannot see her, cannot feel her, yet she's heavier than any sensible thing. The idea alone kills me, perhaps even thrills me, for does the woman live who refuses to give life?

"Everyone knows, though nothing shows . . .

"Alone. Alone. An only woman's lonely, lonely, not alone but lonely.

"Family? Father? Mother? Sister-brother? Friends? What will they say? I can't face them when I can't face myself.

"There's a beast in the woods, a wolf in my heart, a shadow on the altar, a cross on my shoulder. I hear my page turning, watch tomorrow burning, and long for Babylon, Babylon, fairy tale land of my girlish past, where nothing went wrong. And the future? Why speak of the unspeakable.

"It's all unendurably the same, for those who would but feel . . .

"Don't stop now. Hands, don't stop now, don't fail she that he has failed. More drink! More drink! And just one more of these, a painkiller to kill my pain. Hands, hands, do this smothering work, keep agony from smothering me. O hands, hands, all too heavy hands in this all too heavy world, speak for me, for she who longs to be—shut up!"

3.

"A whore to the core, infested with sores as she skips from door to door, led by her lust—"

"Oh shut up. Knock off the fancy talk," Sally said, interrupting Arthur. Arthur had come to her in her cabin and he had proceeded to lay an enormous guilt trip on her. He didn't like his mother's fooling around.

"More matter and less art? Have it your way, you always do," Arthur angrily returned. "So we'll call a spade a spade, a bitch a bitch."

"You make it sound as though I betrayed *you*," his mother said. "Will you please grow up? Your father has known for a long time that I do as I please. I've never lied to him."

"Oh you're a virtuous soul."

"And you're a hypocrite. You sleep around yourself," Sally reminded him. "You didn't think twice about having a roll in the hay with a total stranger, and what's worse is that you made sure *everyone* found out about it. I'm sure your well publicized indiscretion hurt poor Julia far more than anything I've ever done to your father. Or to you. Do you really think it's worse for the wear?" Sally asked, pointing to her crotch. "In your mind, any female who gets around is as evil as Attila the Hun! You should try to be more mature about this, this is the Twentieth Century, not the Sixteenth!"

"And you—"

"I've been fooling around for years," Sally said, firmly. "I'm sorry you had to find out like you did but I guess it was inevitable.

"Why are you making such a big deal out of it?" she gently asked, taking Arthur's hand. "You've always been number one with me where it counts," the mother said, to her son, indicating an area somewhere between her breasts.

"It's just, just," Arthur stumbled, "I mean God, the way you and Dad act, like you're the perfect couple, and I always *believed* that act. Finding out the truth . . ." Arthur's voice trailed away.

"I'm sorry it was so painful," Sally returned.

Arthur was confused. Faltering. He had come to condemn—not to forgive. Could he so easily accept his mother's outlook? Something beautifully primitive then took over. "Forgive me this my virtue," he ranted. "For in the fatness of these pursy times—Virtue itself of vice must pardon beg,—Yea, curb and woo for leave to do him good."

"Christ Almighty," Sally muttered, lighting a cigarette. "The play's gone to his head.

"Get real," she said to Arthur. "This is 1978! ERA! Women's Lib! The Bomb! WW1! WW2! The Space Age! Supersonic speeds! The New Morality! Social Security! Television! Out of the closet and into the streets! Where have you been?! Sleeping? Stargazing? Daydreaming about some romantic past? Wake up!! And though it's bad enough your morals and ideas don't match the times, what's worse is you really are being quite hypocritical, saying one thing while doing another. A hypocrite should—"

Donald then walked in on them.

"Well speak of the devil, here comes the big tough coward himself," Arthur said, greeting his father.

"Huh?" Donald dumbly asked.

"We're discussing, among other things, the difference between the apparent and the true," Arthur replied. "Mom and I were discussing her fooling around and how you've come to meekly accept it."

"Arthur?!? Sally?!?"

"And how do you get your kicks?" Arthur asked his father. "By fooling around with little girls?" he demanded, angrily thinking of the time he had seen Donald with Julia.

"What do you mean?"

"Oh I saw you in Julia's cabin. Trying to—"

"Why you little sneak!"

"You two really amaze me," Arthur said disgustedly. "A whore and a child molester living contentedly under the same roof."

"Arthur, I was just talking with Julia, trying to, to," Donald stumbled.

"What! If you weren't using her to get into her panties you must have been using her in another way, trying to find out something about me," Arthur accused. Donald turned a bright red. "My father!" Arthur exclaimed. "An open book when the world is looking, a closed liar when dealing with his own son."

"That's going too far," Donald protested.

"Not far enough," Arthur returned. "You're always trying to take everyone for a ride. Just like that day in Luxor, in the temples at Carnack, when you beat around the bush while discussing Grandfather's will."

Both Sally and Donald clutched.

"What are the two of you so afraid of when it comes to that will?" Arthur demanded, seeing their reaction. "When the cold old man wrote his will, did he leave you two out in the cold?"

"When I came in, I heard your mother saying something about your being a hypocrite," Donald snapped at Arthur, regaining his composure, trying to draw the conversation away from the terms of the will. "I see she was right. You accuse me of beating around the bush when we spoke at Carnack. But weren't you doing the same thing at the same time, the way you questioned me about your brother's death? You knew he died in the Bronx of a heart attack. Why did you say those things about Queens, about appendectomies. Weren't you checking things out in an indirect way?"

"I—" Arthur stumbled.

"Are you one of those people who imagine they act one way, all pure and proper, when in fact they are as sullied as the rest of us? Is your left hand brother to your right?" Donald demanded.

"Go easy on him," Sally snapped at Donald. She loved her son so very much.

"I need no help from you," Arthur bitterly said to her. "I know myself," he continued, with a shade of uncertainty. Confused, he momentarily thought of confronting his parents with the mysterious telegrams regarding his brother's death. He decided against it, however. "I'll not reveal a scrap of my designing till the plans are complete," he dreamily thought. "Sketches are not to be seen, only the painted masterpiece should be unveiled. I'll find out all before I tell a thing, I'll hide away the pieces till I complete the puzzle. I'll keep playing the part of the moody, love stricken boy, living in a daze, until I learn more about my brother's death and my parents' involvement. Why—"

"Arthur?" Sally gently asked, noting his distraction. "Are you with us?"

"The boy's not steady," Donald muttered.

"Steady enough to see what's unnerving you," Arthur shot back, overhearing him. "*The will leaves me in control of the family fortune, of the family company,*" he then guessed. "Is that it? Did Grandfather leave my parents to his grandson's mercy? Does everything become mine when I turn eighteen? Tell me. Is that why you wanted me to sign those power of attorney papers? Afraid that my uncorralled youth would trample upon your defenseless old age?"

A long pause.

"So you have it," Donald finally admitted, wearily, sitting down. "The will leaves everything, the whole company, to you and your brother. Now that he's gone . . ."

"It's all mine."

"You mother was left with enough to live on quite comfortably," Donald continued. "A modest fortune—"

"That could not possibly feed her immodest desires," Arthur finished, beginning to come of age.

"And I," Donald stumbled.

"A father, left to the mercy of his son's affections," Arthur concluded. He looked, for a while, at his parents. "All this pain and deceit, treachery and woe," he finally murmured. "I know there's evil everywhere, but were you, *my parents*, afraid to count on your very own son?" he asked. Then he thought about what he had said, and laughing hysterically, he left the room.

4.

The S.S. Cosmos sat quietly in Alexandria, Egypt. It was nighttime, and Arthur had snuck ashore to place a phone call to New York. It took him three nerve wracking hours to get through.

It was an uncertain voice at the other end of the line.

"Hello, hello, this is Arthur, David's brother, I'm in Egypt," Arthur began. "You've sent me two telegrams about, about, how my brother died, and my parents," he stumbled, "about my, how my parents may have been involved—"

"You didn't get the whole story," the voice muttered. "What do you really know about your brother David?"

"Why—"

"Did you know that he was a junkie? That he was just like me?" the voice shakily asked. "A fucking two bit junkie."

"A painter, a painter, my brother was a painter," Arthur said, disbelieving.

"Ha-ha, that's a good one, your parents or somebody must have fed you a line," the voice laughed. "I guess Mom and Dad didn't like to tell the folks at the country club that their son had a monkey on his back . . . probably didn't want to face up to it themselves," the voice dreamily continued.

"How do you think David died?" the voice asked.

"A heart attack in the Bronx—"

"Ho-ho, ho-ho. Somebody's been giving *you* the business," the voice chortled. "You took hook, line and sinker."

"What are you trying to say?"

"David O.D.ed, kiddo. He took too long a ride on that big white horse."

"I don't think I believe you."

"I got the proof man. Documents were changed to hide how your brother died," the voice said. "Money changed hands. Somebody didn't want the truth to come out.

"Did you know that your old man saw David the day before he kicked?"

"My father?!" Arthur gasped. "He never told me *that*!"

"Yeah, your old man was at our crash pad the day before Davy boy became no more. Me and David were roommates you see," the voice giggled.

"You know, I think somebody knocked Dave off, gave him a one way ticket," the voice wheezed, coughing. "I heard from a friend at the police station that the guy's last shot was pure smack, one hundred percent H. You don't get that kind of shit unless somebody *wants* you to get it."

"Who? What? Why?" Arthur cried out.

"Slow down," the voice cautioned. "Haven't your folks told you all about this?" the voice sniggered. "I seen your old lady from a distance. Real fine looking broad. Woman like *that* wouldn't hide *anything* from *her* kids."

"I've got to find out more," Arthur demanded.

"It'll cost money," the junkie returned. "Everything costs money. No such thing as a free lunch, no such thing as a free ride."

"I don't care what it costs—"

"That's what I like to hear," the voice interrupted. "You see you're just like me, a man without inhibitions."

"How much?"

"Oh, er, ummm," the voice hesitated, trying to guess just how much Arthur would pay, just how much Arthur could pay. A price, a price, the seller sought the price that the market could bear without collapsing. "Three grand?" the voice tossed out.

"Done I don't care. But I have to see you face to face," Arthur implored. "I have to meet you."

"Make it four and I'll fly to Cairo," the voice replied. "I always wanted to see the pyramids."

"Okay, okay—"

"Wire the money to H. G. Higgins, General Delivery, Bernardsville, New Jersey. I'll meet you—Meet me in the mummy room of the Cairo Museum, on the morning of the 6th. That's three days from now."

"Alright. I'll do it," Arthur agreed. He had no choice. He had to find out everything he could, even if it meant sending thousands of dollars to a junkie through General Delivery.

"Don't talk to anyone about this," the voice warned. "Your parents, your best friend, your lover or your brother. And watch out for your old man! Beneath the plastic coating burns a violent beast. He and David had a big fight the day before David died, the day before somebody, I think, before somebody did a number on Davy. You got it?" the voice wheezed. And then the phone was hung up before Arthur could reply.

It was a queer conversation. Two would-be conspirators, indirectly discussing their conspiring, not sure if they wanted to conspire, wondering if their conspiring was justified, saying they were looking out for the interests of another, when in fact, they may have been looking out only for themselves.

It was a queer conversation.

"The boy is ill," Donald said gravely. "His antics have gone beyond the stage of pranks. He may need help. A rest . . ."

"What do you mean?" Sally asked.

110

"He may need a year, or so, a year or so, *off, away* from the pressures of the world. You've seen how unbalanced he's been lately," Donald stated, matter-of-factly. "The way he walked out on us earlier, laughing hysterically. He was like a madman."

"Are you talking about committing him?" she asked.

"You began this conversation," he returned defensively.

"Well he's been acting so strangely."

"Very strangely. We may have to do something—"

"For his own good," Sally finished, thoughtfully.

Arthur and his roommate Dan slipped on down to the ship's theatre. It was very late at night and the boys were sharing a drink. Or two. As they rambled around on what was becoming one of Arthur's habitual ramblings.

"The stage is set," Arthur said, taking a swig, eyeing the completed props. "Expectant desire shall soon become gluttonous satiation—if the pigs are not too fat to eat."

"And drink," Dan sniggered, sipping on the bottle. Then he began to urinate on the floor.

"How crude—"

"How rude—"

"How rudely crudely human."

"In one hole—"

"And out the other."

"Till we're swallowed up—"

"By the greedy hole that's Time "

"Why you're a poet—"

"Without a poem."

"A fool—"

"Like everyone else."

"Disaster's just a door away—"

"Damnation's round the corner."

"All our futures and all our days—"

"Are lost in life's disorder."

"Where to next?"

"Why ask where you're going when you don't even know where you've been," Arthur chastised. "Why life, life, life's a shattered dream that forever fails us, a deadening sleep from which we never rise. Blindly we go into the future, frightened we crawl from the past, as fleeting desire mocks and teases us in the burning here and now. Don't speak to me of heroes and conquerors when only battered survivors remain. Don't shout of victory when the only conquest allowed is self-defeat. Don't applaud Life when she only ends in annihilation. Fuck it all, it all fucks us!"

"More! More!" Dan encouraged.

"Poetry is dead," Arthur replied bitterly. "Dead, dead, dead. Why I bet she's never even lived, never even existed, unless you count the foolish fancies of sentimental romantics. Come on, let's keep drinking," he ordered. "We've nothing to look forward to and everything to forget."

111

FIVE

1.

"Somebody's got to tell him."

"But who?"

"Not me!"

"He's got to be told."

"There's no way of predicting what that wild man will do when he finds out."

"Somebody's got to tell him. Facts have to be faced."

"Fine. Maybe the facts have to be faced, but that doesn't mean my face has to be around for the facing."

"Mine neither!"

"Nor mine!'

"You can count me out."

"Now wait a second. I thought *all* of us were going to tell him, I thought we were all in this together," Dan protested.

"That was only till it all came apart," a retreating voice called out.

"He's your roommate. He's your friend. You tell him," someone said.

Dan caught his breath.

Arthur was in the Dining Room, eating breakfast, when Dan found him. The room was very crowded. Nervously, Dan tried to convince Arthur to come listen to him in a more private place.

"What do you mean?" Arthur demanded. "Words are words, the time and place in which they're spoken makes no difference. A message is a message, we hear it all the same whether it's delivered in daytime's openness or under nighttime's rock. Speak your peace."

"Arthur! Step outside for a moment, what I have to tell you is very important!" Dan exclaimed. He was trembling. Tears were in his eyes.

"Though the news be crippling I'll take it standing," Arthur returned. "Say it now, for tomorrow you'll have no tongue. The inevitable future silences us all."

"Arthur, please step out—"

"Goddamnit whaddya want!"

"It's *Julia*, Arthur," Dan cried, in a silence, for their ruckus had stilled the early morning conversations around them. "She's she's—"

112

"Julia? What are you trying to—"

"Dead. She's dead Arthur. She fell, late last night . . . down some steps . . . broke her neck . . . Arthur? Arthur?"

Arthur got up from his chair. Glass shattered as his cup fell to the floor. In a daze the boy began to move. The world watched, helplessly, as Arthur felt: "Julia? Julia? Julia? Are you really gone? Answer me, for with your death, I die. My ears, they hear, nothing, nothing more than the sound of my own empty voice. Julia? Julia? Come touch me, my love, bring me warmth, for a sudden cold has crept upon me. Are you really gone? Eyes? Eyes? Can you see the rest of your days, restlessly spent, searching through the endless time of a 'might have been'? Hands? Hands?! Do you feel the 'could have beens' as you carry them through your tomorrows? Julia? Julia? Now that you're gone, where have I been?! Sleeping? Julia! Julia! God. Unhearing, unfeeling God. My sins assault me. My errors mock me. To have sacrificed eternal love for a moment's pride! I must shudder at the sound of a laughter only I can hear, my follies return full force to me—O most grievous homecoming—Once . . . Once . . . I wooed you, pretending Love . . . Once . . . Once . . . I loved you, pretending indifference . . . Once . . . Once . . . I used our love, hiding 'neath it, pretending no need of the very tool I used . . . Oh I was a genius, a pretender who knew everyone but himself . . . A navigator, finding every destination but his own . . ."

"Watch where you're going!" McNulty snapped, as Arthur stumbled into him.

Arthur's right hand balled into a fist. His arm swung. McNulty's face distorted, as his jaw broke, as he crumbled to the floor.

No one tried to stop Arthur when he left the Dining Room.

Arthur didn't even think of knocking.

"I'm sorry about Julia," Sally gasped, frightened, as Arthur stormed into her cabin. She had heard.

"Lies, lies, the only human truth is lies," Arthur raved, grabbing her forcefully by the shoulders.

"I'm your mother, show me the respect I'm due," Sally sputtered, and Arthur slapped her hard across the mouth.

"Lies, lies, the only human truth is lies," he repeated. "Look at you, saying you're sorry about Julia's death, when the truth is nothing could have made you happier."

"That's not true—"

"Bitch!" Arthur ranted, slapping her again. "How come you never told me my brother was a junkie?!"

Sally's face lost color. A touch of fear bleached her eyes.

"And how come you never told me that Dad saw David the day before he died?!" Arthur demanded.

"How—"

"Did I find out. Oh you're a liar's liar. How your sinful deceit was uncovered worries you more than the sin itself. Woman, have you no conscience?!" he begged. "Hiding from me, your only son, the truth about my only brother?"

113

"Oh Arthur," she cried. "I, I, I, your father and I, we just wanted to spare you the pain, and the painful truth, there was no need for you to know . . ." Sally was now sobbing.

"Lies, lies, the only human truth is lies. Quit crying!!" Arthur howled, slapping her again. "Womanly tears no longer blind my manly eyes! The deceived no longer believes the deceiver though the truth kills him! Why you fool. You spared me painful truth, but see where easy deceit has brought us," he hissed, grabbing her by the throat.

"Arthur you're choking me," Sally gasped.

"Just as you choked the life out of my brother," he snarled.

"What? Arthur, you're—"

"How did my brother die? If you value your life, speak the truth about death."

"A heart attack, a heart attack." Sally wheezed, and Arthur clutched tighter at her throat. "His heart failed—"

"Lies, lies, the only human truth is lies!"

"A heart attack, that's what your father told me, Arthur you're killing me—"

"If only I'd finished the job at my birth," her son ejaculated, letting her go. Sally caught her breath. "David, David, my brother, a painter?! A story, a story, he only painted himself, into a corner. A heart attack, a heart attack? Another story, another story," Arthur growled, grabbing his mother by the hair. "A junkie, he died a junkie's death, finding a thrill too pure for weak human blood."

"He overdosed?"

"How truthfully simple, how purely innocent we now sound. You act surprised. Didn't you know?"

"No. Of course—"

"Not. You'd never lie to me," Arthur bitterly finished.

"Arthur—"

"And all that's left to know is who gave the final shot," he said. "Looking surprised again? I don't know if I should believe you. It's murderously clever, the way a murderer can look so innocent when the word murder is spoken. Give me money," Arthur continued. "Since my loved ones go to any price to deceive me, I must run and buy the truth from a stranger."

"Money?" Sally hesitated.

"You brought five thousand cash to buy rugs and furniture with," Arthur snapped. "I know all about it, you're not the only one who can go looking through other people's things. Give it to me."

"No. What for—Arthur have you gone mad—"

Arthur slapped her so hard he drew blood. "Ask me if I mean it and die a meaningless death," he exclaimed. Sally stumbled to a drawer, unlocked a jewelry box and gave him the money.

"You can tell my father there'll be a reckoning in Cairo," Arthur called out, leaving his mother in tears.

"Lies, lies, the only human truth is lies," he then muttered, stumbling out of the room. His mother watched him go as something tore at her heart. She loved him more than anything else she could possibly think of. Yet she was afraid of him. What would he do when . . . *if* and *when* . . . he came into his inheritance. How would he treat her after all of this?

2.

With fear in his heart and guilt on his mind, Donald searched Cairo for his son Arthur.

Try as he might, Donald was unable to locate Arthur. The boy could not be found when he wished to stay hidden and Donald didn't find him until Arthur permitted it, until Arthur let his father know where he'd be through other people.

It was an anxious search. Donald knew of Arthur's violent outbursts and he was afraid that Arthur would do something irretrievably rash. He was very afraid.

Before he left for Cairo, Donald and Sally had had a long talk about Arthur. Once again, they had spoken of confining the boy for his own good. For his own good, and it had been a very serious discussion.

Donald was afraid of what Arthur would do when he came into his inheritance, an inheritance that was the family fortune.

Donald was afraid of what Arthur knew about his brother's death.

It was a very anxious search.

"I hear he's out at the Pyramids," somebody told Donald. A day and a half had passed since Arthur had disappeared.

Donald took a taxi to the Pyramids.

"I seen him around here," a tourist-student from the S.S. Cosmos told Donald. "He said he was going to climb this pyramid here."

Donald gazed at Cheop's pyramid. Age, ever eroding age, had melted its once smooth face into enormous stepping stones, and if one looked hard enough, a path could be found to the summit of this pyramid, the world's tallest.

With some difficulty, the older man began to climb to the top.

Like the silent Sphinx that sat beneath him, Arthur rested mutely atop Cheop's Pyramid. He watched, without a single word, as the sun sank into the desert, as his father completed his painful crawl up the side of the pyramid.

Perspiring and out of breath, Donald finally reached his son.

They said nothing for the longest time.

"Great view you have from up here," Donald finally remarked.

"Of what use is an eagle eye view to a blind man," Arthur muttered.

"Son, I . . ."

"Yes?"

"I want to talk."

"At this point? We've talked too much, said too little," Arthur reminded him.

"Arthur—"

"How could you have lied to me about David? How could you have tried to

115

deceive me about the will? How could you have tolerated the phony marriage you and Mom have had for all these years?" Arthur asked. Demanded.

"Son, I . . ."

"How could you have ever been my father??" Arthur finished.

"We didn't tell you about David—"

"Excuses, excuses, is this the food with which a father should raise a son?"

"I—"

"How did David die? I've got to know," Arthur hissed. "I been thinking about it all day long."

Donald wearily sat down.

"Your older brother was an addict—"

"A junkie, a junkie, you, the highest of the high and mighty, bred a junkie."

"Alright he was a junkie," Donald finally admitted. "You know he never got along well with his mother and me, left home, left us, drifted into the wrong crowd, and well." There were tears in Donald's eyes. "When I finally located him, in New York, he—"

"Had a needle in his arm."

"I only saw him once before he died," Donald choked. "In some unimaginably filthy place. I, I,"

"You what."

"I just took one look at him and walked out the door," Donald cried out, guiltily. "I just couldn't face him, just couldn't bear to look at him, so—"

"You left him. You abandoned him, your oldest son, to the needle and the street. Is that your story, is that the sin you'll tell St. Peter when he asks you what you've been hiding?" Arthur coolly demanded.

"Yes! Yes! I ran away from my own son!" Donald blubbered. With a trace of relief on his face. He looked like a man from whom something had been lifted.

"Can the criminal be trusted to confess all his crimes?" Arthur murmured. "What's one more lie to a liar?"

"Tell me how David died," Arthur firmly said.

"A hear attack," Donald returned, wiping a tear from his eye. "The day after I saw him he dropped dead."

"He was under *twenty*—"

"He was a *junkie*," Donald interrupted. "Your mother told me that you claimed he died of an overdose but that's not true. He had a heart attack, there was an autopsy, an inquest, a coroner's report—"

"I heard he died of an overdose."

"That's not true. Who have you been talking to?"

"You're a fine one to be questioning sources. And you and I both know that overdoses need not be accidental, that certificates and inquests and reports are scraps of paper, bought and sold to the highest bidder."

"What?!"

"The will! The will! The will! What did David know about the will?" Arthur demanded, grabbing his father by the arm. "Did he know that half of the estate was

116

to be his? What did you tell him?!" Arthur raged. "Or did you stay true to form, hiding everything from him to the bitter end?"

"Well, well, no, we didn't tell him, everything—"

"Wasn't he to be told of his rights on his eighteenth birthday?"

"Your mother and I, it's a very big company, alot of responsibility, we couldn't just hand it over to a junkie—"

"Maybe he found out about the will. Maybe he was planning on a homecoming to claim his birthright. Maybe you and Mother couldn't stomach the thought, so maybe . . ."

"Arthur! My God! What are you saying! What are you suggesting?"

"A hideous idea, a hideous idea, but like all hideous ideas, life itself has surely gone to greater extremes. The evil in our hearts is always outdone by the evil in the world, " Arthur muttered.

"Arthur! Answer me! Talk to me!"

"Darkness arrives," he queerly replied. "See how our sun has set? Let's begin our descent, father, before the path becomes even more dangerous. We must seize the moment before the moment seizes us," Arthur said decisively.

Though they climbed slowly and carefully, there were plenty of slips and scares. The footing was treacherous, in the darkness, as a cold wind numbed the hands. Hands that were needed to grip.

Arthur was in a state as they descended. Food and sleep, the staples of a healthy existence, had become total strangers to him. He thought: "Now. Now. My moment is now! It grows dark and cold, the perfect time and place for an accident. A shove here, a push there, and soothing vengeance shall still the beast that rages within me. No one will be able to say a word against it, this foul deed, like so many others, shall be called 'tragedy,' not 'crime,' and with a momentary 'doing,' the eternal 'done' is accomplished. All that remains is to act.

"Of my father's guilt there can be no doubt, no doubt. He has failed me in every way possible, has fallen short of my every expectation, and surely, he killed, he *murdered*, my brother David. No doubt, no doubt, my father's a criminal, criminally capable of the foulest acts, even murder, no doubt, no doubt, it's obvious that I am the hands of God in this most righteous punishment. Destiny has so willed it.

"Of course he's guilty. Guilty! Guilty! Guilty! All that remains is to act, with a momentary 'doing,' the eternal done is accomplished. Death to the murderer!

"God. Have I gone mad? Will I throw my own father off a cliff on the word of a junkie?! Has it come to that? It's only a junkie's word that David's death was an overdose, not a heart attack, and even if he died of an overdose, do I really believe that my father could have done it? Does hatred blind me?? It was to the junkie's advantage to lie to me, to lead me on. I sent him a huge amount of cash on the basis of what he said, sent him gold in exchange for, for, for *information*, and certainly, a junkie will tell you a tale, will tell you any tale, to get his fix. Will the monkeyed man show his evil face in Cairo?! At this very moment, does he count my money and laugh at the fool who counted on him? Shouldn't I wait until, if and until, I meet this stranger in person? He said he'd meet me tomorrow . . .

"Coward. Acting rashly is far better than not acting at all. Shove him, push him, trip him, shall I squander a lasting satisfaction over a moment's hesitation? He's guilty, guilty, guilty, plain as day, kill him and all shall be well. Diseases are only cured when their roots are destroyed. Shove him, push him, trip him,

"But then again . . ."

The two climbed down the pyramid without incident. When they got to the bottom, Donald made a reach for Arthur, but his quicker son ran away into the darkness.

3.

Arthur waited. And waited. And waited. It was the following day and Arthur had an eternal wait among the ancient artifacts of the Cairo Museum.

Morning began, and Arthur was there. Afternoon arrived, and Arthur continued his watch. Evening approached, and Arthur doubted that the man would show. Though the museum would soon be closing, the junkie had not yet shown his face in the mummy room.

Arthur sat down to rest in a corner. His eyelids drooped. The exhausted young man fell fast asleep and no one disturbed him.

The junkie finally appeared, from somewhere, late at night. He came to Arthur as if it were a dream and the boy, the boy was told what he expected to hear.

With the calm of the convinced, Arthur left the museum the following morning.

4.

Backstage, the buzzing was continually constant, constantly continual. It was the S.S. Cosmos' last night in Egypt, and the play *Hamlet, Prince of Denmark*, was about to be performed.

Outside, the ship's theatre was packed.

Backstage, the buzzing was . . .

"Do you think he'll show up tonight?"

"Even if he does, the Director might not let him go on stage. He's missed alot of rehearsals."

"Are you kidding? Arthur knows the part. I don't think there's a better Hamlet to be seen—"

"He was last seen in Cairo."

"The poor guy. It's a shame, the way Julia had to go."

"Did you know today was his eighteenth birthday?"

"I heard the Dean has decided to send him home, that he's caused too much trouble."

"Did you see his mother out there in the audience? I've never seen her looking more beautiful."

"I heard he's loaded. I heard he's a big trust funder, able to fund almost any kind of fun be it good or bad."

"Don't you know who their family is? Yeah, the big steel company. It's *named* after his grandfather who founded the thing."

"Something about his old man has always bugged me."

"He better show up, or the show won't amount to a thing. His understudy's just terrible."

"I loved it when he punched out McNulty. That prick's had it coming for a long time."

"They say he had quite a row with his mother. Mrs. Davis has a cabin across the hall from his parents and she told me that—"

"I've never really liked the guy myself. Sure he's a genius, a great actor, but—"

"He's wonderful. So handsome. So sensitive."

"Poor Julia. I cry whenever I think about it. One of the nurses told me that she was incredibly drunk when she fell, and then there were the pills."

"I've never really understood Arthur," somebody said.

"Oh he's not hard to figure out," Christopher Chirac replied, getting into his costume for the night "Arthur's just another eighteen year old, sitting alone in his Chevy on yet another Friday night, getting drunk on 3.2 beer and listening to Springsteen on the 8-track. The lights of the 7-11 are the only thing he has to go by, and Arthur, good ole Arthur, he's just trying to decide whether he should hit the gas or the brakes. I mean the guy really isn't all the different from you or me, he just happens to care a little bit more," Chirac said, adjusting the whiskers that were supposed to make him look like Polonius.

"Care? Who cares?" Arthur asked. "The only thing people care about is talk," the boy said, in the silence that had been caused so suddenly by his appearance.

"Here's the real thing, here's what you were just discussing," Arthur continued, pirouetting so they could get a complete view of him. "Are you now satisfied!?! Let your curiosity be gorged, though it's a gorging that will only make him hungrier!

"So. Tell me!" he exclaimed. "Am I black or white? Quick or slow? Tall or short? Grey or green? Fat or thin? Rich or poor? We're all actors, we should all be able to see through the actings of each other. Come, come, tell me who I am, I need to know, come, come, come box this unboxable mess called me. I am slave to the man who tells me who I am."

It was quiet. So very quiet.

"Have you no answer?" Arthur asked. "Are you now speechless, you who only a minute ago knew everything? I see every man becomes a mime when confronted with the truth," he finished bitterly. "All of us, all of us, we are all called men, yet not a one of us deserves the name!"

"Last call, first act, first scene, last call," a voice cried out. The play was about to begin and there was a shuffling of feet as the players hurried to their positions. Arthur was left alone.

"Again, again, the tired curtain must rise, revealing yet another staging of life's endlessly petty charade," he murmured. "A farce, a farce. Why must the show go on, it's known that the final act of every play inevitably ends with recurring doom. Is it not a waste to tell this story, a story that's been told and told and told? Is it not an extravagance to live this life, a life that's been lived and lived and lived, and lived? But then again, it's just, it's just. There's not a man alive who deserves to escape his telling moment, the world's a better place for the living when the dying die properly!"

Arthur quietly took his place as the curtain rose.

5.

An atmosphere of concerned expectancy pervaded the audience as the play proceeded. Everyone knew of Julia's death, of Arthur's fighting with his parents, of the instability of the man who was playing Hamlet. Everyone had been told all about it, the voyeuristic beast had been primed, and like spectators everywhere, the audience watched. Secretly hoping for a spectacle, for a vicarious thrill that would erase their own emptiness. The audience willingly played its part, and Arthur performed magnificently for them.

It was the second act, second scene. People stirred uncomfortably in their seats as the temperature rose in the packed house, and sweat, honest sweat, fell from Arthur's brow as he spoke. He was working on the 'rogue and peasant slave' soliloquy which closes that part of the play and a single spotlight, the only lighting then being used, rested upon him.

A new directorial twist had Arthur moving about the audience, off of the stage, as he gave his speech:

". . . kindless villain!" Arthur continued.

"Why what an ass I am! This is most brave,
That I, the son of a dear father murdered,
Prompted to my revenge by heaven and hell,
Must like a whore unpack my heart with words,
And fall a-cursing like a very drab,
A stallion. Fie upon't, foh!
About, my brains! Hum—I have heard
That guilty creatures sitting at a play
Have by the very cunning of the scene
Been struck so to the soul, that presently
They have proclaimed their malefactions:
For murder, though it have no tongue, will speak
With most miraculous organ. I'll have these players
Play something like the murder of my father
Before mine uncle. I'll observe his looks,
I'll tent him to the quick. If 'a do blench,

I know my course. The spirit that I have seen
May be a devil, and the devil hath power
T' assume a pleasing shape, yea, and perhaps,
Out of my weakness and my melancholy,
As he is very potent with such spirits,
Abuses me to damn me. I'll have grounds
More relative than this—the play's the thing
Wherein I'll catch the conscience of the King,"
Arthur spat out, "Yea, The play's the thing Wherein I'll catch the conscience of the
King!"

"Was this to be repeated?" someone in the audience murmured. "This isn't in
the play."

"The real thing, the real thing," Arthur said evenly, pulling that someone in the
audience out of his chair, into the spotlight. The audience stirred. Arthur and his
father Donald now stood toe to toe.

"Arthur!? What do you think you're—"

"Doing? You foul hypocrite. Unless you're prepared to confess what you
yourself have done, don't presume to ask what another is doing!"

"Arthur, this isn't the time or the place to go into—"

"Lights! Lights!" the Director could be heard yelling, from behind the stage,
but no one could find the switch in the confusion.

"Now's the moment!" Arthur hissed, to his father. "I'll be denied no longer.
Tell me and the world about our brother and son David. The truth."

"Arthur, calm down, all these people are watching, you—"

"Should no longer procrastinate when dealing with a procrastinator," Arthur
howled. "The truth must be forced out of this all too free a liar!"

The men grappled. Arthur managed to scissor one of his father's legs. The hair
on Donald's head was pulled. And then there was an awful click, as a knife opened
and appeared in the space in front of Donald's throat.

"The truth! The truth!" Arthur demanded.

"He's crazy somebody stop him!!" Sally hysterically screamed. The audience
looked on in fascination.

"Arthur?!" Donald pathetically began.

"Speak or die!" his son coldly replied, brandishing the knife.

"My son was a junkie," Donald cried, terrified. "I, I, yes I abandoned him, left
him to rot and die, repulsed by fear and loathing."

"And our mother and wife?" Arthur asked.

"She's a whore, she fucks everything and anything in pants," Donald said,
eyeing the knife, willing to say anything.

"And you?" Arthur demanded.

"Why I—"

"A phony! A phony! Death itself looks you in the face yet but still you're falser than
a shadow!" Arthur raged. "Truth! Truth! Admit the truth, you *murdered* your son
David!"

121

Donald was speechless. Arthur glanced and saw the look he expected. In the silence, the knife slashed. And slashed. And slashed!

"Nooo!" Sally screamed.

Several men jumped Arthur and pinned him to the ground. A doctor hurried to the scene. One look at the lifeless Donald was all he needed. He threw his coat over the corpse.

"The proof, the proof, there's papers in my pockets that prove my father's guilt," Arthur shouted, as they wrestled with him.

"There's nothing here," someone said after they searched him.

"Lost? Lost?!" Arthur cried out. "Lost?"

"Arthur. Donald. Ohhh Arthur," Sally howled, as Arthur began to laugh hysterically.

"Blech. Umm. Ahh. This. That. Unnhhh. To be or not to be. The Question. Ha-ha, that's the question, ha-ha, I'm a rogue a rouge and peasant slave, he's a rogue and peasant slave—"

"Take him to the infirmary, tie him up, and heavily sedate him," the doctor ordered. "Obviously he's catatonic schizophrenic."

They didn't bother to finish the play.

GREECE

Land of my fathers, home to my spirit,
Where life loving men drink a wine divine,
I salute you: You who made man the measure of all things,
You who made Beauty the standard by which we should judge.
To the individual you showed the importance of dignity and honor,
To the community you showed the importance of the individual,
And to free thinking men everywhere you bestowed the most im-
                           portant gift of all,
The right of a man to shape his world and his destiny as he
               sees fit.

Why humanity owes you more than a mere debt of gratitude,
She owes you her very existence,
And in the name of those who dare to call themselves 'human
               beings',
This poor shadow of Homer humbly gives thanks.

                    melancholy

                    the sadness comes
                    creeping
                    snuggling close
                    too close to ask
                    the distant question
                    'why'

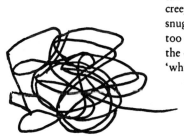

One of those days
With nothing to say
      —or—
Inner turmoil
Hysterically coiled
      —or-
The way it really is
      —or—
The resulting negation
From rampant frustration

pork'n beans

Gimme dem pork'n beans
Make a man feel so clean
Dey turn you inside out
Make me wanna scream and shout
Gimme de pork'n beans

You know dey smooth and greasy
Dey go slippin' down so easy
Nothing cheap cheezy
Nothing fancy sleazy
Jus' dat gooey red sheen
Please gimme de pork'n bean

Hey! Yeah *you*, mudderfucker!
Slimy greeny cockysucker
Dey ain't got no pretence
Dey jus' got de good ole common sense
Why dey so simple
So goddamn simple
Even a fool know how to eat 'em
Yeah you jus' can't beat 'em
Mama's pork'n beans

Ha-ha, Ha-ha, Ha-ha-my man dey de tops
With a flash dey hit de fartin' spot
Dey best when smokin' hot
Smokin' smokin' hot!
And de world would be a better place
If every man jus' stuff his face
Wit' de pork'n beans
—Cause dey so simple
So goddamn simple
It all so fuckin' simple
And de world would be a better place
If every man jus' stuff his face
Wit' de pork'n beans

—No trouble at all then . . .
—Jus' eat 'em cold out of de can if you gots to.

THIS existential agony TH_

Conc
Pan
G

Socrates' Second Thoughts

The Age of Cynicism
Enthroned Skepticism.
But is Wisdom's key
Not to Believe
In Anyone or Anything?
Will we ever hear Truth's ring
Through the Credibility Gap?

NO MESSAGE

'What *is* the Word?!'
We asked the sage.
Smiling he said,
'No message.'

PLANS

'And what do *you* do?' they asked me
Their eyes were small but their teeth were large. And sharp; like fangs
I tensed up; anticipating yet another ego execution
'Nothing,' I nervously replied. With embarrassment
They were shocked and confused
I tried to soften the blow
By saying that I had plans

ption
ic
t born
Be toilet trained
Go to school
Go to play
Back to school again
Get an identity crisis
Get a pimple
Graduate
Go to college
Meet a girl
Go to the movies
Go to a protest
Get fucked
Drop out
Drop back in
Get fucked over
Again
Graduate once more—why not
Get a job
Get wife
Get kid
Get house
Buy color TV
Possess house
Pay taxes
Vote Republican
Play golf
(Get Whore)
Take vacation
Try jogging
Get old
Get old
Play more golf
Get Grey
Get retired
Have a heart attack
Attend a funeral
Receive social security
Be a grandfather
Get senile
Date a teen-age girl
Drop dead
Do it again

In case you haven't figured it out
Life is a snowball
Rolling uncontrollably down
A very steep hill

MELT AWAY

When the fog moves in
Everything's okay
When the fog moves in
I melt away
When the fog moves in
Everything's okay
Because when you can't be seen
When you just can't see
I melt away
You melt away
It all melts away
And everything's okay

IS THIS ALL THERE IS

"Is this all there is?" she asked
I was almost out the door
"Is this all there is?" she asked
I could only glare at the wooden floor
And still I felt the pull of the door

"Is this all there is?" she asked
"You once told me you cared
"Is this all there is?" she asked
Now that all was laid bare
As if she'd earned a fairer share

"Is this all there is?" she asked
My feet they wanted to flee and run
"Is this all there is?" she asked
Though 'n eternity had been said and done
Though long ago it had ceased to be fun

127

"Is this all there is?!" she asked
"O shut up—I've heard it all before," I cried
"Why beat this dog so plainly dead—
"If you must know we bleed till we're bled—
"*And that's all there is*," I said
Closing the door.

LATENT MACHISMO

The black kid told me:
    'A gun is a passport
    A gun is a meal
    A gun is Life; and Death
    It all depends on how you feel'
The days for this nigger
Ticked like a trigger
His street-jungle code
Ready to explode
    The Big Pig Time cut him down
    In staccato like haste
    All the white papers
    Claimed it a waste
    But I watched him die
    With honest fascination
    Violence was his way
    Blood his avocation
    And I was jealous
    Of this cheap hood zealot
Oh I know he wasn't much
He and his impulse-immediate rush
To prove for the mob that he was a man
By dabbing blood on his face, blood on his hands
But way deep within my primeval gut
Down in the cellar where a caveman ruts
Murmurs a vein of truest sympathy
Of reckless six-gun macho empathy
For that savage black who said loud and clear
'The man who is seen is the man who is feared'

KEEPING TIME

Tick Tock Tick Tock
So says the clock
Tick Tock Tick Tock
Again says the clock
But when we stop kicking
He'll stop ticking
Since he only keeps time
For his Creator-Slave, Mankind

NO NEED TO BE FOOLISH

There comes a time
When it's best to retreat
When it's best to be humble
And admit Today's defeat
Since Tomorrow always comes
With Opportunity renewed
For he who but has the patience
To have a beer and think it through

?

We've had enough
F-r-a-g-m-e-n-t-a-t-i-o-n
Alien   Meta   ation
          phor
           +
Ambigu(ity-or is it ousness?)
In our lives.
Must we also
Desecrate our Art?
Apparently so . . .

Of dancing winds and setting suns
Of swaying trees and tides that run, etc. etc.

O you can speak of rivers sweeping
Of stars a' shining, of flowers peeping
But poetry is human art
Man's creation in all her parts
So when you strike the metered rhyme
And beg the Muse to be sublime
Please talk of town and citied ville
Of landscape sculpt'd by human will
For though Nature is a pretty thing
With honeyed bees and larks that sing
The works of Man are non pareil
They soar and swoop and flying fly
To lofty mount no bird can reach
To graceful truth no fox can teach
And they deserve a poet's praise
So much more than the foggy haze

PSALM 69

The river runs a bloody red
The frogs have got the upper hand
The yellowed maggots must be fed
The slimy serpent rules the land
While the flocks and herds are dying
While the buzzing swarms are flying
The festered boils do break and burst
The beating hail does pelt the earth
And locust eat the crops that stand
And darkness awful shade the land
So here's to God and to his plagues
To spirit raging without sense
To he who slaughters helpless babes
To Jehovah, God of Vengeance
The barbaric tyrant who deserves
Human allegiance?

GREAT ART WHERE ARE YOU

The critical rage
In the Modern Age
Is to snobbishly cry
That Great Art has died.
Of this I agree
But 'tis easy to see
Where Great Art has gone
—Where Great Art belongs.
He's a' way back there
In the old land where
His bard can daily breathe
Next to the honored tomb
      Of heroic Achilles . . . .

REASON AND REASONABLE

The philosopher's hair was unkempt;
His pants stained.
His shirt wrinkled;
His shoelaces untied.
His glasses were dirty;
His socks falling.
His distraction was noticeable;
His eyes glazed.
—And still they accused him of logical thought,
Proving that what is reasonable
Has nothing to do with Reason.

FEELINGS

A feeling is a fleeting thing
A teasing wind that blows
A bell that briefly rings
And so I ponder heavy book
With clenched fist and searing look
To try and learn this poet's craft
The words eterne, the verse that's apt
For feeling is a fleeting thing
A guiling touch that softly stings
And I would cage his breezy draft
His siren's challenge, his mocking laugh!

131

My old friend lust.
I see you've come again to visit me. Once again your multi-headed face is on the threshold of my soul, smiling ever so seductively, hoping to disturb my, my, my
Peace of *mind.*
And what would thou have me do,
This time?!
Rape this virgin?
Blacken that name?
Murder this innocent?
Pillage that town?
Begin WWII?
Cry Hell! in the sleeping slumbering night?
Eat the glutton's meal?
Torture the helpless?
Be the vicious tyrant?
Kill!? Kill!? Kill!?
Fuck!? Fuck!? Fuck!? Yes I'll do it.

My old friend lust.
So good to see you once again.
Though I'm far away from home sweet home
Though aged Crete is where I roam
I'm glad to see familiar friend
My familiar friend
My old friend lust.
Well, well, what have we here. What's this I see out the corner of my ever looking eye. A young girl? (A country girl?) A young, young girl? Hah. You bet she's young. And pretty too. With dark flashing eyes and smooth olive skin and full wet lips. And she's eager too. She gives the glance that says you've the chance
To make her!
To take her!
To MAKE her! Rapaciously!
Her eyes they hug the very ground so very discreetly but her heart, her heart, her heart would have the world between her legs. She's a lass forsaking tomorrow for the sake of today,
A virgin
Who hopes to be unburdened,
And she'll dispose of cool virtue
To appease heated desire.
She'll burn her fear
To feed the fire. Softly now.
I see a flash of thigh.
I glimpse a curved breast.

I feel the pointed nipple.
There's a warm moist sigh. The girl she teases me and it's
so much better.
So much better.
So very much better.
Desire is its own reward!
The orange flame of yearning passion burns more sweetly than the dreary smoke of grey fulfillment! Hot pursuit is more thrilling to the touch than the cool hand of conquest! To chase! To chase! It keeps a man lean and hungry, active and alert, while to achive victory is to achieve death. We reach the end when we reach our goal(s).

My old friend lust. And do you know
She is young.
I am much older.
Perhaps it is wrong but I am no philosopher.
A bitch in heat
Is the very best meat
A buck can ever find
And should I waste precious time
Trying to forever find
The elusive lusive line
That stands between right and wrong?
Hah. I leave it to the theologians. They are worms, most suited to suffocate in the mud of 'what is sin' and 'what is grace.' Let them be the ones to crawl in the slime of hesitation and the swamp of conscience. For me the time is now! I seize it and though the pleasure's fleeting the pleasure's real. The earth is dirt but dirt can be worked and what can one say of Heaven. Of ideas! They are nothing. Bread is baked from grain not imagination.
My old friend lust.
The girl is smiling at me!

My old friend lust.
So true and so just
I offer the lass a sip of wine
Of nectar divine
And she *takes* it!
The bota bag is filled to the brim
She squeezes it and licks the rim
You know we just might make it.
And we go for a walk. I take her hand and let the wineskin swing from my shoulder in the warm sea breeze. She keeps smiling and we never say a word for she doesn't speak English and I have no Greek. But who cares.
You see . . .
—My heart is beating, beating,
She is willing, willing,

The world is turning, turning,
The stars are shining, shining,
The cosmos is acting, acting,
Being, Breathing, Being, Breathing,
For better or worse, and the Life, the *Life* is in me,
The Word is speaking:
The chaos of the dark turbulent darkness mingles with the white revealing light—
And the two of us give in. To the inevitable. Like the pebbles that we are we go
rolling down a hillside, down the sweeping hillside, to the shade of the trees that lie
in a valley. It's far away from her sun washed village that lies in the plains and she is
glad. And so am I. Though I never understood how or why.

My old friend lust. The girl is gone now and so are you. My head is clear, my rest is
easy and I'm back in the city. Away from the girl, from what you made us do. I am
relaxed, content, filled with calm—
When a certain scent goes swimming by
I look to see a bright red skirt
Revealing naked thigh
A waist so thin, a smile so true
And lo! I am rocking
The old familiar knocking
Why my old friend lust!
Have you returned so soon?
Will you follow me wherever I go? Oh No!!
My god. My god, my god!
And so.
Like a sin we must regret
Like a dream we can't forget
My old friend lust
Will make of me his pet
From queerest time to queerest time
No easy reasoned rhyme
Will he give
Me
With which to make sense of him
He seems to be
                    beyond
me

RUST

Always creeping never sleeping
Rust moves into the grooves.
Like fires burning, like currents churning,
He forever works and will not shirk
His appointed duty. A diligent beauty
Therefore is he, persevering perpetually,
And I would give my virtues all, my assets large, my credits small,
To have his splendid quality, to own Success's golden key.

HOW TO GET CHICKS

A powerful, confident, dominating and attractive male . . .
—Why it's easy to be one!
Just send $12.95 for my new book with the proven techniques:
How To Pick Up Girls And Get Laid!
—But better still;
If you really want to be
A powerful, confident, dominating and attractive male:
A. Get yourself elected President of the U.S.
B. Invent yourself a foreign crisis.
C. Use military force.
Follow this clinically tested method
And you really will be a powerful, confident,
                    dominating and attractive male.
Why waste your time hanging out in some single's bar
Getting drunk, picking fights, spending
Twenty or thirty smackers a night and still *not* meeting
That certain someone you want to sleep with.
Hurry: Act NOW!
Get your name on the New Jersey Presidential ballot
                    before the filing deadline is up.

ON THE QUESTION OF BEING, EXISTENCE, NECESSITY AND ACTIVITY

To be one must do
                    Sartre
To do one must be
                    Lao-Tse
Do be do be do be
                    Sinatra

(From a toilet stall, author unknown)

135

BURIAL

It took a million men
To put him six feet 'neath the ground . . . .
His coffin was magnesium gold,
Built in Pittsburgh with African ores . . . .
The hearse he rode in was a Chevy,
Constructed in Detroit, powered by Saudi Arabian oil . . . .
A backhoe fiendishly efficient dug his grave,
'Twas made in Canada, designed by MIT, financed in London . . .
And the fellow's epitaph?
Ha. A poet-adman, the best that all of Madison Avenue could produce,
Wrote for him and eternity a most memorable jingle . . . .
Yes, yes indeed, it took at least a million men from this our Modern Age
To bury the singular Renaissance Man . . . .

TWENTIETH CENTURY INEPTNESS

"This is a tool," said the self deprecating,
Self lacerating inner voice.
"Knowing how to use it
"Is one of the things
"That makes you a *man* (you weasel)!"
I obeyed the inner voice. I tried to fix my car . . .
'Twas a simple thing, nothing more than an old fashioned nut
That required a simple tightening—an idiot could have done it—
—All thumbs I wrestled with the socket wrench;
—All ignorance I elected to use too much zeal;
The screw snapped in two at its base
Like a walnut being cracked.

It cost me seventy smackers to get it fixed.
The mechanics were very understanding (while they smirked),
And as I stare at the cancelled check,
I find I just have to wonder
What it was I was paying for:
My pride?
My folly?
My clumsiness?
My foolishness?
My inadequacy?
My honest attempt at being a more complete human being?
O Modern Age, my god, my god, what have you done to me?!?!

136

SWEET SILENCE

The spider plant sprays his web
All greenly thin on window sill
His beauty is a quiet thing
Quite strong enough for subtle thrill
And I'd say more but he once told me
That a feeling defined is a feeling killed

GENERIC LIVING

For a limited time
Save 50¢
On a non-preservative
Dildo
The real thing
May not be inside of you
But if you have a coupon
You can finance a substitute
And get a guarantee
Worth sucking on

COWARD (2)

I stored myself
In distant room
On vacant shelf
In creeping gloom
Where I had the meal
Of bleating sheep
Of vomitted ale
Of poisoned meat
For I had my chance
And gave it up
Afraid of failing
I passed the cup
An' I think my share
Was very fair . . .

2020
20-20

A harmless man with harmless air
Like sheep we bought his covered wares
He spoke to us on even years
When 'Lection Day was drawing near
And he said:
Now do *this!* (though we once did that)
Now do *that!* (though we once did this)
And in our confusion
The modern profusion
We did as we were told
We sold the Truth for basest gold
Polluted streams—obscured the sun
Signed more paper—made more guns
Closed our eyes and worshipped Me
Mouthed our lies like worker bees
As all the while the fog drew near
The killing shroud, the ultimate bier
But we went on. And on. And on. And on AndonAndon—
BOOM!!!
So now. Hacking. Coughing. We reap radioactive breath
Having sowed our soil with Mega-Death
Paying for our dearth of foresight
We live our life cursed with hindsight
For now that it is 2020
At last we see with 20-20

ENIGMA

Painting on my study wall
Silent image saying all
That artist anxious could explain
With colors, canvas, oils and pain
Tell me: Does he live in thee
Has he left you his identity
You who hang in mutest mystery
Or did he father alien child
A separate spirit free and wild
Or are you merely matter dense
A lifeless symbol, inanimate, without spiritual sense
Why speak! O jaded faded print of scars
Say just what and who you are
For weary I be of trying to guess
At who you are, at what is Consciousness . . . .

CONVENIENCE

Pop! Goes the pop top can
Rip! Tears the plastic bag
Hiss! Crunches the tin can compactor
Fizz! Disintegrates hard-to-get-out stains
Trash! Says the disposable this
Garbage! Cries the throw-away that
Suck! Whooshes the abortionst's vacuum cleaner
Sweeping it all away
Burying what's unwanted in the city dump
Making everything nice and clean

THE BIG SALE
(HEY YOU STUPID!)

LADY ULTIMATE® Country Club Stripe, Solid
Color and Lilac Duet Sheets
(WHO CARES® Blah! Blah! Blah! Blah!
Blah! Justwhatyouwant Blah! Blah! Buy it please)

X. Country Club Stripe are fortran/tri-x/cotton
percale with solid hem and contrast piping. Green
or gold combinations
(X. Feed Buzz-Buzz-Buzz-Buzz-Buzz-Buzz)
Y. Solid Color are fortran/tri-x/cotton
percale in black, white, flaming orange or hot pink
(Y. Your Buzz-Buzz-Buzz-Buzz-Buzz-Buzz)
Z. Lilac Duet are fortran/tri-x/cotton
percale in red, white or blue
(Z. Face Buzz-Buzz-Buzz-Buzz-Buzz)

X, Y, & Z Sheets:
(X, Y, & Z Blah-Buzz:)
twin flat or fitted 5.99
(basic scumbag scuzz) .... (CHEAP)
full flat or fitted 6.99
(blech blech more blech) .... ($y^{10}.9^{-10}9^{-10}$)
queen flat or fitted.................................. 8.99
(retch retch more retch) .... ($ $ $ $)
king flat or fitted.................................... 12.99
(for the meglomaniac in the house) .... (charge it)
Behind every comunicated thought
(Lies an unseen desire)

LIFE OF SIN

The frozen man
With buried heart
Who hid his feelings
From the start
Never weeped a tearful cry
Until the day that he died
On that bleak morn he beat his breast
Wailed his woe in deep unrest
Shed his tears and wondered why
Now was the time he chose to cry
'Twas folly; he should bear it like a man
This going to the darkned land
That mortal eye could never see
Whose lock and key were mystery
And yet; he disjointedly pondered
As fleeting life was swept away
If something good had been accomplished
By masking heart till dying day
Had he saved someone by hiding tears
Joys and griefs, the anguished fear
And was the world a better place
Because of his impassive face
Why worst of all he'd left some broken
With his heart untold, his love unspoken
Aarrggh! Suddenly; the last forced breath
He shuddered; 'twas not gentle death
A farewell breaking harsh and grim
An adieu bitter, leaving him
Agonizing; wondering . . . if empty life was life of sin . . . .

the great

Grandeur!
the enticing bitch
Alexander!
had her rich
wet and hot!
but like any whore she left him
to sleep alone
in a foreign grave
where he has to wonder
if she was worth the chase

SWAMPS AND STREAMS

Sweeping stream
At my feet
Running to
Nature's beat
You with life
Troublefree
You who breathe
So easily
Take me with you
Where you go
Let me drift
With your flow
For I would be
Worry free
I who swim
In swampy sea
Where human fish
Drown and wish
Of being like to thee

erasure

i am an erasure
it gives me much pleasure
to correct the mistakes
to wipe clean the slate
of momentary carelessness
after all,
we don't want father time
to get hold of a piece
of passing gibberish;
he might turn it
into eternal nonsense

i am an erasure
i am a human being's
best friend . . .
when used properly
some people call me
discretion
others say i'm
flexible

i am an erasure
too bad i can't be used
on things other than paper
i deserve
a wider sphere
of influence

stolen kisses (2)

stolen kisses
are the best
appetite for life
they surely whet
like unearned gold
like sweet caress
like simple thought
like gentle jest
they soothe the soul
and kill the pest
of murderous arduous
weariness

homeless

the cactus plants upon the wall
are framed within a picture
the shining knight in princely white
has found a niche in scripture
so why can't I, a living human being I
find a place to call my own
find a place to be my home
Am I not worth more than a two
dimensional cactus plant? Than a fictional
character? But then again. Perhaps they are easier
to please . . .

LET ME SLEEP

Morning fell all ugly red—
I moaned; didn't wanna leave my bed.
Angry cold sleeted slivers reached stinging to my bones—
I bit my lip; if only I coulda stayed at home.
Rutted streets oozing black with smelly hot tar—
I clenched at the blare of a horn; why was I driving in my car.
The end of the day . . .a shrouded grey . . . blanketing my tomb—
I nodded my head; knew why they had to drag me from the womb.

PASSING THINGS

When winter's cold has chilled your heart
And stolen *some*one far away
When reaper grim has used his scythe
On one beloved at play in May
Let Father Time do his work
Run his course, have his way
For this is what
The wise ones see
As life is but a passing thing
So should mourning be

HOME WHERE ARE YOU

I asked God how to go about
Getting a home.
God said:
"If you're a fool you'll try to buy one,
If you're a dreamer you'll try to imagine one,
If you're a man you'll try to build one,
If you're a realist you'll never have one,
And if you're a believer you'll wait until you see Me
—And I'll give you one," God promised,
Sounding just like my real estate agent.
My real estate agent. That's one S.O.B. I sure don't trust.

pee

when you gotta pee
you should pee
desire elemental
's not to be denied
it forever takes precedence
over lofty ambition
high-flown words
starried goals
shining somewhere
and that's the way
it should be
first things first, one step at a time
don't hold back, this one's on me
WHIZZZZ . . .

143

PERCH

Squatting on a perch
In a naked black tree
In the thing called me
Away from life's hustle
I watched
A rock that stood tall and proud
Mighty and free
Boldly it named itself
Said it was called Integrity
And there were waters
Smoothly persistent waters
Lapping laughing waters
Mothered by the Sea of Compromise
That always turned back
Agreeably they rolled back
From the monolith Integrity
Yet they returned
Again and again . . .

I studied the contest with passing interest
The thing they wanted was me
They struggled on and on and on
The waves from Compromise Sea
Eating and eating at the bedrock shore
Of mighty Integrity
And though the currents of the bitch
Never ever let up
(Like sirens they wailed on and on)
Integrity's pinnacle continued to withstand
Their eternally soft advances
Their eternally warm advances
Till one day
They asked me to choose between the two of them.

"I make Life itself possible,"
Wooed the washing Sea of Compromise.
"But I, I make Life itself worth the living!"
Grandly stated strong Integrity.
"Come, come, you must choose between us
"And pick *me* if you and Conscience would sleep easily."
—"He'll sleep Forever's sleep unless he learns my art,"
Reminded the Sea of Compromise.

I shrugged my shoulders and pondered

Squatting on a perch
In a naked black tree
In the thing called me
Away from life's hustle
I watched
The contest as it continued
The waters and the rock fought on and on
On and on
For I had refused to choose between the two
I who am shaded by Relativity
And sometimes I wonder
Wonderingly wonder
As Eternity sails by
What it would be like to be different

—BUT—

A telling silence
Is what I seek
To know, to know
I would if I could
—But—
Let the curtain fall
I have no answers
And it is getting late
As the key
Has eluded me
Because of
—But—

WHO CARES

His beer gut
His beery beery gut
Is getting bigger
While he sits alone and watches TV.
Who cares . . .

ANNE MICHELLE

Anne Michelle
    The sweetest bell
        These ears have ever heard
A harmony
    A rhapsody
        Too beautiful for words

Anne Michelle
    A wishing well
        Too deep to ever end
A lullabye
    A sighing sigh
        My heart you melt and mend

Anne Michelle
    A tale to tell
        A rose that never fades
A ton of gold
    I have and hold
        But with you it can't be weighed

My Anne Michelle
    The sweetest belle
        His Hands have ever wrung
A poet's dream
    A sweet sixteen
        For you this song is sung

EAGER TO LIVE, EAGER TO DIE

With eager heart
The young men marched to battle.
Desire drove them on.
Desire for a new experience,
Desire for a chance to prove themselves,
Desire to see, do and be—
But in their hurry to win their medals
No one had the time to tell them
How a lust for life
Leads to early death
And obliviously, they marched into oblivion

THE MALL OF LIFE

On the mall of life
In the womb of dreams
He walked alone
Unnoticed, unseen
With a throb in his heart
The neons were a'blinking
A lamppost held him up
He was thinking
Of what he didn't know
Of who he couldn't tell
While cars went streaming by
A whore was trying to sell
Herself.
So he looked away
Into the thronging crowd
There were no faces there
Just a buzzing lonely loud
And he spoke to no one
In the greying twilight
In an alley he hid
Out of mind out of sight
For he could not bear
Today and today and today
It creeped on and on and on
It was no longer just okay
To endure . . .
As the puzzle was too loaded
The game too large
He was tired of sailing
Ambivalence's barge
Through door after door after door
Without freeing key in sight
In the long dark hallway
In the hot smoggy night
In endless bar after endless bar
A drunk who drinks to die
He never even danced
He was too too shy
To live;
A red light flashed
A tire squealed
A gun was drawn
A bullet had her meal

For no apparent reason
The blood it came in spouts
There was no hesitation
Nor the slightest doubt
For in the human shadow
The blood has always ran
It never has to care
If one can understand
Why?
Grey cracking pavement
The weary asphalt
A television plays
No risk no fault
Is how we live
In comforting ease
In the ultimate supermarket
In the modern breeze
He wanted to run
His soul crying rape
It had been cornered
In the urban landscape
—By itself
And though he was thrilled
By the speeding light mags
By the electric energy
By the non-stop drags
He wanted to fly
Out of here and there
From the friendly acquaintance
From his unseeing stare
And he spoke to no one
In the greying twilight
In an alley he hid
Out of mind out of sight
Waiting—
A long long wait
A vigil of pain and tears
The alley was littered
With semen cheap beer
For nothing else lived
To taste or do-do
All had been sampled
While using him too
And so he sat
On the garbage tin throne

In a dead end land
Where the free slaves roam
Wandering wondering;
While the corners grew tight
The tenement more bare
The wind a little colder
Beauty more rare
In his back street pit
His coffin civilized
A dream coming true
His nightmare realized
Unable to touch
Himself or another
No woman his sister
No man his brother
To leave! But where?
An' he knew he should leave
'Twas sin to remain
The alley was narrowing
He couldn't maintain
When the last open door
Closed out of sight
Sealing him off
Trapped in the night
So he gave it all up
He withered to the root
Reality held no fire escape
Existence no parachute
An' he gave it all up,
An' who was to blame?!?

THE DAY IS LONG

I scratched my dong
        in the grey-lite afternoon
I picked my nose
        in discreet banality
I adjusted my underwear
        with nothing else to do

The day is long
My mind a blank
The day is long
My mind a blank

149

TRUTH

For years I searched Scripture
And many a cold bleary night
I read and re-read dreary Milton, trying to make sense
An' I travelled round the world, round and round
Up to heaven and down to hell
While walking the narrow dusty road
So long and so lonely
With full moon a gleaming
Upon my erratic aching heart, my wild heart
That was sometimes heavy
Sometimes soaring
An' I did this and that
That and this, all to no avail
Like the blind frustrated cat who chases its own tail
Round and round and round
To and fro, fro and to, to and fro
And for what! For what? Hah. For truth
Clear precious truth, I sought 'The Truth'
—But I never found it, never ever
'Twas nowhere, and I had given up hope
Of ever seeing it, of ever knowing it
Till that awesome dawn when I held my first born
And there was truth . . .

THE NOISE

The noise. the noise, the noise
Does it ever stop
Will it ever cease
My ears hear
A silent beauty
But the noise? The noise . . .

Crowding crowds
Choking the air
Filling the streets
With blaring blare
A terrible decibel
Scatters me
And
Routine Anarchy
Edits my spirit
Till   is left

The issue is
Irrelevant
It will make itself
Meaningless
With the turn of a newspaper's page
The flick of a TV dial

The noise. The noise, the noise
It echoes and echoes
Feeding on itself
Till it crescendoes
Into a vacuum
A paralyzing vacuum—

IMAGE

The finer things in life
The blonde blue-peachy wife
The teeny caviar
Good vintage from the Saar
A yacht with purple trimmed
A body young and slimmed
With Paris in the spring
With fingers all in rings
And perfect manicure
And confidence demure . . .
—Why a blue blue blood once told me
That this is what it's all about
The stylish style, the coiffeured hair
"Image! Image! That's what counts!"
But I? I would have the simple things
The grainy bread that Pretence scorns
What use the trappings of a king
When Nobility is truly borne
By itself, without aid of props

EVIL

Judas! Judas! May I call your name?
You who sold our Blessed Savior
You of traitorous fame
Please come and hold this sweaty hand
Please come and steel my heart so tame
For I am plotting monstrous deed
My brother calls me Cain

Hitler! Hitler! Will you come to me?
You who murdered helpless Jew
You who blackened history
My quaking knees they wildly knock
My frightened eyes refuse to see
I need your help to wield this knife
Macbeth is who I be

Nero! Nero! My ears shall hear you play?
You who martyred faithful Christian
You who danced in blood all day
Blast this fear that holds me back
Kill this pause that makes me weigh
Slaves are slaves—they'll not be free
Not while Pharaoh have his say

Stalin! Stalin! 'Tis you I behold?
You who ravaged countless millions
You that burned so very cold
My hate it wavers, heat me up
My faltering step must be more bold
For I'll have blood and blood and bloody blood
Of Jack the Ripper you've been told

Evil! Evil! Now we meet face to face?
You who use so many names
You who move through time and space
My consience is a heavy load
My faith a troub'lin' grace
Give me strength to sin once more
As I am called the human race
And I will do what I will do!
And I will do what I will do!

casualty

perched on a pedestal
i watched life's canvas
i espied dyes of many sorts
as they went by and by
timelessly climbing to nowhere . . .
there were beggars, preachers,
soldiers, sinners, saints,
martyrs, lawyers, doctors,
poets, bankers, mechanics,
greasers, dolls, councilmen,
farmers, fools and niggers,
and honkys,
and they all moved slowly;
slowly, very slowly, like
paraplegics climbing a mountain, cause
they were weary . . .

hmmm. well. ho hum. big deal. such is life's price,
he who would live it
must also be bored by it
must also bear its heavy load
of despair
for justice will be served, she is
a self righteous bitch not to be denied
and my story might well end here
with the parade marching on and on
while i yawn
everything all weary
everyone all teary-bleary
but i had to notice something:
i saw the lowly slave
who was bringing up the rear
of the assembly
who was the most exhausted
of the rag tag human army

and i called to him; for the sake of the story.
i said: "what's your problem boy?"
"why are you the weariest of them all?"
"huh? what the fuck's wrong with you!"

he weakly lifted his woeful eyes
off the endless awful ground

153

weakly he lifted his agonised eyes
—and i shuddered; something was wrong
he was so young to be so weary!
the weariest of them all!
why he had to be in his twenties
—in his prime. his prime!
"you don't belong here!" i gasped
but all he did was groan
moan and groan
"casualty" he managed to mutter
"i'm a casualty" he pathetically uttered
with the whisper of the broken
saying no more
picking up his radio, his light bulb, his
sartre, his tv set, his stalin,
his wwI and wwII
his wwIII perhaps
and marching on. gloom-
ily

PSYCHOLOGICAL SUICIDE

'Tis quite undeniable
That the only thing reliable
Is God
He's forever there
Be it foul or fair
No matter what your cares
—God only knows why they had to kill Him—

154

A TIMELESS STORY
(In Modern Verse)

'Twas by the firelight, late one night,
That Greybeard talked—we all listened,
While winter dropped its snowy white,
Aged sweat upon him glistened. (an' he said:)
"A story is a telling thing,
It starts and ends and goes a-way.
But I've a tale so fine to sing,
You'll not forget these lips of clay.
This web was weaved a long ago,
In time when men knew black from white.
When they would stand at toe to toe
And freely die for what was right.
Heroes then were easily found.
They walked the earth like me and you,
The earth was square not spinning round,
The sky a bright and cheery blue.
Confusion was an unknown thing,
From high to low all knew their place,
Loyalty the binding string,
And slowly stately was the pace.
Oh there were wars—the marching drum,
As men are men they were at odds.
But these warriors were a princely sum,
Were wise enough to know the gods.
Why though they fought in bloodied wrath,
They never hit while one was down,
With chivalry they walked the path,
That soldiers take when glory bound.
Their women were a queenly lot;
Virtuous maids with honor dear,
Becoming beauties for which men fought,
With quiet grace these held the rear.
And cities? O splendor not since matched!
The golden gates, the ivoried towers,
The beggars' rags with silver patched,
Emblems all of regal power.
No mean whining curs where these men!
Their hearts were large, their graces fair,
Their oaths were steel and would not bend,
With honor true they took all dares.
A grand and glorious group were they.
The days they'd feast, at night they sang,

155

They danced and boxed and laughing played,
And rode to court on wild mustangs.
Such was the life in days of old,
The era when all this began,
The wine was sweet, the wenches bold,
And happiness throughout the land,
        —When the stranger appeared— . . . . .
. . . . . Something different about him. He wasn't much to look at. He was small and crooked, with the indirect ways of someone who had something to hide.

They say he was a merchant, was of that lowest class of men who haggle and nigger, cheat and deceive. That's what they say, but I know a few folk who claim that he was a teacher, that he taught Politics.

To tell the truth I don't know what he did, or who he was for that matter. He never did mention his kin or his home or his trade, and that was just like him, his not saying anything about himself. I mean like I say I think he had something to hide.

We treated him better than he deserved. We gave him food and shelter, treated him as the customs of our valley said we should. He refused to drink any wine or liquor however, and that by itself should have told me something. At my age you'd think I'd know enough never to trust a man who doesn't drink—

Anyway, things went okay for a while (Agrippa) . . . . .
. . . . . When stranger meek first showed up
With empty hand, with beggar's cup,
'Twas deep in May all green and gay,
The yearly time for festive day
(That holy week 'f celebration
When men t' gods give due libation.
That timeless Time from time removed
When men breathe deep, their spirits moved,
To leave behind the daily grind
And walk with gods and true life find).
The tournament was gay affair
With athéletes and beauties fair.
In honor of the stranger guest,
The valley folk from East and West
Did come from town and distant farm
In manly dress and female charm.
A gay parade began the show,
A pageantry that finely glowed.
It's forefront graced by champions past
—Society's bulwark hard and fast.
In times gone by they'd shown their might
At contests skill'd, in thick of fight,
Their grayness hid 'n inner fairness:
Deeds accomplished spoke their merit.
By them was claimed the place most blest;

Tradition said they'd earned the best.
The clowns and drums were next in line
And then a band that kept the time
Of music sweet that Muse inspired,
Of tonal grace Apollo sired.
The warriors current were the last,
At them the girls did coo and gasp,
Hot blooded youth who'd have a name
They gave their all for priceless fame.
Their bodies firm, their muscles taut,
Laurel wreaths they desperate sought,
For one thing they could not endure
Was life unhonored, death obscure . . . . .
. . . . . I seen alot of tournaments. We have 'em every year by golly, to celebrate the
coming of spring. An' I tell you it's a good thing, the celebration, the contests,
the women gettin' all prettied up and the men gettin' a chance to prove themselves.

Lysander won the foot race. He always was quick, never could stop him from
stealing out the orchard. Aristotle won the javelin, just like his daddy Brasidas had
done some thirty years ago. Inaros won the boxing and I noticed Clytemnestra
cheering him on. Yep. That Clytemnestra. She looks a little different these days. She
sure is a pretty thing. Puttin' on some weight though. Could be a weddin' coming up
real quick here.

Spring, dadgummit. It sure is a time of year I like (Tydeus) . . . . .
. . . . . The discus was the last event,
Attention there quite keenly bent.
This contest was their pride and joy,
From oldest man to youngest boy
The valley people trained for it;
Proud Agrippa was the favorite.
One by one they took their chances,
Heaved the disc with whirling dances.
The prize they'd earn was four black mares,
A laurel wreath, fame, honor rare.
Agrippa won with splended ease,
The best man there, and all were pleased,
A handsome prince with figure fine,
Conquest belonged to his own kind.
In second place came Atreus,
A bold young man, a feisty cuss,
Who sweated squirming in the heat
Some prickly burr beneath his seat . . . . .
. . . . . and I came in second. I should have been satisfied. Second place isn't bad, my
family would have been pleased, but as I was pacing about after the competition I
grew incensed. Frustrated. Everyone was watching me. It was obvious that they
despised me, that they were completely disgusted with me. It was obvious that the

crowd held me in contempt and I felt alone. Alienated. Disturbed. I felt the intense need to lash out and that was when I saw the stranger.

He was as weak and as miserable and as disgusting as I am. He was a positively revolting example of the human condition carried to its worst possible conclusion. I'm sure he was afraid of me when he first saw me staring in his direction. The puny pathetic shadow of a man. But then he looked at me and I felt a twinge of fear. An attack of angst. A classic case of nausea. I wanted to run. I wanted to hide. I should have thrown-up. Instead I made yet another futile attempt at being a man and a human being. I openly challenged the stranger to participate in our games. I threw the discus at his feet and demanded that he prove his worth.

I was alone. Weary. Disgusted with myself. Contemptuous of everyone else (Atreus) . . . . .
. . . . . And some within the crowd were shamed
That Atreus with spiteful blame
Was trying to humiliate
Their hapless guest with such foul bait.
But mobs are mobs and beasts are beasts,
The majority would have their feast.
To Atreus they gave applause
—They'd throw the stranger to the dogs
Of embarrassment . . . . .
. . . . . Well. If this is the way it has to be—then so be it. Their small minds breed small actions. But why complain. I've always known that every truth must have its martyrs before it will be accepted (The stranger) . . . . .
. . . . . And the visitor picked up the discus. And he nodded to the crowd. And he picked up an axe. And he began to pound the disc into a new shape. And the stranger was a wise man and had spent years conducting experiments and researching ways to improve the design of the sacred disc. And the crowd laughed. And Atreus was goaded on and mockingly asked the weak-wristed man what he was doing. And the stranger replied . . . . .
. . . . . What you see's not deep dark magic—
'Tis only aerodynamics,
The brain child of intelligence,
Of enlightened uncommon sense.
Then he spun the silver platter
Cutting short Atreus' chatter,
As open mouthed the audience stared
At how the discus split the air.
A bird divine from afar
It seemed to reach immortal stars,
Till it landed glory laden
Out of sight, beyond the stadium!
A silence awful then prevailed;
The stranger puny had not failed.
He'd won the game and beat their best
—The crowd was stirred to deep unrest.

158

Atreus loud first found his tongue,
Took it personal, was unstrung.
"That was not fair!" he crying cried,
"The shape—cheat—'twas not fairly tried!"
And many then did sound this note,
Some even said they'd cut his throat,
So hurting was their wounded pride
That scrawny stranger should bestride
Their fairest home grown champions . . . . .

. . . . . And I got to admit; he really wasn't much to look at. All scrawny and dirty and tattered. And it was awful uppity of him to reshape the discus so that it would fly just like a bird. It wasn't very sporting on his part, was hardly the proper thing to do.

For a while I thought all hell would break loose. I thought they might lynch him but with the help of Tydeus, this year's Chief of the Council, I was able to get the worst part of the crowd, the laborers, the serfs, and the slaves who'd been freed, under control.

The stranger got his say when the howling mob had been reduced to a pack of snivelling curs. He wasn't at all apologetic for what he had done. Claimed that our very own rules allowed him to re-shape the discus. He said that the sacred laws that Zeus had handed down only regulated the weight and not the shape of the discus. He mumbled something strange, something I had never heard before, something about his being within his rights when he re-formed the discus.

The crowd was thrown into a frenzy by this new impertinence. They were yelling for his hide but the scribe Aias said that the stranger was right, that he had the Law on his side.

It was a helluva mess. We gave the visitor a bronze tripod as a prize since it seemed as though he had won the contest. Then we sent everybody home. Fast (Agrippa) . . . . .

. . . . . And thus the games abruptly closed
Till spring recur and moistly sow
Eternal life within the land,
And fill again the tourney stands.
Meanwhile folk would find their treasure
In gossip, that perverse pleasure.
Like buzzing bees making din
The mongers talked of what had been,
Of how the stranger won the game,
Fortune eterne, enduring fame.
Some said he was indeed the best
By conquering might with cleverness,
But others said 'twas not well done,
That he'd not earned ' place in the sun . . . . .

. . . . . Bulletin: 'Heated discussion within the valley people's community has reached a new level with the continued operation of Cleon's lyceum. The lyceum, also known by the word 'school,' is a place where people can go to learn to read and write

159

for a fee. The disciplines of geometry, astronomy and debate are also offered at the lyceum, and everyone, be he slave, serf or aristocrat, is allowed to attend.

The lyceum has been in operation for ten years now. Supporters of the school say that it facilitates learning, advances the human condition and provides a service for the valley that it would otherwise not have. Opponents of the lyceum claim that it is a waste of time and money, and some of the hard liners within this faction go so far as to claim that the whole concept of education is dangerous, that the lyceum is a breeding ground for social unrest and that it should be shut down immediately.

Cleon, the man who operates the lyceum, refused to talk to us. Little is known about him except that he entered the valley some ten years ago, impoverished and without a home. In fact, at that point in time he was nameless, and it is the valley people themselves who gave him the name of Cleon. He has operated his lyceum since he first arrived here and the school has been a source of controversy from the day it opened. The Council is once again expected to take up the question of its existence at its next meeting, and whatever the Council decides to do about the lyceum—it is certain that it will be controversial. We'll have more details on our next report. Walter, back to you.'

'Thanks Dan. And that's the way it is . . . . .'

. . . . "In the beginning was Kronos, timeless time, and there was darkness. And the earth was without form and shape. And a raging wind swept over the void. . .

"Mighty Jupiter was the son of Kronos. He came to be when the temptress Desire seduced all seeing Kronos, brother of Chaos. And Jupiter came of age and he imprisoned his father Kronos on the isle of the Beyond. And Jupiter begat the gods and heaven and earth came to be. And men appeared in the image of the gods."

"Very good. Excellent," Cleon congratulated me, after I had finished reading from The Book. I smiled. I was very happy. It was an honor to know how to read and write, to learn what Cleon had taught me. Up until this point in time only the priests and their sons had possessed such magic, had owned the ability to decipher the scrolls. But now, now that Cleon had opened his school, others of us were learning to read and write. We were even getting some math and astronomy.

(The priests and their families hated Cleon. They didn't like what he was doing. They tried to slander him by claiming that he was impious.)

"That will be all for today," Cleon announced, setting the class free. Like always I lagged behind, seeing what this ugly man with the brilliant mind might have to say.

"Sir," I respectfully began.

"Why do you call me *sir*," he snapped.

"Why you are older, you are my teacher, my superior—"

"That's all nonsense," he interrupted. "That way of doing things—come: Recite me your favorite poem."

Flustered, I began:

"The dewey dawn lights up the land,
It brings sweet cheer to every man,
To shepherd gay who tends his flocks,
To women pleased who darn the socks,

160

To farmer strong who plows his fields,
To mother meek who makes the meals.
My tale is one of pastoral joy
Of nymphs who were not very coy
One day they—"

"Enough, enough," Cleon called out, wearily cutting me off. "I have the picture. Your poem—"

"Is a great one, penned by the immortal Diomedes himself," I defensively interjected.

Cleon shrugged, "As you wish, as you wish," he demurred. He was like that. Quiet. Passive. Willing to use persuasion instead of force to get his point across. "Why do you go to school?" he casually asked me.

"That's easy," I quickly replied, on sure ground. "I go to school to learn what the honored poets and the ancient priests had to say about life and reality. When I accomplish this I can repeat to others what I have learned, the things that are important for a sound society and a profitable existence."

"That's very noble of you," Cleon casually returned. "But tell me: Are you not a man?"

"Why yes."

"Are you sure? You sound as though you would go to school like a parrot would. When done with your education will you simply repeat what I have told you? I should be teaching a mimick and not a man if that's the case."

"Well—I—um—err—" Damn that Cleon. He always made me think, was always able to tie me up in knots

"My job as a teacher is not to teach you *what* to think," Cleon said. "My purpose is to show you *how* to think, to show you that there are some thought processes more rewarding than others."

"Huh?" I dumbly asked.

"De-da-de-da-de-da-de-da. This is how your great poet writes. He sounds like a drunken bird. A pleasing pattern but hardly the most accurate way to communicate something. And your Scripture?" Cleon continued, picking up the sacred scrolls and flinging them in the dust. Terrified I looked around, hoping desperately that no one had seen him commit the sacrilege. "A four year old could have written that nonsense," Cleon claimed. "As if reality was a series of discrete happenings that a simple conjunction could connect. The universe was not put together like an alphabet, it didn't go A-B-C-D-E *and* X *and* Y *and* Z, 'in the beginning, and then the middle, and until the end.'

"How do you get at the truth?" Cleon suddenly asked me. I paused. What was he talking about now.

"How do we as humans know the truth?" he continued.

"Well, by faith—" I began.

"Believe in nothing and you can learn anything and everything," Cleon countered, and with that he finished the discourse. I tried to get him to continue but he told me I should spend my time thinking up questions for tomorrow's lessons.

That Cleon. He really was something else (Aeneas, son of Agrippa, a student of Cleon's) . . . . .

. . . . . —sometimes in the night I shudder: What course have I chosen? Almighty God! Why does mortal man dare to be immortal, why do scrawny human beings presume to tread on those lofty heights that even the angels shun. Who? Me? A savior? Hah. 'Tis folly, a god himself has not the courage for that thankless task. To save a man you must first show him that he is wrong, that he is in error . . . why to save a man you must first *condemn* him . . . And what can be more dangerous than that? Why they will crucify me if I persist, they whose minds hold but a single book—they whose hearts tolerate only the one way, *their* way . . . And their eyes? 'Sblood; they are rigid; entombed; have been set to look straight behind them, stonily seeing what the stony past has to offer. They are puppets, never acting, always re-acting, to them the word 'vision' means 're-affirmation,' and they'll behead the man who looks ahead.

But perhaps they are right. Perhaps I really do blaspheme. Why is it not a sin to exchange living flesh and pulsating blood for the creepy comfort of a cold and lifeless idea?!

—Only a demon would barter this earthly 'real'
—For the puzzling mirage that we must dub 'the ideal' . . .
(A fragment from Cleon's diary. All that survives of his writings) . . . . .
. . . . . The spinning wheel that men call Time
Was quickly turned for valley folk;
They soon exchanged sweet peace divine
For angry chaos, for war's yoke.
It all began with one small raid
By foreign men on paltry farm.
They took two hens at point of blade
A worthy cause to cry 'alarm!'
Two nations huge then did battle,
Raised a molehill into mountain,
Slaughtered men like herds of cattle,
Worshipped at Mars's bloody fountain.
Leaders cried they fought for 'honor'
When people weary asked them 'why,'
But cooler heads had to ponder,
If life hinged on willingness t' die.
—But no one talked of rhyme 'r reason:
Spoken doubt was branded treason.
'Twas needless thing, this blood, and death,
That robbed young men of priceless breath.
'Twas plague that Fate had rashly sired
With spiteful gods who did conspire
Against man, woman, child and babe,
Why the land herself felt its rape.
'N the war dragged on. On and on.
Till no one sang heroic song
Of trophies won, victory blest,

'S martial glory seemed pestilence. . . . .

. . . . . When the war had reached its twelfth year, the valley people immediately put Nicias to death on the charge of treason. Although the questions as to whether or not he had really taken a bribe from the enemy were unresolved, and although he had saved the valley people with his leadership at the battle of Platea, the Council was in an angry mood, frustrated by the long war, and they showed him no mercy.

The Council, still in a foul passion after having to deal with Nicias, then turned its attention to proposals that Kornean emissaries were putting forth. The Korneans, trying to act as intermediaries between the valley people and their enemies, the Salatians, had offered a plan to end the war between the two mighty nations. They suggested that the two countries lay down their arms and cease fighting, the terms of the peace to be that things would be the same as they were before the war began. There would be no territory gained or lost because of the conflict, no reparations or indemnities, no apologies would be asked for or given, and the Council sat to discuss the proposal.

Aged Tydeus was the first to speak. He was in favor of the war, had been so from the very first, and he spoke for those who wanted to continue the conflict. He was a hard man and was remarkable among the valley folk for his warlike character. He spoke thus:

'Warriors, comrades and friends. Today we meet to discuss a proposal to bring the war to a close. I myself find this discussion needless and disgraceful since we considered a very similar proposal not more than six months ago. The proposal was defeated at that time, and rightfully so, and I think it necessary to remind the Council that these repeated discussions concerning a negotiated peace are dangerous. They undermine our will and resolve to achieve Victory, for there is not a soldier alive who will do his best on the battlefield if he thinks his generals and leaders are going to sell him out at some conference table. Rather than spend our time hemming and hawwing like weak women, trying to find an easy way out of this difficult war that now confronts us, we should be re-doubling our efforts in the pursuit of Conquest, should be narrowing our vision until we can see only one thing, that thing being Victory. Debate for the sake of debate is dangerous, it leads to confusion, indecisiveness and lack of purpose, and in my mind, to talk of peace now, after all that we have suffered, after all the warriors that we have lost, smacks of treason.

Let me remind you too that we men in the Council are the leaders of our people. We must present a united front to them for the sake of the nation, for if we are seen to be talking of Peace it will show that we ourselves have doubts concerning the conduct of the war and that is the last thing we can now afford. Our people are already weary of this struggle. If we their leaders show an unwillingness to fight they will lose faith in the nation's ability to win the war and they will give up trying, mark my words. We must make every effort to hold fast to our policy, must be ever constant, ever vigilant, and to change policy now would be disastrous. A bad law or policy that remains stable is far better than a good law or policy that constantly changes, and having made up our minds once already we should have the strength and courage to see our decisions through.

—Not only that, but I fear there is a dangerous new element in our society that is encouraging these repeated debates on the question of peace. You all know of whom I speak. This is the group that is spreading dangerous new ideas among our youth and our people, ideas that question the existence of the gods, the right of the landholders to rule society, the place of the individual in regards to the state and the very institution of slavery itself! These people are dangerous, they threaten the very fabric of our way of life, and we should rid themselves of our presence. You yourselves have heard them speak in the courts and the markets, you have seen how the people flock to their lyceums as they are called. These teachers, as some prefer to name them—although I call them for what they are, troublemakers—make an endless maze out of the most simple questions and they should all be exiled. They—'

And thus Tydeus was speaking when a curious thing happened. Gylippus, the town's chiefest idiot, burst into the Council chamber and interrupted Tydeus' speech. The wild looking fool was foaming at the mouth, in some kind of epileptic rage, and he halted the Council proceedings for some time by protecting himself with a sword. He ranted and raved about the most obscene things before he was finally overpowered, much to the discomfiture of all, and since I am duty bound to report all that happened during the course of the war I will repeat some of what the wild mushroom eating Gylippus said although it appalls me:

'—Assholes; virgin raping buttfuckers. Passing dried shit as though it were fresh. They're all after me. There's madness in all your veins—I'm not the one who's fucking crazy—Leeches. You aristocratic geeks. Your blood runs green and gold not red. You could give a flying fuck about people like me, the little guy who has to swim in the shit you expel. Hypocrites. You need oral sex. You need anal sex. War mongering leeches. Why don't you cocksuckers get your cheap thrills some other way, dress up as warriors and ladies and fairies and beat each other up and be beaten while sucking cock and getting buttfucked. You'll kill us all because you can't handle being male without playing with a gun. Maggot headed slimy gargoyles—eat the root you'll understand—maggot headed slimy eagles—'

And thus spoke Gylippus, town idiot, before he was removed from the Council. Tydeus was most distressed at having his speech so interrupted, and the old man complained of being unable to remember where he had left off. Noble Agrippa, most liked and respected of the valley people and their most renowned warrior, gently told the old man that he had just about finished his reasons as to why it was dangerous to even debate the question of Peace before he was interrupted. And so Tydeus continued:

'Very well, having said why it is a bad idea even to debate this peace proposal, let me give my reasons as to why Peace itself is a bad idea. I will be brief—

—Let us not for a moment forget what and who we are. We are an Empire, my friends, much of this nation's substance comes from the tribute that we collect from subject states. If we make peace now, if we fail to defeat our enemies on the field of battle, will not our subjects interpret the negotiated peace as a sign of weakness on our part? Indeed they will, indeed they will, and by making peace with our enemy we risk a new war with our subject states who might well rebel against us. They chafe at the yoke that we have imposed upon them, make no mistake about it, we are an empire and all empires must rule by force, and at all times we must maintain an image of overwhelming strength if we are to control our subservient allies. Nothing so encourages a slave to seek his freedom as the perception of a weak master. And speaking of slaves, let me remind you that the bulk of the population on our very own territory is composed of slaves and serfs. If we at the top of the society conclude this peace the meaner men in this our own country will be encouraged to be disrespectful and disobedient. They will forget who their betters are if their betters show weakness—For in Nature, the perception of who is the best is the same as the perception of who is the strongest—and we cannot tolerate a foreign peace if it will lead to domestic unrest.

In conclusion, let me say that we should hear no more talk of Peace. We went to war because we were wronged in the first place and our enemy deserves to be re-paid tit for tat. Let us hear no more talk of accepting failure, it is not manly to do so. You should follow your instincts in this, your gut feelings must tell you that we should continue the war until we have reached Victory. Remember too that our enemy is totally different from us, his way and ideas are completely foreign to our people, and if this generation of our men does not fight him the next one will surely have to. Finally, let me appeal to your sense of honor as warriors and gentlemen. I do this because I know that as you are men of the very best timber, you will agree with me that it is better to fight an honorable war than to live with a dishonorable peace.' And thus spoke Tydeus, the leader of those who supported the Great War, and the Council was moved for the old warrior had spoken well.

The peace faction was next to speak before the Council. Although it was believed that many supported the idea of peace, few had the courage to come forth and suggest a negotiated settlement. The only man of any stature amongst the valley people who was willing to speak forcefully against the war was Cleon, the teacher, and though he spoke in front of the Council with great reluctance, it was evident that he spoke with some conscience. Although he was a shy man and spoke timidly, the words he gave left a deep impression on many. Yea, it was a deep impression that he made, an impression that would return to haunt him at his trial. He addressed the Council thus: 'An eternity ago, before Time began, the Father of all things deemed it wise and fitting to bring out of the darkness the creature called Man. In His wisdom He made us more alike than unalike, gave all of us hearts and minds, spirits and souls, a love for the earth and love for life, and as the Creator sculpted us out of the dust, the final gift that He saw proper to bestow upon each and every one of us was that glorious commodity we so proudly call freedom of choice. It was the most noble capacity that the Almighty could have placed within us, is the only gift that distinguishes us from the beasts of the land, sea and air, and yet today, as we sat in the Council and heard the arguments for continuing The War, we heard it subtly put forward that this highest of qualities does not exist within us as humans. It was suggested that The War was inevitable, that we had *no choice* in this matter, that it is *impossible* to decide in favor of Peace, and I say to you that you degrade yourselves as men and human beings if you accept these tired and primitive beliefs. We all know that War is senseless, that War begins in fear, continues in fear, is ended in fear. We all know that fear is the most animal like of the emotions we possess. And we also know that to say that we *have* to continue the War, *to say that we have no freedom of choice in the matter*, is to act out of the same fear that began the needless cycle of bloodshed and violence in the first place. Beneath all the so-called reasons that have been put forward to continue the war lies nothing more than an animal like terror, and as a fellow human being I challenge you to put your fear behind you, to stand up and say that you are Men and that you are capable of making a choice in this matter and of exercising your freedom. Once you have done that, once you have enough faith in yourselves to believe that you can decide your own destinies, then I know that you will choose Peace as your way of life since The War exists only because we are enslaved to fear.' And thus spoke Cleon and they wanted to hear him but they were not strong enough. Afterwards, one man said that Cleon and his speech had been a light shining in the darkness, and Cleon, overhearing him, replied that he should look to the light that burned within himself (From the History of Marcellus) . . . . .

. . . . .I was scared shitless; my gut was a knotted ball of ice. I wanted to run away from the whole goddamn thing but I didn't. I stayed with it but a pressure was building inside of me, turning my mind into a blank. My muscles were dead weights; I couldn't move. Then the general took a ride in his chariot in front of the ranks. "Today we claim victory!" he ranted. Breaking a shattering silence. The barbarians charged at that point and we figured if we could withstand the first shock and maintain our ranks we'd cut them to pieces. Time seemed to slow down but they seemed to move faster and faster as they approached. The archers fired a first volley when they came into reach; I thought of some whore that I had slept with a long time ago. Then they hit us. Hard. Fast. Angry. A sword came flashing by—I ducked—I managed to trip one of the sonsabitches to the ground and I speared him the noise was incredible and we were holding up okay till their bloody cavalry came charging down from the hills and then our left flank started to crumble POW! SLASH! CRACK! it was like a wave getting bigger and bigger sweeping the pebbles out of the way DO IT NOW I thought slashing at something moving pulling somebody else off a horse since I knew that to run was to die we had to hold on but I started to think of getting out of there as our wall had been disintegrated by the force of their wave and I got somebody with my shield when I was hit from the rear—(A soldier for the valley people at the last battle of the Great War who survived the defeat, trying to describe the battle) . . . . .

. . . . . I can remember one of the last times I saw Cleon. We were at the lyceum, a month or two after the war had ended, and I had been studying underneath him for a long long time. I had learned so much from him but they weren't things that I can easily repeat here. I mean he never taught a student to memorize anything—he said that they had invented the written word for chores like keeping records—but he always gave a person a new way of looking at things.

I still admire the man for his courage. He saw his beliefs through to the end, an end that wouldn't have come if he'd knuckled under and accepted the majority opinion.

The last time I saw him he gave me something to remember him by. It was a poem of some sort, I think, and he told me to look at it now and then and to think of the things that are beyond myself, my people, my world here in the valley and the very world that lives inside of me as an individual (Aeneas). . . . .

NO EXIT,
NO EXIT

Purpose		Flounder
Goal oriented		Drift
Try harder		Indulge
Discipline yourself		Give in
Thesis		Antithesis

Synthesis
They told me that
Paradise was when
You were able
To balance yourself
But who are they
Kidding
Perfect posture
May make hanging
On the Cross
A little more
Comfortable
But hell;
You're still hanging
On a cross . . . . .

. . . . . and the trial was tumultuous. The entire nation was angry and humiliated at the loss of the war to the Salatians. The valley people had been punished by the loss of their fleet, colonies, right of tribute from their allies and their powers of decision in foreign affairs. The valley people had also lost a large part of their territory and had been forced to tear down the walls surrounding their cities.

Antenor spoke for the prosecution. He tried to sway the 500 man jury by linking Cleon and his teachings with the defeat that the nation had suffered. He also emphasized that Cleon was a stranger, had not been born in the valley, and he tried to suggest that Cleon was somehow or other in league with their enemies. And Antenor was an eloquent young man, had in fact been trained in the art of demagoguery by the very man he now prosecuted, and by appealing to the people's baser instincts he so moved them.

Cleon spoke in his own defense. In addition to his unimpressive appearance his small shy voice also hindered him, and more than once he was shouted down by his adversaries as he defended himself. He also at times seemed to be rather disinterested in the trial, though it was his own, and after the jury returned with a verdict of guilty he spoke to them thus as they considered his penalty:

167

'Tomorrow, tomorrow. And tomorrow:
How much we so cheerfully sacrifice
To prolong the agony! The days they
Go . . . as they will . . . on . . on . . . chained together
Like the dull dead weights they so grossly are,
Hanging, hanging, hanging to each other,
Hanging down from our cursed aching necks
As tar that tortures blistering bare feet,
And a sane man must wonder: Do the days
Cling to us? Is it we who clutch at them?
Or is it mutual strangulation?
It would seem that as we thirst for life, Life
Ad nauseum thirsts for us, would devour
A man until he become one more notch
On Time's endless belt . . .
—Why continue this frantic grab for fleeting life
When eternal death is oh so easy!!
Come. Do with me as you will. I'll not beg.
Though I cherish life more than any man
I freely accept its most heavy price
Untimely death. Here. Take me. Feed your base
Desire, eat my flesh, drink my blood, it is
Written: He was sent into the darkness
That they might escape the light. . . . .

    And thus spoke Cleon before they took him and passed the death sentence
(From the History of Marcellus) . . . . .
 . . . . . And so they strung him to a tree,
A crowd did watch with frightful glee.
His death was slow, a lifetime long,
A minstrel played a sad sweet song.
He showed them courage as he died.
With quiet gaze he held their eyes.
He did not falter, did not cry,
And never did apologize . . . . .

 . . . . . It was not a pleasant death. Since I was this year's Chief of Council I had to oversee the execution. They left his body exposed, after it was over, for the vultures to pick at, tried to make an example of him . . . . .

    It wasn't a very good show, our using him for a scapegoat because *we* had lost *our* war. And I think Cleon was right, that the war was a bad thing, but he shold have toed the line and supported his people anyway.

    But maybe it's for the best, his being executed. He was a dangerous man. The ideas he had—he would have changed *everything* around—and I think that for all his great intellect, Cleon never did understand human nature. For some strange reason he expected that the rest of us could be as good and as pure and as strong as he was, that we could be more human than animal, but the human race just isn't like that; it's mean, base, petty, greedy to a fault, motivated by evil as much as it is by good.

I guess he had to go. He really was undermining the very things that hold this society together, that keep us from degenerating into a dozen different factions that would be constantly tearing at each other's throats. He was especially persuasive with his young students, and sometimes when I look into my son Aeneas' eyes I see some very strange things (Agrippa) . . . .

EPILOG

The story finished all gave applause
To him we held in frightful awe,
To cunning Greybeard, master bard,
With ease he'd played his tune most hard.
His tale had found its fitting end;
Its course had been a skillful blend
Of magic, fact, truth and beauty,
'N he'd upheld artistic duty,
By telling it as best he could
And shaping it as craftsman would.
By using every tool he'd needed,
He'd placed Message in its medium
While knowing that the human race
Has deep within it special place
For mighty deed, for vision bold,
For story grand that's been well told.

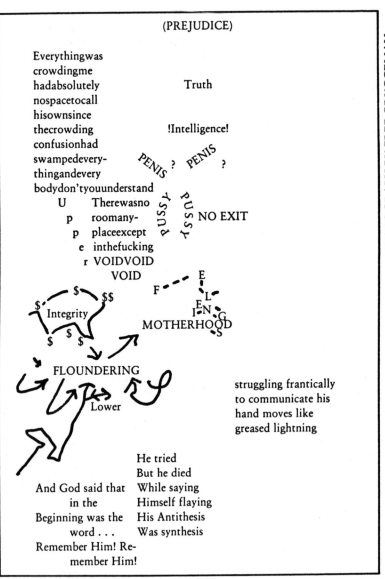

(PREJUDICE)

Everythingwas
crowdingme
hadabsolutely   Truth
nospacetocall
hisownsince
thecrowding   !Intelligence!
confusionhad
swampedevery-   *PENIS* ? *PENIS* ?
thingandevery
bodydon'tyouunderstand
     U   Therewasno *PUSSY PUSSY* NO EXIT
     p   roomany-
     p   placeexcept
     e   inthefucking
     r   VOIDVOID
            VOID   E
                      F - - - • L
                                I•N• G
                      MOTHERHOOD   S
     $ $$
  $ Integrity
   $ $ $

FLOUNDERING
          Lower

                              struggling frantically
                              to communicate his
                              hand moves like
                              greased lightning

                    He tried
                    But he died
And God said that   While saying
     in the   Himself flaying
Beginning was the   His Antithesis
     word . . .   Was synthesis
Remember Him! Re-
     member Him!

WORDGRAPH BY FRED BRUGGEMAN

The searching poet amid all his options

Warning: The Surgeon General Has Determined
That Cigarette Smoking Is Dangerous To Your Health

170

HAPHAZARD

Chapter One

"You must go to Marrakech," the grubby little man said. He was a shabby looking fellow in a shabby type business.

Adrian paused. They were on the Spanish Riviera. Everything here was nice and clean and modern. But Marrakech? That was Third World. Disgustingly Third World.

—But at least it would be different.

"I will go to Marrakech," Adrian Post agreed.

The medinah was dark and cramped and narrow. It smelled of poverty and sweat and death. Very little had changed here in the last thousand years. But Adrian waited impatiently.

"The living—" the words, harshly whispered, jolted him.

"Dead—"

"Will be—"

"Resurrected," Adrian finished, completing the verse from the Book of Truth. He turned to meet his contact.

"My master will meet you—" the fellow began. Adrian grabbed him by the throat and began to squeeze. Who did they think they were dealing with?

"I am the King's man," Adrian growled. "Tell you master that I am to be treated with respect. Tell him that I do not deal with servants. Tell him to meet at 4 in Casablanca at Ticos," he finished, squeezing a little harder. The djellabah clad figure began to faint. But in the netherworld of the medinah, no one took the chance of seeming to notice.

The fellow ran like the dickens once he let go of him. Adrian grimaced. He was starting to get alienated from this whole line of work. He checked the time. Then he pushed his way through a crowd and got the hell out of the medinah.

The ride on the tube to Casablanca was fast and clean. It went hissing by the famine and the poverty and the overpopulation at five hundred insulated miles per hour. Adrian sighed. He was glad of this luxury. Though he had always found the Third World colorful it was now beginning to lose some of its appeal for him. He was getting older.

171

He ran into his first and only wife when he disembarked in Casablanca. It was a freak meeting. She was in transit, on her way home to the sea farms that lay off the coast of South Africa.

"Everything's just fine," he said for openers. He looked at her beautiful face and her beautiful body. She was still quite desirable but there was something about her shape that had changed.

"I've remarried and had two children since I last saw you," she gushed, eagerly and awkwardly. "We're raising our own," she added proudly.

"Congratulations," he returned, meaning it. He did not live in the past and all the hard feelings had been put to rest.

"And you?" she asked. "Married? Children?" she said, in a hopeful tone of voice.

"I'm still a reckless bachelor," he admitted, grinning. "I still have my commission and I'm still sailing the S.S. Cosmos X.

"But I am thinking of getting married again and of settling down," he added. "Who knows, I might even take a chance and try to raise my own."

She gave him a big hug. "You won't regret it if you do I just know you won't," she burst out. "I know it's alot of trouble and there's times you'd rather be without the responsibility, but it's worth it Adrian it really is."

"The psychologists say the state does a much better job of child-rearing," he teased.

"Oh hogwash—"

"According to the statistics, over seventy percent of the civilized world seems to agree with them," he pointed out.

"They're adolescents," she flared. "Trading the joys of having a family just so they can spend their time fooling around!"

He laughed. Living in a society which permitted the family unit meant renouncing the joys of polygamy and infidelity. The lifestyles of liberation and familial responsibility just didn't seem to go together.

The beeping of a buzzer signalled a sudden end to their re-union. They looked at each other for what would probably be the last time. They tensed up a little, it seemed so premature. But later on, when they thought about this meeting, they would realize that it had always been like this for the two of them. "Good-bye," she was crying out, as she stood on the steps.

"Good-bye," he returned, waving. He wondered if it was foolish to wish that their then could have had a chance to happen now. And then he felt a sadness, and he knew that it was indeed foolish, quite quite foolish.

"The ending—"

"Of intolerance—"

"Is the beginning—"

"Of the end," Adrian completed. He felt a twinge. This was one verse from the Book of Truth that he did not like.

His contact was a Bedouin, well manicured and obviously rich. He apologized effusively for having sent a subordinate in Marrakech. Adrian waved him off. He was in a better mood now, surrounded as he was by the lush opulence of Ticos. Outside, however, the crowded squalor continued to heave like an angry storm.

"The King?"

"Is well and sends his greetings," Adrian said re-assuringly.

"I would like to go to the kingdom," the man started up.

"Request for transfer denied," Adrian responded summarily. The man stiffened. In a place as volatile and as poor as Morocco he could never secure his position. That was why he wanted out, why he wanted to emigrate to the kingdom. There he could be a duke with all the comforts of a secured place in civilization. There he could be something else besides a precariously positioned proxy for a foreign power in this poverty stricken land.

"You don't understand!" he whined.

"I understand perfectly," Adrian interrupted. "You have to stick it out here. Period."

"I—"

"You should be concerned with improving the welfare of your people and not with saving your own skin," Adrian chastised. The man faltered. "Things are getting *better* for the Third World," Adrian continued. "Food production from the seabeds is way up. Fusion plants for energy are being built at a rate of one per month. Per capita income, World GNP, economic growth rates, they're all on the rise. Soon—"

"Soon is not soon enough," the man bitterly said. "When hundred of millions of people are starving they look for someone to blame."

"You should enjoy your position of privilege in a poorer nation such as this," Adrian retorted. "Wealth among poverty is the most treasured wealth of all. A meal is most savory when the man next to you is starving."

"Bahhh—"

"I did mean what I said about eliminating poverty," Adrian said soothingly. "With all the advances that have been made we may soon put an end to hunger and deprivation. Another twenty years, a little more luck with population control . . ."

"I'll believe it when I see it," the Bedouin snapped. He had once been poor and he did not want to be poor again. He believed in Poverty as something that would always be there to catch and smother him if he should stumble. "Something will go wrong," the man muttered. "Something always goes wrong and I want to be in the safest place possible when it does—"

"Request for transfer denied!" Adrian exclaimed heatedly. He didn't want this fellow to get any ideas about taking some of the kingdom's gold and making a run for it. The Bedouin shrunk back in fear. He understood.

"Yes sir," he whispered.

"And keep calling me 'sir,'" Adrian hissed, not wanting the man to forget his place in the hierarchy. Adrian had earned his place in the scheme of things and he didn't want this inferior to become too familiar.

"Yes sir."

"We both know why I am here," Adrian gruffly continued, getting to the point. "What has happened to our North African supply of lotus?"

173

"We don't know sir," the man meekly whispered, now openly afraid. The Kingdom of France was not noted for tolerating failure. "The soil on the farms has somehow or other been polluted . . ." his voice dribbled off.

Adrian winced. He had heard that line in the last three places he had visited. Something was wrong. Very wrong. "Get out of here," he told the man. He did not want to hear the details. The fellow scurried off.

Chapter Two

The airship ride was slow and beautiful. The weather was clear for the whole trip and he allowed himself a draught of lotus to unwind. He drank freely and when he opened his eyes there was the Mediterranean . . . sparkling . . . flecked with tiny boats . . . the coastline framed with white puffball clouds . . . he laughed . . . though he was thousands of feet above them he could clearly see the vineyards in bloom . . . punching the flight attendant button . . . 'Yes?' a voice pleasantly asked (A voice trained to please the ears of first class passengers with a strange mixture of deference and efficiency) . . . 'Send in two (Not one) courtesans!' he heard himself demand . . . living it up . . . expensive pleasures were his right, his right, his right as what? A twenty second century buccaneer? He laughed again and again . . . the girls came and went . . .

He sobered as the zeppelin approached Paris. He wanted to be on his toes. He had sent word ahead of himself that he was bringing bad news. And he knew what that meant.

He was met at the airport by no less a personage than the Minister of Finance himself. Adrian wanted to get back on board the zeppelin when he saw who it was. It was one thing to bring the high and mighty good news. It was another to bring them bad.

They took a ride in the Minister's 2067 Cadillac, an enormous classic of a gas guzzler that only the rich could now afford. Smaller electric cars, cramped, slow and efficient, struggled to get out of their way as they roared along. Adrian tried to keep it as brief as possible, as if by shortening bad news he could somehow or other make it better. The Minister sat quietly for the most part. Adrian was not surprised. He knew that the man was a Genius. Such men were not known for their small talk when dealing with the rest of the population.

". . . so I think someone is trying to corner the market on lotus," Adrian summed up, giving his opinion as to why so many of the Kingdom's lotus fields had been polluted. "Natural causes cannot account for our having lost four fields to erosion this year alone."

"And *who* do you think is behind this?" the Minister asked.

Adrian shrugged. "Someone who wants to make a profit," he suggested. "Someone who wants to make unthinkable amounts of money."

The Minister smiled. His mind in one billion, a product of genetic engineering, totally agreed with this fool's analysis of the situation. Adrian saw how the man was smirking at him and he had a sudden impulse to seize the Minister by the throat. He could kill him in a matter of seconds. Though the Genius had an I.Q. of well over 200 he was no match for Adrian physically. He was frail, weak and thin, doomed to die by the age of 40, and Adrian was glad that as a species the Geniuses were dying out. A benevolent act of God had made them unable to adequately reproduce themselves. Only one Genius in ten was able to leave even a single heir and in another fifty years they should all be dead.

"You hate me, don't you?" the Minister curiously asked. Adrian started. He prided himself on being street-wise, able to camouflage his true feelings. How had he known—

"No matter," the Minister laughed. "We both have our jobs to do. Mine is to run the kingdom's finances. Yours is to handle field operations for the production of lotus. Unfortunately for you, you haven't been doing your job very well lately."

Adrian had a reply ready. He had had plenty of good years. He had done as he had pleased and been well paid for it. He had lived the life of a pirate, ostensibly sailing the S.S. Cosmos X around the world as an educational tool while in fact using her as a device of plunder, and he was not afraid. "I hereby offer my resignation," he said. The time had come. He was more than willing to get out if they wanted him to.

"If it was up to me I should accept it," the Minister murmured. He disliked this man and looked him in the eye. "You've lost a step," he challenged. "According to the principles by which we rule this kingdom you should therefore be removed. The King has a soft heart, however, and he wants to give you another chance.

"Let me see here, you have accumulated an estimated credit of forty thousand talents with the National Bank," he said, shuffling some papers. "We also estimate that you have another sixty hidden away from us that you made on the side, on things other than the King's business. That gives you a net worth of one hundred thousand talents—a very nice nest egg, I might add—"

"Get to the point," Adrian snapped. "What's mine is mine," he added fiercely. Though the Minister was a powerful man he was not above the law. Adrian wanted to remind him of this.

"I am aware that the kingdom does not have the right to expropriate a single ducat of your wealth," the Minister retorted. "The point is that our fool of a king has ordered me to offer you another hundred thousand talents if you will stay in his service long enough to clean up this little problem of his. For some reason His Majesty has great faith in your abilities, *Sir* Adrian," the Minister sneered.

"A *hundred* thousand?" Adrian asked. That was a tremendous amount of money.

"That's what he thinks it's worth to him," the Minister replied. "The lotus fields are the largest source of his income. Well, will you stay on or not?" he impatiently demanded.

"At those rates hell yes," the freebooter replied.

The Duke of Shell Oil kept putting an arm around him at the cocktail party. Adrian kept backing off. To hell with this one. The Kingdom of France was mostly hetero. This guy was going nowhere.

The Baron of Mercedes-Benz was preaching in a very loud voice. He was a definite comer. In the last year alone he had doubled his profits. People crowded around him. ". . . statistics show that we have almost completely recovered from the last two world wars," he was crowing. "Our real per capita income is now equal to the U.S.A. standard circa 1970," he boasted. He wanted very badly to be a duke. And the Council, if he kept his profits up, would almost certainly have to kick him upstairs at its next session.

"Bringing back the nobility has been the key to our success," the baron smugly continued.

"And the people?" someone questioned.

"They are as they are," the baron arrogantly proclaimed. "What do they care, they share in the profits. Through their labor unions they own much of the common stock in the major corporations. And they retain the right to abolish the whole system with a ¾ vote . . ."

"They say the King is in trouble," somebody whispered. Adrian groaned. This court chatter could be exhaustingly nauseous. "He's got trouble with his lotus fields," someone added, and Adrian tensed. His self confident aloofness evaporated. Were they talking about *him*?

The Baron of Airfrance-Lufthansa sat brooding in a corner. Rumor had it that an eager vice president was bucking for his job. The baron stared gloomily at the floor. It wasn't that he was all hung up about his title. But he really did like the castle and the thousand acre estate that went with it.

The blare of a trumpet silenced their thoughts and their chatter. The King was now arriving. They all bowed. It meant a year in jail if they didn't. Not death or enslavement, but a year of confinement was enough to make even the most arrogant hop to.

From the top of a grand stairway, the King surveyed his court in all its splendor as his trumpet blasted on. Here beneath him was the supposed flower of what used to be called Western Europe. He wondered. Did the ability to turn a profit make one worthy of being called a baron? A duke? A king?

The Minister of Finance was lurking in a corner. The King pretended not to notice him. He hated, feared and respected this man. He knew that the minister wanted his place. And he knew that someday he should probably have it. And what was it that that apocalyptic piece of trash, the Book of Truth, said? "From beggar to king all hold their place—but 'tis for another they hold it."

"All hail the King," his herald cried out, shattering the silence.

"Hail to the King," came the roaring reply. But the King was troubled and the acclaim did not please him. Perhaps he was even a bit scared. Though his title was shallow it was more than anyone else had and he wanted to keep it. Badly.

176

"As you were," the King permitted, coming down the stairs. The noisy festivities started up again.

They had re-built Paris in splendid fashion after the War of 2070. The wide boulevards. The huge trees. The fountains and the parks and the delicate architecture. Not one stone had been left un-renewed.

Versailles itself had been completely restored. Though the phaser attacks had wiped out everything, thirty years later the palace stood as it once had. Incurable romanticism had refused to be denied. As it was, the forms of the past now made up a divine trinity with the economics of the present and the technology of the future, and everyone was happy. It had been a long rocky road, but at last, Science, Chivalry and Materialism walked hand in hand.

This was Paris. This was the Kingdom of France. This was Adrian Post's home.

Chapter Three

He had a helluva time getting to Aspen. The capital of the New Mormonism could only be reached by horse or foot. The New Mormons did not permit any type of machinery in the area that they controlled, an area comprised of what used to be known as Colorado, Utah, and parts of Wyoming, and it took Adrian three whole weeks to ride on in from the nearest airport in New Mexico.

He had plenty of time to think as he travelled. Plenty of time to curse himself for not having resigned his commission when he had the chance. This chasing after the lotus was not always easy. Still, the mountains were beautiful, forever beautiful, and his sleep in the meadows was sound, sounder than it had ever been in civilization.

He was careful about who he spoke to and what he said as he went along. He avoided people for the most part. The story that he gave to those he did meet was that he was a tourist from California. "I'm just curious to see how you folks live," he would say in a friendly twang. The people, in their simple farmer's dress, would nod in reply.

He got nervous as he approached Independence Pass. Something had changed since he had last been here five years ago. That shopkeeper in Durango had given him a very strange look when he passed through. Of course, everything in Durango and this land still *looked* the same, would always look the same in a land where they fought Change and Progress tooth and nail, but there was still the queer feeling that something had *happened* since his last visit.

So he took to looking over his shoulder and to being cautious as he rode along. He watched the shadows and the corners, the nooks and the crannies. Nothing came of it however, nothing at all, and the miles kept adding up. By the time he got to Josh Parker's place most of his uneasiness was gone. It was now early June, all clean and green and fresh, and the snows were melting and the streams were running. He was at peace with himself, was at peace with the budding aspen on the valley floor and with the blue blue sky that was their roof, and it came as no surprise when they caught him flatfooted. He had gotten careless.

"Josh ain't here," a voice said, from behind a shotgun. "We done cleaned out all the renegades, Mr. Civilised."

"You better come with us," a calmer voice commanded. There were several of them. He did as he was told.

The Aspen jail was old. Authentic. Built of real brick and real pig iron. Romantic that Adrian was he would have liked it from the outside. But from the inside it was depressingly efficient. It held him securely for two weeks.

He chafed as he waited. It was election time and not many people were paying attention to him. The Conservatives and the Moderates were at it once again. The Conservatives were reminding everyone of the past, of how they had come here from Salt Lake City to escape the atomic radiation caused by the Third World War. They cried out against the evils of machinery and of how they had to be ever vigilant to protect the community from heresy. They talked about how bad it was out there, out where they had Sex and Civilisation and Godlessness, and when they got done frightening the people they won in a landslide. The moderates, who for their part had advocated a dangerous change in the uniform dress code and who had wanted to let women go bareheaded in public, were soundly defeated, and order was preserved.

The day after the elections, the newly elected Proctor heard Adrian's case. A surprisingly large crowd was present, causing Adrian to wonder what the big deal was all about.

". . . so this here fellow seemed suspicious like when he was down round Durango way," the shopkeeper reported. "Me and a couple of the men followed him all the way up here and sure enough he went straight to Josh Parker's place. Sure enough he's one of them lotus traffickers come to see how the growers are doing. We nabbed him when he got to Independence Pass and brought him straght here Your Honor."

The Proctor nodded. They had done well. They had been vigilant.

"You gonna hang him?" one of the men who had captured Adrian asked. Adrian nearly gagged. What *were* they talking about. He had been expecting a small fine and his immediate release.

"He's subject to our laws when he's here on our land," the shopkeeper added. "I think we should hang him. Make a good example. These lotus traffickers ought to be taught a lesson. Took us years to get rid of Josh Parker and the rest of those growers. We don't want to lose ground now."

"Hang him," another agreed.

"Now wait just a second!" Adrian Post objected. He hadn't realized just how

178

much had changed here in the past five years. The Conservatives had gotten *very* conservative. "You can't—"

"Silence!" the Proctor ordered and several men grabbed Adrian. "You are on our land and you are subject to our laws, the laws of God," he pontificated. Adrian swallowed, held his peace and tried to keep from fainting. "Now we are a righteous people," the Proctor continued, "and you may have your say in due course. Let me first impress upon everyone here, however, just how serious your crime is. The lotus is an evil plant and it cannot be allowed. It is not God's Will that a man be permitted to forget that His Earth is a place of torment and suffering. The lotus brings a false paradise, it is not the true paradise that we shall find when we die and become as gods, and all who partake of the lotus must be swept away."

"Hear, hear," everyone present cried.

"Have you anything to say in your defense?" the Proctor then asked him.

Adrian knew when to be humble. "I could say that I am an outsider, ignorant of your new harsh laws against the lotus, but instead let me say that I acknowledge my sin and am sorry for it. I repent and I throw myself at the mercy of the community," he said meekly, keeping it short and sweet. He hoped he had mollified the community but he had his doubts. These people had gone totally theocratic on him and there was a righteous blood in their eyes . . .

"I will retire for an hour of prayer before I pass sentence," the Proctor concluded, standing up. Adrian was taken roughly back to his cell to await the verdict.

He tried to sleep. He couldn't. He was too afraid.

"Mercy? It is not to be shown as Nature, who is our Father and our Mother, is a parent who is forever just, forever true and forever merciless." So the Proctor, dressed in black, read to Adrian from the Book of Truth when they brought him back to hear the verdict. He then sentenced him to death by hanging and the next morning they carried out the sentence at the base of Ajax Mountain. They erected the scaffolding on the spot where Little Nells used to be, in the area where the ski lifts had used to run, and it poured rain. Across the street from where they hung him sat the tiny church that they had erected in the year of Our Lord 2000, the year they had first come here, and a big crowd turned out for the hanging.

Chapter Four

"Well he certainly fucked up," Aaron Roberts mused, reading through Adrian Post's report. The New Mormons had allowed him to write it the night before he was hung and had forwarded it to the King as a courtesy. They had also warned His Majesty to cease and desist from pursuing the lotus in their land.

"He was getting old," the King murmured. "Pity. He was the best in his day. He should never have been so careless.

"But we have other things to discuss. You are now in charge of field operations for the lotus. Your appointment to this office is being guarded with the utmost secrecy. I expect you to find out what is happening to the supply of lotus, why so many of my fields have been polluted and destroyed. You will be rewarded significantly if you succeed," His Majesty promised and Aaron Roberts hopped to. He was very eager. The King watched him as he left and gladly noted his youth, his leanness and his hunger. He was depending on him to save his throne and he hoped he would do better than his predecessor. "Pity," he mumbled again, thinking about it.

Aaron Roberts was a mercenary man. He would do anything for a dollar or a thrill. He was not like Adrian Post, was not getting middle-aged and sentimental and complacent, was not thinking in terms of settling down and raising a family. Aaron Roberts wanted more and he wanted it now. He would stop at nothing which was one reason the King had picked him for the job. He had all the necessary qualifications.

As soon as he left the King, Aaron packed a bag and got on the next flight to San Francisco. It seemed like the logical place to begin. Tucked away in Marin County were some of the kingdom's most prized lotus fields. They were in perfect condition and Aaron wanted to be sure of what he still had before he started worrying about what had been lost.

The fiercely hetero and pridefully individualistic Aaron was not happy about having to travel to San Francisco. California had been destroyed twice in the past one hundred years, first by the Russians with atomics in the year 2000, then by the Japanese with phasers in 2070, and as far as Aaron was concerned it should have stayed destroyed. It was now a stagnant society, run by a socialist bureaucracy that did its almighty best to cater to the pleasures of the masses, and Aaron was repulsed by everything that existed in that part of the world. As usual the airport was overrun by fags, as usual the entire city was overrun by fags, as usual the fags were everywhere, and the Book of Truth had something to say about a place like this. He repeated the verse to himself: "Awareness breeds Thirst; Thirst breeds Activity; Activity breeds Accomplishment; Accomplishment breeds Expectation; Expectation breeds Disappointment; Disappointment breeds Death—and thus is written the epitaph of Modern Man." Well. That was one way of putting it.

He closed his eyes and tried to isolate himself as he rode along in a cab towards Marin. It didn't work though. California's strange mixture of brassy hedonism and pretentious brotherly love was too powerful a combination to ignore. It was a way of life that was sweeping the entire world. 'Everyone belongs to Everyone, Everyone is responsible for Everyone,' ran its creed, and like some brave new world it forged ahead despite its many opponents. In this society it was law that child rearing be handled exclusively by the state. Sex and the first person pleasure principle was the goal of all effort, and to top it all off they somehow or other managed to throw in some Christian Brotherly Love to give it a little *meaning*. It really was a vile place—

At a stop-light two fairies jumped into his cab. "What the hell do you think you're doing," Aaron demanded, slightly panicked. He felt threatened by this entire culture and this intrusion did little for his mood. Were they here to rob and beat him? He tensed up, getting ready for a fight.

"We just needed a ride, brother," one of them replied. "You know."

"What?" Aaron exploded. The nerve. He was tempted to beat their brains out.

"There's a paarhhty we just caaann't be late for," the other said.

"Share and share alike, guv'nor," the cab driver interjected. "If they wants to ride you have to let them."

"Who asked you?!" Aaron demanded. "Get out," he ordered his uninvited passengers. They took a frightened look at him and complied at the next stop light.

"You shouldn'ta done that," the cabbie offered as they fled. "We have Good Samaritan Laws here. There's not really much of what you'd call 'Private Property.' Just cause you paid for this cab doesn't mean someone else isn't entitled to use it if'n they have to. They'll report you to the police, brother," he warned.

"I'm not your brother," Aaron snapped. "Shut up and drive."

The cabbie meekly did as he was told. He was a little scared. They didn't get many of his sort around here anymore.

The overseer wanted to sleep with him. He was about fifty and was dressed in some very wild colors. He was a middle level bureaucrat who spent most of his time ingesting the lotus. Aaron was disgusted.

"I didn't mean anything—" the man said nervously, after Aaron had knocked one of his hands away from his thigh.

"I know exactly what you meant and I'm all hetero," Aaron snapped.

"I only wanted to see if you wanted to go to the feelies—"

"Buzz off or I'll break you!" Aaron threatened violently.

"You won't get very far around here with *that* kind of attitude," the overseer sniffed. "You know, you people from the Kingdom, with all your capitalism and machismo, are really quite out of date."

Aaron slapped him in the face. "Stop that," the fairy whined. "You just can't act like that in this part of the world. The police will come and get you."

Aaron smiled. The police didn't bother him. They were as weak and passive and docile as everyone else in this god-forsaken land. "I see the fields are still intact," he said. They were standing at the base of a hillside. On the slope above them and on all the surrounding mountainsides the precious plants grew.

"Yes, yes," the overseer agreed. "We haven't had any trouble here."

"Double the guard," Aaron ordered worriedly. These fields were important. More than a third of all the King's lotus production came from them and they would be incredibly easy to sabotage if someone wanted to. 'Incredibly easy,' he mused, and something puzzled him. If a private entrepreneur was behind all of this, was behind the destruction of the fields in Morocco, Italy and India, why hadn't he started here. With a single stroke he could have inflicted twice the damage he had already done. With a single stroke he could have cornered the market for lotus if that was his ultimate aim, yet whoever was polluting the King's fields was going after the smaller, less important fields. Why?

"Any other orders?" the overseer asked him. His nasally voice broke Aaron's train of thought.

"No, no," the King's man returned. "There is one thing though. I won't be able to get a flight out for another six hours. Could you tell me if there are any real women left in this country?"

"What do you want one of them for?" the overseer asked in reply, puzzled.

Once he got back to a sleazy part of San Francisco it was easy to pick up a girl. There were many women down there in that part of town, and all of them were dying for a hetero encounter.

"Thank you," she kept saying, over and over, as they lay naked in a hotel room. "Thank you, thank you," she hosannaed. She was quite beautiful and very horny.

Aaron stroked the long curves of her hip and thigh. It had been alright. Hell why not. A fellow had to do something between flights. And though philosophy and psychology were not high on his list of interests, he had been curious. That was one reason he had made an effort to sleep with the girl. He wanted to know what made the females in this part of the world tick. "You seemed to enjoy yourself," he commented, continuing to stroke her thigh. "Why don't you emigrate to a place where hetero is the accepted form?"

"Oh I don't know," the girl replied. "I do like it in groups . . . and I like not being bothered with pregnancy and raising children . . . and I do like other women, terribly . . . and I don't like having to worry about taking care of myself, finding a job, that sort of thing . . .

"I don't know," she repeated realistically. "I was brought up here. I just couldn't fit into a society that emphasized raising a family or hetero or fidelity or assuming responsibility. I guess I like to take it easy," she concluded dreamily, "as easily as possible."

"Well then have another on me," Aaron pleasantly chided, pouring her a draught of lotus. The Californian took it without thinking twice.

Chapter Five

"You will proceed immediately to Fiji," the telegram said. It had been placed in his hands just as he was about to board a flight for Paris. It was signed 'Royal' which meant that it was a direct command from the King.

"The old boy must be getting nervous," Aaron muttered to himself, changing his reservations. Passage was booked and a half hour later he was winging across the Pacific at supersonic speeds.

It turned out that the King had good reason to be afraid. Upon arrival Aaron discovered the the Fiji lotus fields had been polluted. A brown skinned Polynesian told him that they were very very sorry. In fact, they were more than sorry, they were panicked. "You know," the fellow began excitedly, without bothering to say hello, "the lotus is our only cash crop. We were using it to support our entire economy. Everything you see here on the island, why the very food we eat, the g-strings that we wear, it's all bought with the money from the lotus. What *are* we going to do?" he wailed.

"You can always go back to working for a living," Aaron said gently. He took a deep breath of warm muggy air.

"The tribe will never go for that," the fellow said. "That's not our way," he exclaimed.

"We all have problems."

"You don't understand," the fellow earnestly continued. "We just can't go back to work. We'd die. We haven't had to work since the year 2000, when we overthrew the whites and re-took our island.

"We had a helluva gig going until the fields were ruined," the fellow continued, moaning. "Somebody's going to pay."

"Any ideas as to how it happened?"

"None."

"Any strangers been hanging around?"

"None."

"What exactly is it that destroyed the plants?" Aaron asked.

"We sent a sample of one of the fouled plants to a laboratory in Hong Kong. They wired back that it was some parasite they'd never encountered before that was doing the damage."

Aaron nodded. The midday heat and humidity bore down upon him and he understood why these people were so terrified of work. The smart thing to do in this climate was to find a chilled drink, a cool breeze and a little bit of shade on the beach. "We had it all set up," the fellow moaned. "We had gotten our population under control. We had the women doing all the work again. We had broken down all ideas concerning monogamy, technology and capitalism. We were keeping out-siders off the islands and we were getting all the dough we needed from the lotus and man things were going *great*," the fellow bitched. "Something like this . . . shit. We'll have to start letting tourists back on the islands to make a living. And once we let those outside influences back in everything will get screwed up again."

"Too bad," Aaron said sympathetically. "Couldn't you folks start to live off the land again? Mangoes? Pineapple? Fish?"

The Polynesian spat in the sand. He didn't think this was very funny. "I've gotten so inept that I couldn't spearfish if I had to," he complained. "I'm used to getting my tuna out of a can."

Singapore was ultra ultra modern. Everything here was as up to the minute as possible. There was not a single crumbling ruin that had been left standing to mar the path of Progress. There was only titanium and chrome, polyplastic and euroylathene.

The entire city, with its monorails and spires and geometric architecture, had been designed by computer. Aaron looked at some incomprehensible piece of machinery and knew he had come to the right place. He had wanted to get the best scientific analysis possible of a polluted lotus plant that he had brought with him from Fiji.

A white gowned technician escorted him to a waiting room while the analysis was being completed. The Singaporean was young, male, clean shaven and energetic. Aaron was not surprised. Singapore was 90% male, was filled with scientist and engineer types who were selflessly dedicating themselves to the pursuit of knowledge. Along with a few women, these men had forsworn the luxuries of carnal desire and easy living so that they might be better able to serve the god of Truth. They had made of Singapore a center for Science, Technology and Space Exploration, and though they had to live like ascetics while they pursued their goals, to them it was worth it.

Aaron scratched his nose. He was glad that there were people like this. It made things easier for less noble sorts like himself. He heard the roar of a rocket as it blasted off somewhere in the distance, watched the intense, self contained technician as he re-entered the waiting room, and had the urge to ask the fellow what he did for relaxation. He decided against it though. The man seemed to be gritting his teeth.

"The assistant director would like to have a word with you about your plant," the man said. Aaron grunted. He didn't want to waste his time with some small fry scientist. He only wanted the answers. But when the technician indicated he should follow he complied.

"I'm in a hurry," Aaron began, when he entered the assistant director's office. He slowed down when he saw that there was no one else in the room.

"Welcome to Singapore, capital of the Malayan Federation," a tinny voice said. Aaron stared. The voice had come from a small grey box. "Do sit down," the voice invited. "I am XJ-3."

"Pleased to meet you," Aaron murmured, taking a seat. He felt a little uncomfortable. It was a large room but there was nothing in it except himself, the chair and the box. It was a metallic thing and was mounted on a pedestal that elevated it to the eye-level of a seated person.

"I am in charge of public relations for the Malayan Federation," the computer began. Aaron gave the thing a funny look. "Please don't be startled or upset," the computer continued, apparently observing his reaction. "In our society computers are programmed to perform many of these bureaucratic functions. It frees the humans to concentrate their efforts on more important things, things like Science."

"You don't say," Aaron replied.

"Oh yes," the computer returned. "In fact, very little of what you call 'Govern-

184

ment' is left in human hands anymore. Here in Singapore we computers take care of such trivial things. And we do our job very well, do it quite logically," XJ-3 added.

Aaron listened closely. Was that a hint of pride he had heard in the box's voice?

"That was an interesting specimen you brought us," XJ-3 observed. "The lotus plant appears to have been contaminated by a simple fruit fly carrying a parasite of unknown origin. We have never encountered such a species in our research."

"You learn something new every day," Aaron joked in reply. The computer did not laugh.

"We do not like mysteries here. We will re-double our efforts," XJ-3 said tersely.

"You don't have to be defensive about it—" Aaron said.

"That is not in my programming," the p.r. computer interrupted.

"Okay, okay. The King will be most generous if you find out anything of value," Aaron hinted. Then he winted to kick himself. Bribing a computer would be most difficult.

"Money is only of secondary interest here," XJ-3 smoothly returned. "We try to isolate ourselves from such mundane considerations. We are, however, looking forward to the return of our deep space probe," the computer enthused, changing the subject. "We finally managed to launch it last month."

"I read about that," Aaron eagerly said, and he wanted to kick himself again. Was he now trying to impress this thing?

"We sent it to the star system nearest our own," XJ-3 informed him. "We hope to find new life forms there."

"Wasn't that supposed to take a long time to get back here?" Aaron asked curiously.

"Only three hundred years," XJ-3 replied. "We will see the original astronauts' great, great, great, great, great, great, great grandchildren when the probe finally returns, if everything goes as planned."

"I see," Aaron said, rising to leave.

"We will continue to investigate your lotus plant," XJ-3 reassured him. "The limited shall know the limitless," he said, quoting the Book of Truth.

"What's that?" Aaron asked, surprised.

"That is how we say 'farewell' here," XJ-3 informed him.

"Well, good-bye," Aaron mumbled, wanting to kick himself for the third time. Damn these Singaporeans.

Chapter Six

The girl entered his life when he went to Moscow. She had dark hair, a rich mouth and a sleek full body. A temperamental streak ran through her very black eyes and Aaron wanted her. Badly. He was infatuated and could not help himself.

He was in Moscow because he was on his way to the Ukraine to check up on some more of the King's lotus fields. He met her at a party and soon thought he had her. She was an elusive thing however, and before he knew it she had him. Her mere presence was enough to distort his better judgment, and he soon forgot all about the lotus plant, his job, the King's commission and his future prospects. For the time being everything took second place to her and her whims.

"Dahhlingg," she would say, in an outdoor cafe in the moonlight. "*We* are pehhfect for each other. It must have been fate that brought us together."

"Then sleep with me," he would demand. And she would smile. She was fairly certain that if she did that he would lose interest in her.

"I can't," she would moan plaintively. "My lover would be so hurt. I must tell him everything."

This was driving him crazy. The thought of another man having her was too much. And he had never met this other lover of hers. He wondered if she had simply made him up to hold him off.

"I know we'd be so happy if you'd only sleep with me," he begged, once again blurting it out uncontrollably. She smiled teasingly and patted him on the thigh. He wanted to die.

It went on like this for two weeks. He would be persistent and charming while she would be elusive and desirable. He could tell she was a high strung girl with lodes of passion. He wondered where she found the self-discipline to say no. At times so did she but instinct told her she was doing the right thing. She knew that once a man became sure of you you lost him. You had to keep them guessing at all times. And even if she did consent to go to bed with him she would still have to find a way to make him unsure of himself. There would always have to be some mystery about her, some chance that he wouldn't be able to hold onto her, if she was to ever keep him. All in all she was a very instinctual female, a fact which came as no surprise since she lived in a very instinctual land. The Soviet Union and Eastern Europe had fragmented into a hundred small countries after the Third World War. The Communist Bureaucracy had been wiped out by the total devastation that the United States had inflicted upon it with their newly invented phaser weapons in the year 2000. What had been the Soviet Empire disintegrated into petty nationalist states, and civilised life had never really recovered. In this part of the world scientific research had stopped, education of the public had taken a step backwards, and unemployment, inflation, counterfeiting and intrigue had become commonplace. In order to survive here people had learned once again to go at it day by day, toe to toe, with no holds barred. Russia was now a wild and woolly place and some people went so far as to claim that Eastern Europe was degenerating into some kind of Dark Ages. For his part Aaron didn't know. He didn't even care. What difference did it make if there were bombs falling and gunfire echoing. All he could think about was the girl. And if chaos and confusion was what it took to produce such a creature, then so be it.

He received many messages from the King during this period. They asked him how the work was going, what he had found out about the lotus fields. He ignored them.

The affair, as it must, finally came to a climax. She called him up on the phone one day and used some very heavy breathing to get his attention. "I've *got* to see you," she panted. "I can't stand it anymore. Get a room at the Lenin Hotel and then meet me in the lobby. I don't care what people say. Dahhhling I *love* you," she cooed, hanging up on him.

He felt the fire. This was it. Fulfillment was at hand. He did as he was told and was nearly pushed to the breaking point by the excitement of it all. After renting a room his eyes eagerly searched the lobby of the hotel where they were to meet, but he didn't see her.

"Are you Aaron Roberts?" a handsome man called to him from across the room.

"Why yes," he admitted, startled.

The man, who looked like a Spaniard, walked up to him and slapped him in the face. "I am Teresa's husband," he announced, "I should like to kill you."

"Well," Aaron stumbled, caught off guard.

"However, I will let you live," the man graciously offered.

"Teresa never said she was married," Aaron shrugged.

"It is no matter," the man moaned, with dignity, tears coming to his eyes. "She took her life this morning. In the note she left she said she would rather die than have to choose between the two men she loved."

"I don't believe you," Aaron sneered, figuring that the man had concocted this story to move him out of the picture.

The man, now crying hysterically, refused to pay any more attention to him and walked away.

Aaron didn't give up all that easily. Upon leaving the Lenin Hotel he tried his very best to find her. He left countless messages for the girl with her answering service. He went by her apartment a half a dozen times but was told that she had moved. He contacted the police and reported her as a missing person. He made every effort to re-locate the Spaniard who had claimed to be her husband. Each night he went by their old hang-outs in search of her, and he even took out a huge half page ad in the Personal Column of the classifieds in the Moscow Press, proclaiming his eternal love for her. But alas, it was all to no avail. He never heard a single word. She had left him. Left him cold. After a week of this he gave up, having never known the bliss of her naked body next to his, and there was a funny taste in his mouth when he left Moscow.

Chapter Seven

He was back in Malaga, on board the S.S. Cosmos X, when he received word that his father had passed away. It was a sudden thing. They had been forced to hold the funeral without him because of his absence. Aaron Roberts felt hollow at the news. He and his family were on good terms. He wished he had been there. It would have given him a sense of renewal, of the orderliness of the natural process, if he could have seen his father off. It was—hell why brood about it. Hell. There was some news from home to be cheerful about. His younger sister had given birth to her first child. He tried to smile.

"Sir?" someone quietly asked. For the second time.

"What?" Aaron mumbled, startled out of his distraction.

"I said there's someone here to see you sir," a crewman said. The visitor was shown in.

"Greetings from His Majesty," the man began, flashing a ring with the royal signet. Aaron tried to concentrate on business. He didn't want to. He wanted to mope around and brood and feel sorry for himself and the rest of the world. But this fellow had come directly from the King. Aaron tried to pull himself together. "His Majesty is most curious to know the results of your travels," the fellow mouthed. Aaron noted that he was cheerful and well fed. He probably held a high position in the royal court.

"The fields in Fiji have been polluted," Aaron reported laconically. "I sent one of the damaged plants to Singapore for analysis. They were able to tell me very little.

"The lotus fields in San Francisco were okay as of three weeks ago. I doubled the guard around them.

"I was unable to reach the Ukraine to inspect His Majesty's fields there," he concluded. He saw the sycophant regard him suspiciously. He wondered if the King had heard of his little affair in Russia.

"You were unable to reach the Ukraine?" the man pleasantly questioned. "My, my."

"Travel is becoming very difficult in that part of the world," Aaron hastily added. "All those tiny countries with their petty dictatorships. It's hard to move about. I got as far as Popol and had to turn back."

"Tsk, tsk," the messenger sympathized. Aaron studied his face carefully. Did the King know that he had never even made an attempt to get out of Moscow? Damn that girl. He had risked everything for her and received absolutely nothing in return.

"That's all I have to report," Aaron nervously finished. The man casually lit a cigarette and Aaron suddenly relaxed. It was becoming quite obvious that this fellow could care less about his romantic escapades, about what he had been doing for the last three weeks, about the fact that his father had just died. It was evident that this joker didn't give a flying fuck about anything exept the maintenance of his own bloated gut.

"I shall repeat what you have told me to His Highness," the fellow blithely replied. "Here are your new orders," he said, handing Aaron an envelope. "Good day," he called from the door, excusing himself, and he was gone.

Aaron half-heartedly opened the envelope: "Proceed immediately to New Jerusalem," the message read. "Continued Singaporean analysis of insect carrier from polluted plant indicates Palestinian origin. No new information concerning type or origin of parasite that insect carried. On arrival check in at Peace Hotel, United Nations Plaza. You will be contacted."

Aaron destroyed the communication, repacked a satchel, sucked up his gut and was on his way.

Chapter Eight

That I am a man and that life is worth living as a man.

That my neighbor is my brother and that he may live as he wishes.

That I will do my best to be happy in the society that I was born into.

That if necessary I will migrate to a society that will make me happier.

That I will not construct atomic weapons, phasers or other implements of Armageddon and that I will not engage in biological warfare or genetic manipulation.

That it is my duty to keep others from doing these things and that I will report to the authorities and to the general public any such activities.

That I am a man and that life is worth living as a man.

So ran the words of the seven commandments that all men were to follow. They were inscribed in a huge bronze plaque that was set in an obelisk located in the center of the United Nations Plaza in New Jerusalem. Aaron re-read the commandments that were the duy of every human being to obey and of the U.N. to enforce. He pretty much agreed with them. He was certainly in favor of outlawing the weapons that had made such holocausts of WWIII and WWIV. And he also thought that people should live in a society that made them happy. Or move to one with a way of life that did. It was all part of the Great Re-Location scheme, a plan that tried

189

to place people in societies that made them happiest. It was supposed to reduce tension and friction among human beings and had been implemented after WWIV in 2070. For the most part the plan seemed to be working. If you didn't like state socialism in San Francisco you could always become a New Mormon in Colorado. If you didn't like being a royalist capitalist in Paris you could always try being a scientist-space explorer in Singapore. And if your only objective in this life was to cause trouble and be an agitator, you could always migrate to what was left of the Soviet Empire with its hundred nation-states. The people there were forever at each others' throats. A man could raise as much hell as he wanted to in that part of the world and harm a minimal amount of people while doing it.

Aaron reread the seven commandments for a third time. He felt good after he did it. Maybe the human race was finally getting things under control.

"The eternal dawn—"

"To end all dawns—"

"Is breaking first light—"

"If we but have the vision to see it," Aaron Roberts finished, completing the verse from the Book of Truth. He and his contact were standing in the lobby of the Peace Hotel.

"I am Rabbi Goldstein," the man said by way of introduction. Aaron was surprised. He was speaking with a big wig from the United Nations.

"Aaron Roberts, in His Majesty's Service," he replied. They shook hands.

"I have been ordered to offer you whatever assistance I can," the rabbi said. He was short and dark and seemed to be able. "We have heard of His Majesty's lotus problems. Since the Kingdom of France is one of the United Nations' largest contributors and since the King is a personal friend we are pleased to help you."

Aaron nodded. He wondered just how big a donor the King really was. "Thank you," he replied circumspectly.

"Right this way," the rabbi offered.

It was the first time that Aaron had ever been to New Jerusalem. The rabbi gave him a little tour and he was impressed. New Jerusalem, the home of the U.N., had been rebuilt from the ground up after WWIV. It was on a much smaller scale than its predecessor and much of it was done in a classical style that borrowed heavily from the Greeks. Everywhere one looked, in the courtyards, the parks, the public buildings, the commercial and the private sectors, one found a sense of quiet assurance and easy grace. There were no grandiose carvings on enormous buildings, no fifty lane boulevards with skyscraper fountains, no anxious attempts to make an impression. There was rather an aura of peace and order and simplicity, as if a man could plant himself down in any one spot of the city and still feel at home.

"It's beautiful," Aaron murmured appreciatively, somewhere towards the end of the tour.

"That was our goal," the rabbi replied. Aaron nodded.

They got down to business once the tour was finished. With the combined resources of the United Nations and the Kingdom of France they tried to find out

190

who was causing the King's lotus problem. It was an intensive effort. They used computers, satellites, data banks and human informants. They went over the dossiers of any people who would have both the means and the motivation to pollute the King's lotus plants. They checked up on hardened criminals and entrepreneurs anxious to make a buck. They watched ports of entry and searched all kinds of laboratories. They resorted to strong arm tactics where they felt it would do some good, and when it was all over they had nothing. The fact that the insect carrier of the unknown parasite that fouled the lotus plant was of Palestinian origin didn't amount to a hill of beans.

"Maybe the Singaporeans made a mistake with their analysis of the bug," Aaron grunted wearily, after a week's effort. He and the rabbi were having a cup of coffee. He was tired and depressed.

"Who knows," the rabbi returned queerly, almost fatalistically. "After all, it was only a fruit fly."

They were on their way to the airport when they spotted the stranded vehicle. It was pulled over to the side of the road with a flat tire. Rabbi Goldstein, who was giving Aaron a ride, pulled over to lend a hand.

It took them less than five minutes to change the tire. The motorist they helped was a sparse man and effusively thankful. He drove off in a hurry and the rabbi headed his own vehicle back towards the airport.

"I think you should turn around and head towards the city," Aaron suggested, after a minute or two of driving.

"What's that?" the rabbi questioned.

"I should like to know what my country's Minister of Finance is doing in New Jerusalem," Aaron replied, referring to the motorist who had had a flat tire. "He usually travels with a little more pomp and circumstance," Aaron mused, deciding not to fly back to the Kingdom of France just yet.

Chapter Nine

And God created man in his own image; in the image of God he created him was crudely engraved on the archway. Aaron recognized the verse as coming from the Book of Truth. But the rabbi, holy and devout man that he was, knew it as originating in Genesis, out of the bible of old that people seldom read anymore.

The heavy oak doors that denied them access were locked from the inside with a bolt. But above them was an ancient porticullis, brown and rusted, and the cement

191

that held it in place was weak and crumbling. They procured a ladder and after several minutes of banging on the thing with a sledgehammer, Aaron knocked the porticullis to the ground.

"I wish we could have been more quiet," Aaron murmured, as they clambered into the castle. It was a medieval thing, dark, gloomy, romantically exhilarating. "We don't want to let the mice know that we're coming," he continued, as they stood in a foyer that led into a great receiving room. They were now inside the Minister of Finance's vacation home on the outskirts of New Jerusalem.

"If anybody is here they must have heard the racket we just made," the rabbi offered.

"Probably," Aaron replied. "But we're here; let's go ahead and take a look."

"It's a creepy place to have as a vacation home," the rabbi muttered.

They moved out of the foyer and began a search of the fortress from top to bottom, starting with the upper chambers and continuing with the main floor. They found no people and more importantly, no sign that anyone lived there or used it as a vacation home. It was all quite empty and very dusty, and Aaron felt a rising sense of anticipation as they went along. When they had worked their way through the kitchen and were approaching the stairway to the basement he found that he was glad he had armed himself before coming. It was likely that there would be trouble.

They moved as quietly as possible now. They took the basement steps one by one and at the bottom of the stairway they found a single large room of perhaps a thousand square feet. Judging from the racks that lined its walls it had once served as a wine cellar. The rabbi let out a disappointed sigh as their flashlights swept the darkness. "Looks as though we came up empty," he murmured, perhaps somewhat relieved. "Maybe—"

"Unn-uhhh. Shhh!" Aaron quieted him. His flashlight beam had found a doorway in a corner of the far wall. "One more place to look," he whispered. They nervously tiptoed across the room in something of a fright. They walked in starts and stops and when they got close their flashlights found something else. Above the doorway, on a crudely lettered sign, was written: "And they ate of the fruit of knowledge; and they became as gods, knowing good and evil; leaving only one possible result . . ."

They shuddered when they read the inscription. No one had ever figured out what the last verse in the Book of Truth really meant. They had a sudden impulse to turn back and run for it. But what else could they do but open the door.

Chapter Ten

"Come in, come in," a weak voice murmured. They were standing on the threshold of an enormous room, temporarily blinded by a searing incandescent light. "Do come in," the voice urged.

They entered. Aaron had his gun ready just in case. It didn't look like he would need it though. There was only one person in the room. He was a smallish figure and was seated with his back to them. He was bent over what appeared to be some kind of microscope. "Minister?" Aaron softly queried. His voice echoed throughout the spacious laboratory.

"Of course, of course," the Genius mumbled. "Just as I thought," he murmured, squinting into a microscope for the last time. "One more moment please."

"What sort of research are you conducting down here!?" Rabbi Goldstein of the U.N. demanded, trying to sound authoritative, finding his voice at last.

The Genius arrogantly laughed. "Genetic manipulation," he said, haughtily, as though speaking with inferiors. "I am developing a human being so superior he won't really be human. He'll have mental abilities that will be the envy of mystics and computers. He'll be . . . something beyond us.

"I watched you two making your way through my castle on a video system," the Genius casually added. "How did you find me?"

"Aaron Roberts, in charge of field operations for the lotus plant, in the service of His Majesty," Aaron said, by way of introduction. "This is Rabbi Goldstein from the U.N. We—"

"I remember," the Genius interrupted. "You helped me fix a flat tire two days ago. Is that what put you onto me?"

Aaron nodded. "It was all wrong, your being down here alone, on your own, fixing a flat tire of all things. I just knew you had to be up to something. Once I looked into things it didn't take a genius to figure out that you were polluting the King's lotus fields in an effort to overthrow him. The Board of Directors meets next month. The King would not have had enough profits from his lotus fields to retain his title. I checked up on it and found out that you had had a very profitable term of office and would be next in line for both the throne and the lotus fields. And so ends the mystery of who has been polluting the King's lotus plants with a Palestinian fruit fly carrying an unknown parasite.

"But all this," Aaron said, indicating the laboratory, "comes as a total surprise. I never dreamed—"

"Of course you didn't. Probably couldn't have if you had wanted to," the Genius bitterly interjected. "And I'm so close," he lamented. "So damnably close. When I began polluting the lotus fields I thought that I would need the power and the money that goes with the throne to complete my experiments. But it's gone much better than I had planned. All I need now is a little more *time*. You see, I'm just about ready to produce my—"

"You're *what*!?" the rabbi cried out. "A new race of inhuman superhumans!? You know this sort of thing is forbidden. Outlawed. After what happened with WWIV! Damn you. Damn you!!"

"Your friend is puzzled," the Genius said, indicating Aaron. "He doesn't understand the reference."

The rabbi hesitated. The real causes of WWIV were hidden. History had been completely re-written. Only a few men alive had the privilege of knowing what had really happened.

"What was the cause of WWIV?" the Minister asked Aaron.

"Control over the world's supply of gold," Aaron replied, giving the textbook answer. "Japan had wanted the Australian and South African gold mines for her own. The United States refused. So the Japanese constructed their own phasers and launched a sneak attack on the United States and other selected centers of civilisation. A 49¢ transistor on one of their two main phaser banks failed them, however, and they were totally destroyed when what was left of the U.S. counterattacked."

"A very good story," the Minister applauded. "And all of it is true—except for the reasons you gave as to why the Japanese launched their sneak attack. They didn't give a damn about the world's gold supply. What they really wanted—"

"Be quiet!" the rabbi exclaimed.

"Was to be able to continue with their genetic experiments," the Genius blithely continued. "If you will recall, by the year 2065 Japanese scientists produced the first batch of genetically engineered human beings. My father was among the first hundred. Increased intelligence was the primary criteria the scientists used for their DNA selection and they liked what they saw. By the year 2070 enough advances had been made to the point where they wanted to produce another breed of humans that was even more advanced than the first group—

"It was at this point that the moralists and the do-gooders and the politicians got scared," the Genius bitterly spat. "The powers that be of that time, all of which were located in the phaser guarded U.S., decided that they would put the question of genetic engineering up to a vote of the general public. The Japanese scientists decided that it was too important a question to be left to an election—"

"So they built their own phasers, launched their sneak attack and were finally destroyed," Aaron completed.

The Genius shrugged. "A flat tire here. A 49¢ transistor there. The most important decisions that face the universe being made by such things. It almost makes one believe in fate . . ."

"Or in God!" the rabbi shouted.

"As you wish," the Genius demurred. "Myself, I too believe in God, though I see him differently than you do."

"Enough is enough," the rabbi said decisively. "You have broken the laws of mankind," he accused the Genius. "Your laboratory and your work will be destroyed and you will be executed."

"The continued progress of what we call 'Knowledge' will hardly be stopped by such doings," the Minister challenged. "The wheels of Time never stop. Today's Inquisitor is tomorrow's Heretic."

"You're a devil who brings us Armageddon," the rabbi spat out. He turned to Aaron. "And we are so close to creating the New Jerusalem *everywhere*, throughout the world! Food production is up. Population is under control. We have all the energy we could ever think of using. At last, we can conquer poverty. More importantly, the Great Re-Location program is working beautifully, is settling people in societies where they will be happiest. Interpersonal conflict is on the decline. And finally," the rabbi said enthusiastically, "we are seeing a change in the very heart of Man. The human race, after four world wars, is tired of death and destruction. People are upholding the seven commandments and they eagerly uncover and denounce men like our friend here, men who would bring us more misery."

"You paint a very rosy picture," the Genius murmured.

"The New Jerusalem is here to stay!" the rabbi rejoiced.

"Baloney. Totally unrealistic," the Genius returned. "Human beings will never create a Utopia . . . as long as they remain human."

"You are devil—"

"And you are a fool! What do you think we're doing here, on this planet, in this time and this place!?" the Genius demanded. "Eh? What is our purpose?! What is the meaning of all this," he shrieked, indicating everything there was.

"We are human beings, created in the likeness of God, here to do His Will, here to be happy, here to live with dignity and in peace, with love and brotherhood . . ." the rabbi faltered here, fumbling for an answer. In a sense he knew he was muttering tired platitudes and though he sincerely believed them he felt uncomfortable mouthing them. But then again, at least he was sure of one thing: The Genius was wrong and had to be stopped at all costs.

"Do you know the last verse in the Book of Truth?" the Genius demanded. "Well I do, and I should since I wrote the damn thing. The verse goes: 'And they ate of the fruit of knowledge; and they became as gods, knowing good and evil; leaving only one possible result . . .'

"Didn't you ever wonder what that one possible result was?" the frail little man shouted, now in a total frenzy. "Don't you know that the logical climax of evolution is when a species assumes control of its own development!?! Can't you see that all the rest of it is chaotic bullshit, that nothing will change for mankind until he sees this truth and acts upon it?!"

The laboratory fell silent. Both the Genius and the Rabbi temporarily held their peace. Fascinated, Aaron watched them, feeling as though he had been an audience to some great debate, feeling as though these two men had been trying to win him over to their respective viewpoints. And why not. What was so surprising about that, Aaron suddenly realized. After all, he was the only person in the room who held a gun in his hand.

"Enough of all this," the rabbi said. He turned to Aaron. "We have a duty to perform here. We must turn this man over to the authorities and destroy his laboratory—"

"Why must you do those things?" the Genius interrupted, giving Aaron a meaningful look. "What's in it for you?" he slyly asked.

"Don't listen to him!" the rabbi ejaculated.

195

"I can make you *King*," the Genius ran on smoothly, pandering to the man with the gun in his hand. "It may take four or five years but I can promise you a dukedom right away—if you play along with me."

"Aaron," the rabbi said sharply. "Don't listen to him. You have a duty as a human being. Who knows what this man is doing here in this laboratory. Who knows what the results may be. There is unheard of danger here. Think of your fellow man," the rabbi implored.

Aaron tightened his grip on the gun. "Don't worry," he said to the rabbi. "Of course you're right. I have him covered."

The Genius faltered when he heard this. He made a move towards a coat pocket. Aaron saw it and squeezed the trigger without thinking.

And Rabbi Goldstein fell dead to the floor. There was a silence.

"The two of us ought to be able to cover this up," Aaron finally said to the quaking Minister.

"You had me worried there for a while," the Genius muttered. He was as pale as a ghost.

"Philosophy is not one of my strong suits," Aaron replied. "What you do here is your business," he continued, gesturing towards the laboratory. "But I do want to know how soon I can be King," the opportunist demanded, as they picked up the warm bloody body.

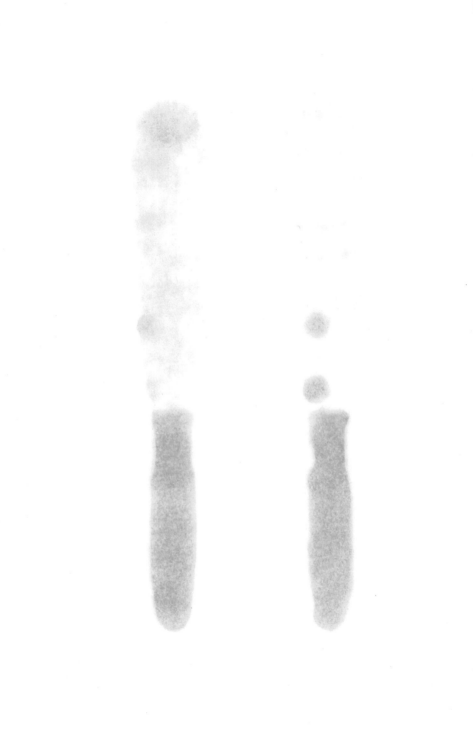